DARK PLANET WARRIORS

ANNA CARVEN

CHAPTER ONE

Abbey

I'm sitting in one of the window booths of the Meteorites Café, staring out through the thick glass. There's movement below me as processed Armium metal is loaded onto a freighter bound for Earth. I sip on my expensive imported coffee, inhaling its comforting aroma. So freaking good. I have missed this stuff so much. Here on Fortuna Tau, luxuries like coffee are a rarity.

Its delicious smell reminds me of Earth.

I glance across at my friend Jia, who's also savoring her coffee. "This is heaven," she sighs, taking a slow sip. "I can't believe they got some in at this time of year. The Earth shipments are usually too full to take luxury items on board."

"Bree's got connections," I shrug, winking at the cafe's manager, who's standing behind the counter. She's too far away to hear me, but she smiles back all the same. "And, did you hear they brought in chocolate?"

"No way. You mean the real stuff?" Jia's eyes go wide. "Where? Who? I need it now."

"Relax. I know a guy who works in stores. I'd reserved some way back. Asked him to put some aside for you, too."

"You're the best, Abbey. How come you always know about the contraband before anyone else?"

"Connections," I reply with a deadpan expression. I taste my coffee, enjoying its smooth, slightly bitter taste. "By the way, you missed a spot."

"Huh?" A look of confusion spreads across Jia's delicate features.

"Right cheek, grease monkey," I say. She rubs at her face with the sleeve of her coveralls, wiping away a black smear.

"Occupational hazards." Jia rolls her eyes and I laugh.

We're a sight for sore eyes, sitting in this super clean café dressed in our work uniforms. Jia's got her grey mechanic's jumpsuit on, and I'm wearing my green scientist's scrubs.

"You've got plant bits in your hair," Jia observes. I run my fingers through my short locks. Sure enough, a few bits of twig and some scraps of leaf come free. I groan.

"Man, I can't wait to get back to Earth. I'm sick of this damn gardening work."

"Yeah, but without you guys, we don't eat and we don't breathe. You bio-sci guys literally grow the station's entire food supply. I'd hardly call it just 'gardening.'" Jia pops a cube of recombinant strawberry between her delicate pink lips. "How much longer do you have on this junk heap anyway?"

"Two years," I sigh. "When I applied to the Federation, I didn't think I'd end up on an asteroid mining station of all places."

"Same here," Jia shrugs. "But you take what you can get, huh?"

"True. It's impossible to get a job on Earth these days without off-planet experience. So I just need to do my time, then boom, I'm out of here." As I shovel a spoonful of pudding into my mouth, a red light flashes from the loading dock below, and the huge airlock doors start to open. "Incoming," I mumble between mouthfuls of artificially flavored vanilla mush.

We both look down, staring at the giant space below. The grey floor of the loading dock gleams under the impossibly bright lights. A squad of peacekeepers runs across the floor, taking position beside one of the landing bays. They're fully armored, their bolt-cannons drawn.

"What the hell is going on?" I put down my coffee, my attention captured by the unfolding scene. The doors of the airlock are fully open now, and a sleek black spacecraft glides into the dock.

The thing is huge, easily the size of one of our freighters, but where the freighters are built for stability, this thing seems designed for speed and destruction. It's all sleek, aggressive lines, and it has some mean-ass looking artillery bristling from all sides. It's like nothing I've ever seen before. It's definitely not Human.

"You recognize that thing?" I turn to Jia, who is gaping. Her mouth is actually wide open in shock. I've never seen her wear that expression before. Normally, she's as tough as nails and totally unflappable.

For a moment, she says nothing.

"Jia," I say slowly, a bad feeling rising in my chest. "Who the hell are those guys?"

"What are they thinking, letting them in?" she murmurs, staring at the sinister looking craft with an expression of mild horror.

"Who, Jia?" I don't like the way she's gone all quiet.

"That's a Kordolian battle cruiser," she says. "Alpha class. They're packing so much firepower in that thing that they could blow Fortuna into oblivion if they wanted."

"Kordolians?" I shudder. "You mean those scary silver skinned guys? What the hell is command thinking, letting them in?" I shake my head, echoing Jia's thoughts. "They're a long way from home, aren't they?"

"Hey, look closely." Jia points to the craft. "It's taken damage. Two of the thrusters are out and there's a tear in the hull."

"You're right." I shake my head, trying to piece it all together. "But who would be stupid enough to attack a Kordolian ship?"

"Beats me." Jia shrugs. "Space pirates get a bit trigger happy sometimes. Maybe they didn't know who they were messing with."

"Or maybe they're insane." I watch as the peacekeepers get into a defensive formation around the ship's hatch. The doors start to open, revealing the muted glow of the interior.

The air around the craft shimmers with blasts of heat, and for a moment, nothing happens.

Jia and I are glued to our seats, as if we're watching a suspenseful movie. We share an astonished glance as the Kordolians appear. They walk down the ramp with their weapons raised.

"Those are Kordolians?" I whisper, trying not to sound too awed. Everyone's heard of Kordolians. Because of their warlike tendencies, they've somehow ended up owning half the galaxy, but for some reason, they've never bothered with Earth. Most Humans, including myself, have never seen one in the flesh.

So why haven't they colonized us?

There are lots of random theories out there. Earth's too far. Too insignificant. We're not a threat to them. They can't afford any more expensive incursions. We're an important trading partner. Blah, blah, blah. They have analysts on the Network debating this stuff all the time. I've never paid much attention to it all. Interplanetary politics isn't exactly my area of interest.

Are they a threat to us? Hell, yeah, they are if they want to be. They have the most advanced military in all of the Nine Galaxies, and judging by the looks of these soldiers, they don't mess around.

There are around a dozen of them, and they sure as hell look intimidating. They're clad from head-to-toe in some kind of form-fitting black battle armor. Their features are hidden under menacing looking helms, with even their eyes covered by a black visor, and they're packing some serious looking artillery. There are weapons strapped to their bodies that I've never seen before. I squint. Are those freaking *swords* sheathed at their backs?

"Um, is this about the time we initiate an emergency distress call to Earth?" I watch them with a mixture of horror and fascination. My coffee's starting to go cold, but I don't care. I've lost my appetite. "Is this where our backup arrives three months later and finds Fortuna Tau empty? Are we about to become another episode of 'Great Space Mysteries of the Twenty-Fourth Century?"

Before them, the peacekeepers somehow look small and not very threatening. If it came to an all-out shitfight, they'd be no match for the Kordolians.

But it seems the boss peacekeeper has some sense in her, because she holds up a hand, signaling to her soldiers to lower their weapons.

"Good call, lady." Jia sighs with relief. "Lucky they sent Sergeant Varga and not some irrational musclehead jacked up on growth hormones." She rolls her eyes. "Peacekeepers. You know how they are. Varga's different, though. She's got a cool head on her shoulders."

"You know her?"

"Yeah. She runs security for us in the grease pits sometimes. She's a good sort." A look of mild relief crosses Jia's delicate features. "And now it looks like the Kordolians aren't going to kill them after all."

As the two groups lower their weapons, the Kordolians do something that seems to make their headgear melt away, revealing their faces.

"Nano-armor?" I mutter, grimly fascinated. It's scary how advanced these guys' technology is.

Without the helmets, we can see their features clearly.

Jia and I exchange a look of wonder. Of course, we've learned about Kordolians. We've all studied Universal Planetology in school. But seeing them up close is a shock.

"Wow," Jia whispers. I throw her a sidelong glance. Is that a blush spreading across her porcelain cheeks?

I sort of get where she's coming from. I hate to admit it, but these Kordolians are oddly attractive, in a surreal, alien kind of way.

I'm glad for the thick one-way glass windows of the café, because I'm staring like crazy. The Kordolians have light grey skin that appears almost sliver under the harsh lights. They're too far away for me to see their eyes, but I can make out strong, aristocratic features and hell, are those pointy ears? Impressive physiques seem to be a characteristic of their species. They're all tall and athletically built. Under that freakish black armor it looks as if there's a whole lot of muscle, but that's probably to be expected, because this seems to be some sort of team of super soldiers. I bet not all Kordolians look like these guys. There are probably imperfect looking ones somewhere back on their home planet. At least, I hope there are.

A race of perfect, deadly super-beings is just too overwhelming to think about.

But of all the aliens I've come across in the galaxy, these guys are the most humanoid looking I've ever seen. They have the same number of legs and arms and eyes and everything. No slimy bits, or scales, or tentacles. At least as far as I can tell. It's hard to know with all that armor. But they kind of remind me of big grey-skinned evil elves. I say evil, because they sure as hell don't look warm and cuddly.

One guy stands out amongst the group of Kordolian soldiers. He's obviously their commander, because he's the one doing all the talking. I squint, trying to get a better look at him. To my surprise, I can't tear my eyes away.

This guy commands attention. It's in the way he stands; arrogantly, threateningly, looming over Sergeant Varga as if he's expecting her to kneel or bow down in front of him.

He looks like he's used to being the biggest, baddest thing in the room, but even though he's intimidating, Sergeant Varga doesn't back down. She stares up at him, her body tense and rigid.

I haven't met the lady, but I decide I like her.

But this Kordolian boss is exactly the kind of guy I can't stand, alien or Human. I don't get along with arrogant jerks.

Jia draws my attention, a luminous expression on her face.

"Jia," I breathe, shaking my head. "Don't say it."

She looks back with wide eyes, her peachy lips slightly apart. "I've gotta say it, Abbey."

"Don't go there, Jia," I warn, my voice low and threatening.

Jia raises an eyebrow, ignoring my warning. "Gotta admit, they're kinda hot."

I resist the urge to drop my face into my hands. She went there. "They're killers."

"Sexy killers."

"Shut up, idiot." I make a face and gulp down the rest of my coffee, which has gone cold. I don't know why Jia's joking around irritates me so much. I slam the cup down, shovel in a few more mouthfuls of vanilla protein sludge and stand up, refusing to look at the Kordolians again. "I'm going back to work," I announce. "Break's over, anyway. And even if we're being invaded by evil elves wearing nano-suits, the bio-plant won't run itself. Meet you here same time tomorrow, if we're still alive?"

Jia blinks in confusion. "Elves? What?"

"You should read the classics. You know, Tolkien and so on." I wave my hand in the air as I slide out of the booth, turning my back on the scene unfolding below. As I exit, I tap the register with my hand, leaving my bio-print. It'll go to that nonexistent place in the digital ether and take payment from my already depleted account. "Come tomorrow," I call over my shoulder at a perplexed Jia. "I'll bring chocolate."

Then lunch break, with all its weirdness, is over, and I'm rushing back to the bio-plant, trying to forget about the Kordolians.

Damn mean-looking, pointy-eared, scary alien-elves. I just hope they don't try to kill us.

Tarak

I STARE DOWN at the Human soldiers, trying to ignore the growing ache pounding inside my skull. The bright artificial lights of the dock don't help, but at least they aren't ultraviolet. This is only the second time I've been to this planetary system, but I'm already dreading facing the star Humans call the Sun.

My kind aren't used to such conditions. We're sensitive to ultraviolet light. It's one of our few weaknesses.

"I told you," I growl in Universal, looming over the female soldier who has identified herself as the head of this rabble, "we are not assuming control of this station. We have no interest in Humans. We only require that you provide us with the resources and personnel to repair our craft. You will also clear this dock of any unnecessary Human workers while repairs are underway."

My team surrounds me, tense and ready to burst into action if needed. So far, this Human female has been sensible enough not to threaten us. For that at least, I have to applaud her instincts.

"With all due respect," she snaps back in passable, heavily accented Universal, "you and your men represent an unsanctioned arrival, and that is a breach of security protocol. There are procedures we need to follow before we can assist you with anything. I don't even know who you are. You could begin by at least having the decency to identify yourself."

I glare at her. Are all Humans this entitled? Is this female somehow confused? I'm a General of the Kordolian Empire. I don't have to explain shit to any species in the Nine Galaxies. Beside me, Rykal, our newest recruit, bristles, raising his plasma cannon. "Respect, female. Would you like me to remind you what it means?"

Underneath her ridiculous oversized helmet and bulky armor, the female soldier stiffens in outrage. "Is this how you Kordolians rule your empire? With threats?"

It's true, but I ignore her taunt. I hold up a hand, motioning for Rykal to stand down. "Patience," I murmur in Kordolian, too low for any of the Humans to hear. "Let me handle this. Fighting will just waste time, and we don't have much time."

I'm irritated as fuck, but I make the effort to soften my tone. "I am General Tarak al Akkadian of the Kordolian First Division. We have experienced an enemy attack and request temporary refuge on Fortuna Tau to repair our battle cruiser. We have been engaged in mid-space warfare and have arrived here unintentionally. We are *not* here on hostile terms."

The woman clearly doesn't believe me, because her expression hasn't changed. "You threatened to blow up the station if we didn't allow you to dock. How is that not hostile?"

I take a step forward, and a few Human trigger fingers twitch. They don't know that I can smell their fear. Even though we're outnumbered three to one by the Humans, they seem to recognize their natural predators.

Once upon a time, our ancestors might have considered them a food source.

The Humans are a strange looking species. Their skin comes in all shades of brown, from very pale to very dark, and their eyes are odd colors. Blue, green, brown, black. The soldiers before me are wearing old fashioned non-symbiotic combat gear. It doesn't suit the wearer's needs as well as our exo-suits.

I size them up and find them to be little of a threat.

I tower over their female leader, staring down into her blue eyes. To her credit, she doesn't flinch.

"Make no mistake," I say softly. "We *can* be hostile, if we wish. I am offering you the easy option. Are you going to waste my time, or not?"

"That's not my decision." There must be something in my voice, because she steps back, holding up her hands in surrender. "I'll take you to the Station Boss, but you all need to disarm."

I smile then, showing my fangs. Humans don't have fangs. They have straight, flat herbivore's teeth. "How about we keep our weapons and you take us to your boss?"

"But protocol dictates that—"

All this talk of protocol and rules. It's making my head hurt. The headache has crept behind my eyes, turning into an insistent, stabbing pain.

I'm out of patience.

"Rykal," I mutter, making a discreet signal with my hand. He knows what to do. Before the Human can blink, he moves, becoming a black blur of motion. He comes up behind her and disarms her. The Human's simple weapon drops to the floor with a metallic clatter. Her soldiers raise a sea of guns against us, but Rykal has a Callidum dagger pressed against her throat.

"Any of you so much as twitch and your boss dies. And so do

you." It's not an idle threat. We're bigger. Faster. Stronger. Our technology is better. They're outmatched, and they know it. "As I said before, it's not a request. It's a demand. And I am not interested in your 'protocol'. We will not disarm. We are not going anywhere."

The Human captive glares at me with her odd icy blue eyes, but she's smart enough not to resist.

"You stay here," I add, "as security. Any one of you decides to do something stupid, she dies. Rykal, that's your responsibility."

"Sir." He nods in assent.

I point to another Human, a male. He stares at us with a look of dismay. No doubt the ease at which Rykal took their commander hostage has shocked him. "You. What's your name?"

"Uh, Jacobs."

Such strange sounding Human names. Such fear and hesitation. We don't have time for this shit. I resist the urge to close my eyes and drop my face into my hands. My headache is getting worse. "You will show us the way. Call ahead and warn them not to mount any resistance. Any attempt to attack us will be met with consequences. Do not try my patience, Human. The rest of you stay here, and drop your weapons."

A muscular Human steps forward, outrage twisting his features. "Fuck you, alien. Think you can just enter our territory and do whatever you want?"

"Yes." My response is matter-of-fact and honest, but it sends him over the edge. He raises his cannon.

"Stand down, private, stand down!" The female commander shouts at him, straining against Rykal's strong arms. "They're fucking Kordolians. What do you expect to achieve here? You want to get all of us killed? Stand down. That's a direct order."

The Human looks at us, then at his boss, then back at us. There's anger in his eyes, but he can't disobey her command.

He lowers his weapon, laying it on the floor. Reluctantly, his comrades follow suit.

I issue orders to my troops in Kordolian, selecting two soldiers to accompany me. The rest will stay behind to guard the ship and keep an eye on the Humans.

A nervous silence has settled over the Humans as they watch us, fearful and unsure of themselves.

It's a look I'm used to. Our reputation is well known throughout the Nine Galaxies, even in this shitty backwater of the Universe. Luckily for the Humans, they seem to have above average intelligence, or at least their leader does.

Some species would have attacked by now, inviting all-out slaughter.

"Jacobs." I motion to the Human I've randomly picked out.

"Sir?" His response is instinctive, an automatic reaction to my commanding tone of voice. Military personnel are the same, the Universe over.

"What are you waiting for? Lead the way."

He looks back and forth between me and the female commander. She signals for him to move with an irritated flick of her head. Underneath his armor, he looks young. I don't know much about Human lifespans, but he seems to be little more than an adolescent.

With small, hesitant steps, he starts to lead us out of the dock. I come up behind him. "I'm impatient today, private," I whisper in his ear. He shudders and picks up the pace. Two of my soldiers, Arkan and Kalan, follow behind, their plasma cannons ready.

If anyone tries anything, we will set them to vaporize and blow a hole out the side of this fucking rust bucket.

"Speed it up," I growl, taking position at the back of the formation. It's my preferred location in any team. I like to guard the back and see what's going on at the front.

My headache is pounding now. It's almost unbearable, but I grit my teeth and force myself to ignore it.

We're running out of time.

In the middle of a speedfight with enemy Xargek, we were accidentally sucked into a wormhole, and it spat us out in this remote corner of the Universe. Now, the unstable wormhole is collapsing. We need to get off this station. Somewhere out there is a ship full of Xargek monsters that I need to hunt down and kill.

And I'll die before I end up stuck on some poorly maintained Human outpost in the middle of nowhere. The sooner we're gone, the better.

Abbey

ON THE WAY back to the lab, I hear footsteps behind me. Because we've just been invaded by terrifying aliens, I'm a little bit on edge, so I whirl around and come face to face with the very last beings I wanted to see.

Three Kordolians glare at me. They're accompanied by a very scared looking peacekeeper. The poor kid looks barely seventeen, his eyes nervous and wide in a pale, freckled face.

The alien commander looms at the back of their little convoy, silent and scary. He wears a thunderous expression on his face. I freeze in shock, taking in his otherworldly appearance. Up close, he's even more striking, his luminous grey skin almost shimmering under the artificial light. His eyes, I realize, are a deep shade of red, the color of wine. They're hard, brutal eyes. He has the look of a killer, and he looks pissed off.

These Kordolians are huge. They tower above the kid and I, filling the wide passageway, making it seem small. A claustrophobic feeling works its way into my gut, and I press my back against the wall as they pass, trying to appear as insignificant as possible.

I hope to hell they don't notice me. I pray that they're too busy with whatever it is they're doing and that they'll just get on their merry way.

But at the last minute, the commander turns, his harsh gaze fixing on me. My heart sinks. He gives me a quick up-and-down, and I do my best to keep a neutral expression on my face.

Stay calm, I tell myself. I figure these guys are like most predators. When they smell fear, it only encourages them.

The Kordolian narrows his eyes, his nostrils flaring slightly.

Why do I suddenly feel as if he's the hunter, and I'm dinner?

It's making me squirmy. I get an overwhelming urge to sidestep him and scurry off back to my lab, but I don't think he'd take that too well.

Don't make any sudden moves.

I don't want him to think I'm about to try something reckless. The last thing I want to do is end up as Abbey mincemeat, splattered across the service corridor.

The Kordolian inclines his head. He really does have pointed ears, like an elf.

A stupid, irrational giggle threatens to burst from my lips. I suppress it with all my might.

Wrong place, wrong time. Being scared out of my wits is probably making me delirious.

Stop it, Abbey. Don't make the big, bad alien angry.

Is this what happens in life-or-death situations? I think I've read about something like this. Detachment from reality. Inappropriate hysterics. These are the symptoms of temporary insanity.

Say something. Make him go away.

"Er, hi there," I say in Universal. Everyone who goes into space has to learn Universal. It's a Federation requirement. "You guys seem to be in a hurry, so I'll just get out of your way." A tiny, nervous laugh escapes me, and immediately, I'm kicking myself.

Seriously Abbey? Was that the best thing you could could come up with?

I hold my breath, waiting for his reaction. I try not to stare at his pointy ears and menacing red eyes and rather overwhelming, muscular torso. Because that nano-armor stuff is quite, ah, sculpted. It doesn't really leave much to the imagination.

"Is something amusing, woman?" His deep voice resonates in the confines of the corridor. It's exactly how I was expecting him to sound. Arrogant. Authoritative. A guy who always gets his way.

If he weren't so intimidating, I'd find him annoying, but the only word that comes to my mind is *scary*. I hold up my hands in what I hope is a placating gesture. "I'm not amused," I blurt. "Far from it. I was just thinking about all the things I have to do this afternoon. You know, DNA splicing, plasmid engineering, cleaning oxygen filters, that kind of thing. So I may have come across a little preoccupied." It's half-true. I *was* thinking about those things, but I was somewhat distracted by the fact that we've just been overrun by some of the most dangerous beings in space.

He stares at me blankly, saying nothing.

As if he has no idea what I'm talking about.

"I'm a scientist," I elaborate. "Cleaning biomeric oxygen filters isn't glamorous, but someone has to do it."

Still, he says nothing. I have a bad habit of saying too much when I'm nervous. It's gotten me into trouble on occasion.

His deep red stare never wavers. He narrows his eyes, reaching out with a black-gloved hand. I flinch.

You've gone and done it now, Abbey.

Then his fingers are plucking something from my hair. It's a piece of greenery; a bit of leaf from a passionfruit vine. It probably got stuck there when I crawled through the hydroponic vents, looking for fruits that had been missed in the harvest.

He stares at the leaf critically, then at me, then back at the leaf, shaking his head. He mutters something under his breath in his native language.

Then, in a rush of weapons and armor and sharply issued commands, they're gone, storming down the passageway, disappearing from view. And once again, the service corridor feels empty, as if their departure has left a vacuum. It's as if our little encounter never happened.

Relief rushes through me and I let out a deep breath.

On a positive note, at least I didn't get killed.

"Crazy Kordolians," I grumble, running my fingers self-consciously through my hair. Why should I care about what some muscle-bound, galaxy-colonizing, silver-skinned asshole thinks?

Why is my heart still pounding?

I sigh, shaking the tension out of my body, blowing a puff of air through my lips. I don't know what they're doing on our station or what they want, and I really don't care.

I just want to get back to work. As long as they're not here to colonize the station in the name of the Kordolian Empire and ship us all off to some remote outpost for nefarious purposes, then I'm fine. They haven't blown anything up yet and they haven't shot at anyone, so I'm secretly hopeful that they're just passing by.

Maybe they just want a place where they can fix up their battle cruiser before taking off to carry on with whatever they were doing in the first place.

They sure as hell aren't here because they *want* to be here. We Humans and our little planet don't rank very highly on the intergalactic desirability index, and ever since the Nine Galaxies were mapped, we've come to the realization that we're actually not the center of the Universe. Far from it. Most aliens consider us a far-flung, underdeveloped backwater, not worth even fighting about. We've already damaged enough of our own planet without the help of aliens, thank-you very much.

I've never even heard of Kordolians traveling this far out of their way. Has a Kordolian even set foot in the Solar System before? I sure as hell hope they're just lost, because with every-thing that's happening on Earth right now, the last thing we need is a dominant alien race coming and recruiting us under the guise of benevolent rule. Maybe their Galactic Atlas malfunctioned.

I shudder a little before pulling myself together, catching my errant thoughts before they spiral downwards into full-on scary panic-mode territory.

No point in worrying about things I can't do anything about.

On the other hand, the oxygen filters won't change them-selves, and I have chocolate stashed in my locker. It always does wonders for curing feelings of imminent doom.

Just the thought of it is making me feel better already.

CHAPTER TWO

Tarak

The boss of the mining station occupies a floor high above the Human workers' factories and offices. There's a reception type area at the entrance, and for a utilitarian industrial station such as this, it's surprisingly opulent.

The polished floors are made of rare black Jentian stone, and there is green vegetation trailing up the glass walls, attached to metal trellises.

Again, the lights are irritatingly bright, serving to perpetuate my headache.

Humans must have poor dark-vision. It has to be the only reason they insist on illuminating the entire place like a flaring star.

The space is seemingly empty, but from a distance, I hear something.

Footsteps. Arkan and Kalan sense the same. We're at a kind of junction, the passageway stretching out in both directions in front of the cavernous space.

"They're trying to cut us off." Kalan hefts his giant plasma cannon over his shoulder and gets down on one knee, pointing it down the empty corridor.

I sense tiny vibrations. The disturbance is coming from dozens of Human footsteps.

Arkan takes the other direction, drawing his twin rapid-fire plasma rifles.

It seems as if the Humans are stupid enough to try and ambush us, after all.

Their loss.

"Full armor," I snap, and the nanites of my exo-suit whirr and click, forming a helmet that protects my face. I get some relief from the harsh lights as the combat visor covers my eyes, its datafeed throwing up numbers and graphics in my vision. It tells me Human enemies approach from both directions.

Just as we'd sensed.

I grab Jacobs' arm and he whirls to face me, in a panic. "If you don't want your comrades to die, get your ass up to wherever your leader is hiding and tell him to call off this death wish. Otherwise the fifty or so Human soldiers who think they're about to get the jump on us will end up painting the walls. Don't you know that your weapons can't penetrate our armor? There's nothing your soldiers can do."

"I have nothing to do with this," he stutters. "I swear."

"I don't care. Get your Station Boss down here now. I'm out of patience." I turn to my subordinate, who is now similarly decked out in full battle armor. "Kalan, fire a warning shot. You know the drill."

"About time you decided to go hostile, general," Kalan replies. "These Humans are just fucking around." He steadies himself, and pulls the trigger. A loud boom follows, and screams echo down the corridor.

Jacobs looks back and forth in alarm.

"Run, Human," I tell him. He wastes no time, scurrying off to enter an elevator.

Although the visor has dimmed the effects of the harsh lights, it hasn't helped my pounding head at all. A small part of me wishes I could retreat to the cruiser and pop a few of the pills I normally take to help me sleep. I squash that weak, pathetic voice in disgust.

We're running out of time, and I need results, fast.

Cold logic tells me I should kill all the approaching Humans. But death is a punishment best saved for last, when there are no other options left. I need the Humans co-operative, because I need their machinery, their resources, and their expertise.

We're soldiers, not mechanics.

Basic military strategy dictates that I should gain cooperation of the leadership first. Only once that option fails do we go on the offensive.

I need these Humans to understand that one does not make an enemy of Kordolians.

The female soldier down in the dock understood it.

The strange female scientist I encountered in the corridor understood it.

This so-called Station Boss had better understand it. For their sake, and for ours.

We need to repair our battle cruiser and get back into the wormhole before it collapses. Otherwise, we'll have to return the long way, stuck on a six-cycle long roundabout trip across the outer sectors of the Nine fucking Galaxies.

I don't have time for that shit. There's a Xargek warship floating around out there, and we need to hunt it down.

"What in Kaiin's name is taking so long?" The pain is in both of my temples now, insistent and merciless. I'm in a mood to fight, but I need a worthy opponent, not some slow, feeble Human.

Killing these weaklings would just be a waste of plasma cartridges.

We wait, tense and ready, and the footsteps of the Human reinforcements become louder. They're approaching.

Still, that damn Jacobs doesn't appear. Perhaps he's run off to hide, like a coward.

I clench my teeth in frustration. "I'm going up," I announce, drawing my twin Callidum blades from where they're sheathed at my back. They're better for fighting in close quarters. There's a staircase to the left of the elevator. I head towards it. If the

Station Boss doesn't want to come out, I'll hunt him down. "Hold the position."

Kalan and Arkan nod in agreement. We've done this sort of thing a hundred times before. As a crowd of Human soldiers converges on us from both sides, I disappear into the stairwell, taking the steps four at a time. I use the synergistic movement of the exo-suit to my advantage, passing four or five floors to reach the top of the stairs.

I figure the Station Boss will be hiding at the top. Most leaders like to position themselves high up. I'm assuming this Human won't be any different.

Throughout all the galaxies, intelligent lifeforms tend to behave in the same manner.

The doors at the top are sealed with some sort of security code. I stab my blade into the glowing panel on the wall, the sharpened Callidum slicing through the components with ease. A shower of sparks flies out and an alarm goes off, bathing me in red, flashing light.

Oh, for fuck's sake.

I kick the twin doors and they shudder open, sliding to reveal a dimly lit hallway.

There's thick, plush carpet underfoot. I snort in grim amusement. It's a wasteful, indulgent choice. As I make my way down the corridor, a faint hum causes me to turn. I raise my sword and slice through a flying drone, a shower of sparks cascading to the floor as the cut halves of the machine drop noiselessly onto the dark carpet.

In the same motion, I turn and bring my sword down through a second drone that has approached me from behind.

Sparks go everywhere, spitting onto the dark carpet. Small fires start to burn, emitting chemical smoke.

I start to run, heading for the big, ornate doors at the end of the passage. Two Human guards are stationed at the entrance, and they start firing at me with their laser weapons as I approach.

Their shots glance off my armor as if they're nothing. I hold my blades low and close to my body as they raise their weapons for another shot.

"Don't," I order, running straight past them, kicking open the wide double doors. In a place where space is at a premium, they're the old-fashioned swinging type.

Swinging doors. On an industrial station. Really? These Humans are crazy.

The guards fire half-heartedly after me, but my exo-suit absorbs the shocks. I pull a Callidum throwing dagger from a sheath at my thigh and flick it over my shoulder. I don't look back. It must have done something, because the irritating firing stops.

I glance around the space I've entered.

Two pale Human faces stare back at me in shock. I'm standing in the center of a spacious room. It's framed by wide windows that look out onto the vast emptiness of space. Of course, one of Humans is Jacobs, and the one beside him must be the Station Boss.

Jacobs' face has turned an odd shade of red. Humans have this strange thing they do when they're upset. They change color. It happened with the female scientist too. Her cheeks turned a shade of light pink.

With Jacobs, it makes him look ridiculous. But with the female, I found it strangely endearing.

She was small and delicate and smelt incredible, a mixture of exotic blooms and fruits from far-off planets. For a moment, when I was with her, my headache disappeared.

I vanquish the memory from my mind. What a ridiculous thing to think about right now. I wonder if being around Humans is making me stupid.

"Stop right there, Kordolian!" The Station Boss takes a step forward. Unlike the soldiers we encountered in the dock, this Human looks older, his thinning hair shot through with traces of grey. The skin beneath his eyes is loose and dark, and he carries excess fat around his waist. "You are under arrest. Trespassing on sovereign Federation property is an offense."

"Under whose jurisdiction?" I move forward, looming over the sweating Human.

"You're on a Federation station, Kordolian. We are still governed by Earth Law. I have two squadrons of peacekeepers on the way. You're outnumbered. I would advise you to stand down."

"Peacekeepers?" I stare down at him through my visor. The datafeed tells me his heart rate is high, his breathing is rapid and his temperature is rising. He's afraid. "Your peacekeepers aren't coming. You really think you can win a siege against a fully armed Kordolian Elite Division?"

I pick up the sound of movement behind me and realize the two guards are approaching. They think to surprise me. I pretend not to notice.

"I'm out of patience, Station Boss." He stares in wide-eyed horror as I turn, my movements enhanced by my armor. I execute a wide slash that takes off the head of one of the guards as he raises his laser weapon at me. The second guard is frozen, unable to move. I've plunged my other blade into his chest. Crimson blood erupts from his lips as he falls backward onto the carpeted floor.

So Humans bleed red. Strange creatures.

"I need your cooperation, Station Boss." I reach the fat Human's side before he can escape. "I need access to the supplies and materials on your station, and assistance from the Humans who operate your spacecraft repair service. I'm tired, Station Boss, and for that reason, I'd rather not kill any more of your people, but if you continue to make stupid decisions, that's what will happen. I'm offering you a choice. But you're the one in charge, so it's your call. Will you cooperate with us, or will you continue this stupid resistance?"

Fear. It's one of the most useful tools in a war. The first thing we were taught in the military academy was how to instill and manipulate fear.

Create fear. Dominate. Rule.

It's what we Kordolians do.

The Station Boss will fold. I can tell from his stance. They always do.

"W-we'll help," he stutters, looking at me as if I'm a monstrous Xargek. I might as well be, with my full Callidum exo-armor in place. I'm sure the battle suit was designed to intimidate as well as provide the wearer with protection.

"Wise decision. I will send someone with a list of our requirements. If the idea of fighting us enters your thick skull again, think about what just happened to your guards."

"Uhh," he makes a low-pitched sound of shock, as a low boom reverberates through the walls.

"Oh, and you might want to call off your troops downstairs, before any more of them are killed." I turn to leave, sidestepping the bodies of the two guards. As I reach the doorway, my comm buzzes.

"Rykal. What is it?"

"Uh, General, we have a problem down here."

"What's the problem, Rykal?"

"We just saw several Xargek larvae escaping our ship."

I drop several colorful Kordolian expletives. "How the hell did they get on board? I thought we left them on the other side of the wormhole. Did you kill the larvae?"

"Shot three, one got away. Disappeared into a vent."

"Get a team to scour this station. We have to find it before it grows and starts to reproduce." I don't really care about the fate of the Humans. But there's no way I can allow the Xargek to survive. All it takes is one larva, and suddenly half the sector will be swarming with the creatures. And if their warship has made it into this sector, then it's only a matter of time before they find a habitable planet.

And then, they'll start to multiply. I can't afford to let that happen.

Eliminate them at all costs. Those are our orders.

"Sir." Rykal grunts in agreement, and logs off. I turn to the Station Boss, who has managed to assume position behind his desk. He's on some kind of comm, issuing orders in another

Human language. I make a slicing motion with my hand, and he cuts the communication, dropping the receiver onto his desk.

"The situation's changed," I inform him. "The station's going on lockdown, as of now. Tell all Humans to return to their quarters and stay there until we've found and killed every single last one of those Xargek vermin. Anyone who disobeys our orders does so at their own risk. I won't be responsible for any harm that occurs as a result."

"Xargek?" The Station Boss' pale eyes go wide, the color draining from his face. 'There are Xargek on Fortuna?" His voice has dropped to a whisper.

"Lockdown," I repeat. "Right now, we're your only hope of survival, so don't fuck things up."

Abbey

I'M in the outer dome of the oxygen filter plant, a huge structure that stretches over the sun-facing side of Fortuna Tau, when the announcement crackles through the speakers.

"All workers return to your quarters. I repeat, all workers return to your quarters. This is a state of emergency. Full lockdown commencing now. Do not, under any circumstances, leave your quarters unless directed to do so. This is an order from Station High Command."

I pause mid-scrub, flicking phytogel from my gloved hands. A droplet of goop lands on my safety goggles, obscuring my vision. I rub at it, but that only makes it worse, as I accidentally smear viscous slime across the lenses.

I'm about a hundred feet above the floor of the biomeric facility, stuck between rows of oxygen filters. Every day, millions of liters of carbon dioxide is pumped through the filters, and fresh oxygen is generated through photosynthesis, to be recirculated throughout Fortuna Tau.

That's where the green slime comes in. It sits in the filter cartridges, absorbs a bit of sunlight, and basically photosynthesizes.

In theory, it's genius. In practice, the filters often become blocked. That's where I come in. Amongst the bio-sci staff, I'm pretty much the only one crazy enough to climb a hundred meters up a flimsy ladder and dodge in and out of the complex maze of filters and pipes like a monkey, scrubbing at the caked green slime.

The fact that I did gymnastics as a kid probably helps. I'm not afraid of heights and my balance is pretty good.

It sounds like an awful job, but I actually like it up here. It's quiet. I can see glimpses of the stars through gaps in the machinery. And the soft, rhythmic hum of the filter plant is actually quite soothing.

It also helps that I'm short. My body was designed for navigating small, twisty spaces.

A shrill alarm follows the announcement, along with repeated blasts of "return to quarters," in a pre-recorded, robotic voice. I groan. I've just climbed all the way up here, and now I have to leave?

I peer down through an opening in the machinery, but all I can see is the green canopy of the biosphere below. My co-workers have probably forgotten that I'm even up here.

And if I don't clear out the blocked filters now, there's a chance the whole system could become backed up, resulting in a build-up of pressure in the CO_2 pipes.

Pressure equals explosion. The last thing we need right now is a circulation malfunction.

No doubt the Kordolians have something to do with this lockdown order. But for some reason, I feel a little less scared now. Maybe it has to do with the fact that the boss alien actually stared me down in the corridor and didn't kill me, even though I'd somehow offended him with my smirking.

I pull my goggles off and wipe them on my pants, removing the smear of green slime. The rickety metal ladder stretches down the wall behind me, disappearing into the leafy thicket. I reach up with my sleeve and wipe sweat from my forehead. It's humid up here under the thick glass panels, and now and then, beads of condensation turn into fat droplets of water, catching me in the face or hair.

It's the closest thing we have up here to rain.

I really miss Earth.

I decide I'm going to ignore the evacuation order and finish my work. It's so quiet and isolated up here that I doubt anyone is going to find me. And I don't expect the Kordolians to show any interest in the biomeric facility. Even if they do, they'll never find me. I know every nook and cranny of this maze-like place.

I don't want to go back to my sterile, windowless sleeping pod. What am I going to do there for the next several hours? Watch NetCom and chill?

Boring.

I grab the brush and hose, spraying a jet of cool water into my mouth before I point it at the oxygen filters. This is thirsty work. As I hose off the area, bits of caked, greenish-brownish slime start to dislodge, and the wastewater falls to the forest below, feeding the trees.

I smile to myself. While everyone else is stuck in their prison-like quarters, I'll just hide out here, and carry on with this rather enjoyable work.

Hopefully, when I'm done, the Kordolians will be gone.

I start to whistle an old Earth tune, not worrying if I'll be discovered. Because up here, no-one can hear me.

Tarak

I FIND Kalan and Arkan in the lobby below, with the Human soldiers nowhere to be seen.

"Tactical retreat on their side, apparently." Kalan shrugs. "We got the all-clear?"

"An agreement has been reached. The Humans will cooper-ate." We break into a rapid jog, returning the way we came. As we turn down another narrow passageway, a shrill announcement in some Human dialect blasts from hidden speakers, unintelligible to us.

It must be a lockdown order.

The warning is followed by a shrieking alarm, blasted at incredibly high volume.

With my headache throbbing at full force, it's almost too much for my sensitive hearing. Pain shoots behind my eyes, blurring my vision. I slow down.

Kalan and Arkan glance backwards in alarm, sensing my drop in pace.

"Return to ship," I bark over the noise of the siren, not wanting them to see my weakness. "I have something to do here. Tell Rykal to prepare a list of requirements for the Humans and get them to work. Dissolve the Human soldiers, but keep their female commander as a translator. She seems to have some sense. I will join you afterwards."

"Sir!" Without another word they take off, not sparing me a second glance. That's what I like about this team. They follow my orders to the letter.

And there's no way I'm letting them know that all I need right now is a rest.

I need something to ease the fucking pain in my head. When will that Kaiin-cursed Human noise stop? Why do they have to make it so loud? Are Humans partly deaf?

I will my helmet to retract, taking a deep breath, suddenly needing fresh air.

There's that scent again.

It's exotic and fragrant, carrying with it a hint of mystery. It's like nothing I've ever smelt before. It's complex, with hints of sweetness and bitterness combined.

It smells of *her*, the female scientist. That strange, tiny Human, who turns a delicate shade of pink when confronted and babbles nonsense through her tiny lips.

The infernal siren wails on and on, and I'm about to go to my knees with the agony of it. I close my eyes, following the scent, allowing it to lead me as it becomes stronger, more intoxicating.

It's as if the Goddess Kali has wound her ephemeral tendrils around me and I'm powerless to resist as she pulls me along. I'm almost forgetting my headache as I find myself outside a glass doorway.

A pair of terrified Humans stumble past, glancing up at me in horror as I walk past. They make no effort to stop me as I stride beyond the entrance.

I travel down a narrow, brightly lit corridor and come out in a space I can only describe as impossible.

The scent is overwhelming here, surrounding me and filling my lungs. The air is cooler, cleaner, and all around me are signs of life. The place is filled with vegetation. There are strange, exotic fruits, the likes of which I've never seen before. Bizarrely shaped flowers appear amongst the foliage, revealing colors I never knew existed.

Things like this could never grow on Kythia. There's not enough light.

The space is housed in a giant dome-like structure, lined with orderly arrays of panels. Real light from the sun filters through the gaps between the panels, causing me to squint, the bright, ultraviolet light blurring my vision. I command my nanites to form a pair of light-goggles, shielding my eyes. But I leave the rest of my face uncovered, savoring the clean, fresh oxygen.

The infuriating siren has finally stopped. I exhale slowly, trying to force the tension from my body. My head is still killing me, but it's not as bad as before.

I just need a moment, to close my eyes and forget the noise and pain.

Just a short moment, away from it all.

Even I have my bad days.

I need to rest, even if it's just for a few *sivs*. I spot a bench type structure alongside a winding path that leads into thick vegetation.

I'll lie down until my headache is less severe. I can't afford to be walking around with blurred vision, sensitive to every alarm because of this ridiculous pain. I can't afford to take sedatives, either. Not when there are Xargek larvae crawling around the station. I have to be alert.

I need to restore my level of functioning. This vegetation dome seems as good a place as any for that purpose. The Humans have all left, and it's mercifully quiet. If any Xargek appears, I'll be able to hear its insectoid skittering long before it can attack.

I lay my swords on the floor beside the bench and lie down, closing my eyes. I allow the sun-goggles to dissolve, because the mild warmth beating down on my face from the bright star above is actually quite pleasant.

It's a rare moment of weakness, but for me, it's necessary. Lately, my headaches have been getting worse and worse.

The scent of the Earth vegetation and fruit seems to have healing properties. Because my pain starts to melt away. And as I slow my breathing to its lowest possible rate and force my heart rate down, I hear something.

Strange Human sounds. An odd, wordless type of singing, soft and uneven.

It should be irritating. But somehow, I don't mind it at all. It's imperfect and uniquely Human.

I open my eyes just briefly, and squint. The sound's coming from the roof of the dome. Between the panels.

It's *her*. Her scent reaches my sensitive nose, mingling with the smell of chemicals and sweet fruits and fragrant blooms.

I thought all Humans were confined to quarters. Is this one defying Station orders?

The panels are suspended high above the vegetation. I can't see much. Is the female really up there? There's no way I'm climbing the flimsy looking structure to find out.

Instead, I close my eyes, waiting for the pounding in my head to subside.

CHAPTER THREE

Abbey

After I finish cleaning the cluster of blocked oxygen filters, I'm covered in green gunk. The mush has a strange leafy smell, like chopped celery. My hair is matted with sweat, and my protective goggles are smeared with the green stuff. I pull them off, stuffing them in the top pocket of my scrubs.

Grabbing the narrow rails of the ladder with my gloved hands, I balance precariously, making a slow descent. The ladder creaks a little as it takes my weight.

My late father would have had a fit if he saw me like this. As the chief scientist of a big biotech company on Earth, he was big on the whole occupational health and safety side of things.

Here on Fortuna? They're not so big on safety. What happens in deep space stays in deep space, right?

Station Boss Emin runs a tight ship. Rumors are he cuts costs and skims a little on the side for himself, depositing it in a secret off-planet tax haven.

Apparently, that's the reason they've started enforcing lights-off during the night-cycle. In order to save electricity, we have to walk around the dark corridors with freaking headlamps on.

Tightasses.

Cost-cutting is part of the reason I have to manually clean the filters up here. A robot cleaner has supposedly been on order for *months* now. It's turned into a bit of a running joke amongst the bio-sci people.

I reach the floor and make my way down the narrow winding path that takes me past a row of hyper-productive fruit trees. In the biomeric facility, we've got supergrafted Earth trees jacked up on plant growth factors. The current growth cycle for apples from bud to fruit is one week. The trees supplement the oxygen filters, cleaning the air.

That's why it always smells fresh in here.

The outside, especially the quarters, can get a bit stinky at times. When you have thousands of human beings crammed into a giant floating rust-bucket, it's to be expected.

That's why I'd much prefer to hide out in the biomeric dome during a Kordolian takeover. Not to mention there are all the apples, peaches and cherries I can eat.

As I reach the little bend in the path near the front entrance, I freeze.

Someone is staring at me.

"You!" I gape at the Kordolian. He's sitting on the bench we jokingly call the loveseat. "You're not supposed to be in here!" This place is off-limits to the general population. Only authorized workers are allowed in here, but station protocol would mean nothing to a hard-faced warrior like this Kordolian.

"Human." A look of displeasure crosses his face. He's wearing funny little blacked-out sun-goggles that look like an extension of his freaky nano-armor. "You were ordered to return to your chambers."

He stands up, grabbing a pair of menacing looking blades. He secures them at his back as he approaches. "Why have you disobeyed the orders of your Station Boss?"

"I was in the middle of a critical task." To my relief, my voice is steady, even though my heart is racing.

"You would disregard your own safety for the sake of your work?"

I study him for a moment, then take a calculated risk. Something tells me that fear and meekness won't get me far with this fearsome alien. I have to appear confident and in control. I have to convince him of the importance of what I'm doing. "See those oxygen filters up there? I was cleaning them. The dirt buildup can cause a critical malfunction if it isn't attended to promptly. My *work* ensures a clean air supply. So I'm sorry if you were upset I didn't rush back to my pod, but other things took priority. Like making sure everyone has air to breathe." I narrow my eyes, taking in the Kordolian's intimidating appearance. He's good at looming threateningly, this one. His grey lips are pressed together in disapproval. He takes another step forward and I shuffle backwards, scoping out the nearest escape route from the edge of my vision.

If I had to, I'd probably climb back up into the filter plant. He looks too heavy to go up there.

I hope his nano-suit doesn't allow him to fly. That would complicate things.

Do Kordolians fly?

"Do all Human females have such little care for decorum?" He looks me up and down critically, my reflection flashing in his black goggles.

"Decorum?" I stifle a laugh. The word sounds so old-fashioned, even in Universal. I must look terrible with green gunk staining my work attire and my hair tousled like a bird's nest, but when has that ever bothered me? "This is a mining station. We're here to work. You know how hard it is not to chip a nail when you're scrubbing caked-up phytogel? That's why I keep these babies short." I wriggle my gloved fingers. "I don't know what you expect of your ladies back home, but this is the twenty-fourth century. I'm not out to impress anyone."

"Hm."

"Anyway," I hesitate, trying not to squirm under his implacable stare. "Er, how should I address you?"

"You may call me General," he says haughtily, s if he's giving me *permission* to address him.

"General, then." So we're not on first-name terms just yet. Or even surname terms. It's just 'General'. "Are you claiming

Fortuna Tau? Are we now under Kordolian rule? Is that what this takeover is all about?"

He inclines his head, his expression completely unreadable. A gentle shaft of sunlight beams down from above, making his silvery grey skin glisten. His hair is a shade lighter than his skin, almost white. Soldiers the universe over seem to have the same regulations, because his hair is done in a neat crew-cut.

So quickly I almost miss it, his pointed ears twitch.

What does that even mean? Is that some kind of Kordolian tell for being pissed off?

"Would it bother you," he asks softly, "if that were the case?"

"Of course it would," I reply without thinking. "I don't want to be shipped off to be some alien's pet on a distant planet somewhere." If he's going to strip me of my freedom, there's nothing much I can do except make my feelings known. Some might think me crazy. Perhaps I am. My bravado is born of anxiety, fear, necessity, and a little bit of defiance.

"Hm." He stares at me again, in that quiet, serious way of his.

"You don't give much away, do you?"

Infuriatingly, he doesn't say anything in response. It's like trying to get information out of a brick. Instead, he lifts his gaze to the arrays of oxygen filters attached to the domed ceiling. He changes the subject. "These devices. You say they are important for air quality, and they require ongoing maintenance?"

"Yes and yes. I've only finished one cluster. I was just going for a chocolate break. Then back to work."

"What is this 'chocolate' you speak of?" He inclines his head, the unfamiliar word sounding strange as it escapes his lips. Of course, there's no word in Universal to describe chocolate, so I've used the English equivalent.

"General," I gasp in mock-horror, unable to resist the chance to take a jibe. Do aliens have a sense of humor? Little by little, I'm taking my liberties, wondering when he's going to lose patience and reel me in. For some reason, his demeanor —more curious than threatening—tells me I can do this. "Until you've eaten chocolate, you have not lived. I'm happy to share my stash with you."

I receive a blank stare in response. "I doubt Human food would be palatable to our kind."

Okay, so the guy's sense of humor is pretty much nonexistent. Can't blame a girl for trying to lighten the atmosphere.

"You will carry on with your assigned task," he announces imperiously after a brief silence. "You will be assigned a guard."

"Guard?" Taken aback, I stare at him. "That's a bit extreme, don't you think? I'm not going to run away or start an underground revolution, I promise." Besides, what could *I* possibly do against a squadron of invading Kordolians?

"As you your role is important for the function of this Station, the guard is for your protection."

"Protection? Against what?"

I'm met with a stubborn, cryptic wall of silence. He regards me silently for a moment, completely ignoring my question. Then he walks away, leaving me to stare after him. Damn his well-built, muscular, tightly-armored ass. I have never met such an infuriating person, uh, alien, in my life.

"Doesn't want to try chocolate," I mutter under my breath. "You don't know what you're missing out on, Kordolian."

I swear his ears twitch a little bit as he disappears around the corner.

Tarak

I RETURN to our battle cruiser, aptly named *Silence*, to find work commencing on the damaged hull. Even though the metal the Humans mine here is far inferior to Callidum, it will be suitable for a temporary patch that will hopefully last for the duration of our journey back to Kythia.

Human workers swarm all over the ship like insects, operating small droids that are busy cutting, welding and hammering. The noise echoes throughout the expansive dock, and I'm thankful I've had time to rest. It's done wonders for my pounding headache. To my surprise, the pain in my temples is almost gone.

I find Rykal in the middle of a tense exchange with the female soldier he took hostage. Now that the Station Boss has seen reason, there's no need for further threats, and he's allowed her to walk free, at least for now.

She's removed her heavy armor and oversized helmet, revealing cropped golden hair.

Despite the tone of their conversation, Rykal looks relaxed, almost amused. I signal him and he strides over to my side.

"Did you find the Xargek larvae?"

"No sign of it yet, boss. The rest of the boys are scouring the Station. They've left me here to keep an eye on the repairs."

I swear under my breath. Time's running out. I don't want to leave this place without exterminating the remaining Xargek, but the wormhole will collapse soon. If there's a Xargek ship floating about, they'll gravitate towards the nearest source of food sooner or later. That just happens to be the Humans. We can't leave without destroying the Xargek, but we can't afford to lose the wormhole. This little dilemma is starting to give me a headache again. I decide to worry about the problem later. It's better to focus on what can be done now. "How long until repairs are complete?"

"The Humans have told me half of one of their daylight cycles, which equates to approximately one-half revolution."

"That's longer than I expected."

"Their tools are primitive."

"So it seems," I grumble. A Kordolian tech team would be useful right now, but *Silence's* usual crew are back on base in Sector Three. I'd left them there for a reason, using the short weapons calibration run as an excuse to bring my inner circle—my trusted First Division—into the silent zone, away from any potential Empire spies. My intention had been to debrief them on highly sensitive matters, but now my plans will have to wait.

The fucking Xargek had come out of nowhere.

It was almost as if they had anticipated us.

"It appears there's nothing we can do to speed up the

process," I say softly. "We just need to let them work and hope that the others eliminate the Xargek in time."

Rykal grunts in agreement, his amber gaze flicking across to the Human female.

"And Rykal?"

"Boss?"

"Don't get too friendly with the locals," I warn. "This isn't a recreation stop. The High Council looks down on inter-species mating."

"What happens off-planet, stays off-planet, right, sir? You know we've all indulged in a little 'exotic fruit' from time to time." His voice is filled with dark humor.

"Rykal," I growl, shooting him a glare. He dips his head in assent. "Any trouble on your watch and I'll put you on cleaning detail for the next five orbits."

"Understood." He slinks away, unable to completely suppress his smug expression as I make my way into the battle cruiser. I navigate the dimly lit interior, passing racks of ammunition and weapons until I reach the medical bay.

The First Division's healer is sitting in front of a holocell display, flicking through data. As I enter, she looks up, raising an elegant lilac eyebrow. "Headaches again, General?"

"Zyara." I lower myself into the observation chair, allowing my exo-armor to retract, leaving my torso bare. "This one was worse than usual. I need to you take a look."

"So you're finally giving me a chance to examine you. You should have come sooner, you know." Zyara rolls her eyes, snorting softly. "Males. You always think that if you ignore it, it will go away." Her slender hands attach lines and monitors to my arms and chest, and she brings up a small holoscreen. Numbers and charts flicker across the display. To me, it's just meaningless medical data.

Zyara frowns.

"What is it?" I study her reaction impatiently, but Zyara says nothing. Whether it's in the midst of battle or navigating *Silence* through a meteor storm, nothing shakes this female.

It's why she was chosen as the medic for the notorious First Division.

She reaches out and presses a sensitive point at my temple, just above my hairline. I wince. It's unexpectedly painful. "Your horns are regenerating," she says dryly. She pulls a light from a belt at her waist, shining it in my eyes. I wince.

"A little warning next time," I growl. We Kordolians have always been sensitive to light. It's the reason we see so well in the darkness.

Zyara gives me a critical look. "You're more photosensitive than usual. Add to that faster regeneration, irritability and those headaches." She starts to unhook me from the monitoring equipment, a thoughtful expression on her face.

I grow impatient. "Spit it out, medic."

"You need to mate."

"What?" I glare at her. *I need to mate?* That's the last fucking thing I want to hear right now.

Zyara shrugs. "Mating fever. It happens to some of our males. Hormone levels increase, arousal is heightened, and you're in a perpetual state of irritability."

"And what happens if I don't mate?"

"The symptoms will become more severe. The headaches will get worse, and you'll turn into one grumpy bastard, excuse the language, Sir. Good for battle situations, because any release of aggression will dampen the effects. Bad for, say, a long trip home, confined to ship." She pauses, giving me a strange look. "There's also a chance your judgement might be affected, *especially* if you come into contact with a compatible female."

"There's no chance of that," I say, a little too quickly. "Is there any other way to cure it?"

"It's not an illness, General. It's nature. Mind you, this doesn't happen to all males of our species. Just to the more, ah, dominant ones."

"Isn't there a drug you can give me to suppress the symptoms?"

"Normally, I might use a low dose sedative. That would only lessen the symptoms, not get rid of them. But in your case, you can't afford to be sedated or have your concentration impaired in any way, so the only solution for you is to find a mate."

"Fuck." I step off the examination chair, willing my armor to return. The nanites swarm over my torso, forming an impenetrable exoskeleton. After years of rigorous training, the exo-armor is an extension of my will, shaped by my mental commands.

What am I supposed to do, stuck at the other end of the Nine Galaxies, so far away from my home planet, when the medic tells me to mate?

Follow Rykal's lead and take a Human?

What am I supposed to do when I return to Kythia? I've always found the majority of Kordolian females to be delicate, pampered creatures, present company excepted. They're not suitable for a battle-hardened soldier like me. But that's what happens when there are so few of them. We shelter them.

And we go off-planet to fight any race that threatens the survival of our people.

Zyara is looking at me strangely, as if she's concerned. As I rise and pick up my weapons, the dull ache behind my eyes returns.

"If anyone asks, I'll be out hunting Xargek." I feel the sudden urge to kill something. I decide to head back to the vegetation dome, where one crazy, stubborn Human female is climbing above the canopy with no care for her own safety.

My soldiers are all out hunting, and I promised her a guard.

I don't know why I feel the need to guard her. If she wants to disobey orders and get herself killed, that's not my problem.

But there was something oddly noble about her insistence on carrying out her duty, even in the face of danger. There was something compelling about the way she clambered through the structures above, unafraid of the dizzying heights.

Absence of fear.

How very Kordolian.

And in the vegetation dome, I realized something. The intoxicating scent I had caught in the corridor wasn't from the plants and trees, but from the female herself.

Underneath the dirt and the shapeless garments, the Human is oddly attractive. Some Kordolians might consider her ugly. She's no statuesque Kordolian beauty, but there's something undeniably feminine about her. She has delicate features and pale, flawless skin. Her eyes are strangely colored, shining brown or green, depending on the angle of the light.

And her scent seems to lessen my infuriating headache.

It would be a shame if this exotic, stubborn creature were killed by some filthy Xargek.

So I suppose the guard is me. I have my own selfish reasons also. I want to watch her again, and see if the effect she had on me was simply my imagination.

Aroused by a Human; an inferior species? Impossible.

So why am I drawn back to the garden?

I tell myself it's logic. Xargek like humid, densely vegetated habitats, which makes the bio-facility an ideal environment for larvae to grow and reproduce.

If one of those infernal creatures has gone in there, I have to get to it before it harms the female. So far, the Human scientist has shown me that she's courageous, attending to her duty at all costs. She might be odd looking, and she might talk too much, but she's brave.

But against a Xargek, even in its larval phase, she'd stand no chance. I doubt she's ever held a weapon in her life.

Humans are so fragile. How they have stubbornly managed to cling to life in this remote part of the universe is beyond me.

Abbey

I FINISH the last square of my precious chocolate, savoring it as it melts slowly in my mouth. Then I grab my gloves and goggles and head for the roof. The maintenance panel shows me there are two more clusters of oxygen filters that need cleaning. One of them is starting to show a slightly concerning pressure buildup.

I haul myself up the narrow ladder, and by the time I get to the top, I'm breathing heavily. The sun is at an angle now, casting irregular shadows across the oxygen plant.

As our orbit is farther away from the sun than Earth's, we get a skewed version of the daytime cycle. This is supposed to be our 'afternoon'.

I peer down into the canopy below, searching for signs of movement, but I can't see anything through the thick treetops. The *General* told me he'd be sending a guard, but from here, I can't see any signs of life down there.

I don't like the idea of some unseen alien watching my every move from under the cover of the trees.

That's kinda creepy.

And protect me from what? That infuriating Kordolian didn't tell me anything. What could be more dangerous than the Kordolians themselves? I'm still half surprised they haven't tried to enslave us and ship us off somewhere.

From what I hear on the Networks, these guys treat the Nine Galaxies like their personal playground, but strangely, our black-clad invaders haven't gone to town on us just yet.

Maybe we're really just not that important. Maybe we have nothing they want.

I clamber over the railing, setting foot on a narrow metal walkway that stretches across the length of the oxygen filter plant. It creaks and sways as I regain my balance, but that doesn't bother me. I know these walkways like the back of my hand, and I'm steady on my feet.

I don my goggles and gloves and find the nearest hose, retrieving my bucket and brush from their little hook.

Then, I get to work. The physical exertion is good. It helps take my mind off other things; disturbing things, such as a certain grumpy alien General who acts like he owns the place.

I decide I don't like Kordolians.

Still, Jia was right. They have a certain, er, magnetism about them. Standing before the General, I couldn't help but notice a few things.

His features were striking; strong and elegant, completely alien, and yet somehow familiar.

His size was impressive, and I found myself a little overwhelmed by the sheer, intimidating force of him. His physique was lean and muscular, and I wouldn't mind seeing what's under that seamless black armor.

His eyes were blood-red and piercing, and like nothing I'd ever seen before.

Shit. Don't go there, Abbey. I can't believe I'm fantasizing about a Kordolian. I have to remind myself that he's a vicious killer; a conqueror, and that he doesn't care one bit about us feeble Humans.

As I scrub at a particularly stubborn bit of gunk, I hear a faint tapping sound.

I look around, but don't see anything. I can't pinpoint where the sound is coming from.

Taptap.

There it is again, louder this time. I look up beyond the bits of metal and glass to the surface of the outer dome.

That's where the sound's coming from.

There it is again, ominous and insistent.

What the hell? I move closer, trying to locate its source.

It seems to be coming from *outside* the dome, but that's impossible. Nothing can survive out in deep space. Not without life support.

Maybe its a blocked water pipe? I *pray* it's just a blocked water pipe.

The tapping is slower now, becoming rhythmic and methodical. But at the same time, it's become harder and louder.

I peer up towards the thick, impenetrable glass of the outer dome. A crack has appeared. I stop dead in my tracks.

What the hell?

The surface that can withstand incredible pressure has cracked.

There's something out there, trying to break the glass. Where's that guard when I need him? The General said he wanted to protect me from something.

Is this what he meant?

Dread courses through me as fissures start to appear in the super thick glass, widening and lengthening. It's all messed up now, like crazy paving, so I can't see clearly through it anymore.

I start to back away, the skybridge wobbling beneath my feet.

There's an almighty tearing sound, a rush of air, and then the whole panel of glass caves in. I scramble out of the way as massive chunks fall all over the place. A sharp, irritating pain flares across my forehead and cheeks. I think some splinters have caught me in the face. Suddenly, I'm grateful for my protective goggles and gloves.

The breach in the outer surface has exposed me to the vacuum of space, and air starts to rush out, accompanied by shards of broken glass. It's trying to suck me out. I grab onto the railing and pull myself across the bridge, dragging myself further and further away from the breach.

The sucking air whips at my hair and makes the cuts on my face sting. I'm sure I'm bleeding somewhere, but I don't have time to assess my injuries. I cry out with the effort as I continue to drag myself away from the huge, gaping hole, not daring to look back.

And bit by bit, it becomes a little easier, the pressure lessening.

I start to run, the metal bridge clanging underfoot. I run until the sucking force has lessened and I'm standing at the top of the narrow ladder, looking down.

I curse Station Boss Emin to hell for being too cheap to install a freaking hoverlift. And that's when I hear it.

That sound. A low-pitched, *chchchchch*; an insect-like chittering.

"What the hell is that?" I groan in dismay.

I shouldn't look back right now. I really shouldn't look back. But I can't help myself.

I turn and see something straight out of a twentieth-century horror movie.

It's an oversized cockroach. At least, that's my first impression. But then I realize it's black, with two giant claw-like limbs for arms and several pairs of long, spidery legs. It has a head of sorts, a rounded ovoid shape that pops out of its hard carapace to reveal a giant gaping maw. Two triangular black eyes stare back at me.

It's about twice my size.

I freeze. This is not good. As I make eye contact with the thing, it lets out a shrill shrieking noise. Its multiple lower legs start to retract. It's sort-of crouching down, and I realize in horror that it's preparing to jump.

At me.

I have barely a second to weigh up my options.

One, I could try to climb down the ladder, but that will slow me down. The thing will probably get me before I reach the second rung.

Two, I could rush at it and try to fight it. With what, exactly? A bucket and brush? This thing just cracked the supposedly impenetrable outer dome of the facility. No, I don't want to end up skewered on its serrated claws.

Abbey shish kebabs is not an option right now.

Three, I could…

Oh, hell no.

I look towards the thing, then back, then down. Then at the thing again. Bridge. Ladder. Down. Me. Thing.

Jump.

"Shit," I whimper, not liking the options before me. Climb ladder and die. Stay here and die. Jump and die.

One has more chance of survival than the others.

If I'm lucky, I'll land in a tree or in a compost heap. There are a hundred things down there that can break my fall.

The insectoid thing opens its mouth, revealing strings of viscous mucus. I don't hesitate for another second.

"Fuck that," I whisper. There's no way in hell I'm letting that thing bite me.

So I close my eyes, and jump.

Tarak

AS I ENTER the giant vegetation dome, an ear-splitting rushing sound reaches me. The air is moving.

It's being sucked out of a break in the structure.

Movement draws my eye. At the top of the flimsy ladder, a figure is falling, and screaming.

The Human.

I start to run, willing my nanites to push my legs faster, harder. She's dropping like a stone, and after her comes an adult Xargek, its spindly legs flailing in the air.

The Xargek must have breached the glass of the dome. Only a Xargek could survive for so long in pure space without oxygen.

I jump over bushes and garden beds and containers of fertilizers and harvesting machines. I will myself to reach her.

But she's too far, and no matter how hard I try, I just can't make myself go any faster.

Fuck.

I let out a grunt of frustration as she gains velocity. The sucking air has become a roar, and a wailing, deafening alarm starts up. Bits of leaves and sticks are flying around, and I bat away a small branch as I sprint towards her.

An emergency shutter is sliding down over the dome, cutting off the light and restoring normal pressure. As I whip through a grove of trees, I see her crash down into the foliage, a cry of pain coming from where she's landed.

Then, silence.

I curse out loud in Kordolian as the Xargek flutters its small, useless wings, landing next to her.

Moments later, I'm reaching the spot beneath a fruit tree where she's landed. Round, sweet-smelling pink fruits are scattered all around, some squashed on the floor. Beside her, the Xargek is raised on its hind legs, its claws poised, ready to strike.

Yellow venom drips from its maw as it shrieks, carrying on with its incessant death cry.

Blood lust overcomes me and I draw my twin blades, my

armor extending to protect my face and hands. I have to kill it. As it descends, I move in front of the Human, my blades meeting its sharp foreclaws with a metallic clang.

It emits a piercing cry of anger.

It's engaged me now, forgetting about the Human. As I deflect its vicious blows, I draw it away from her, towards an area stacked with barrels. It's focused on me now, and it's irritated.

I need to get in close. Even Callidum can't pierce its tough carapace. I need to find the weak spot at the top of its head, or I need to sever its neck.

The Xargek swipes at me with its claws, and one of the strikes catches me in the torso, sending me skidding back several paces. The exo-armor absorbs most of the impact, but the force is enough to slow me down. As it goes for the second strike, I drop to the floor, evading it. It hits again and again and I roll out of the way.

Deep gashes are left in the synthetic floor where it has struck. Only a Xargek's claws or a Callidum blade could cause such damage.

I'm lying on my back, about to jump to my feet, when the Xargek swarms over me, dripping acidic venom onto my armor. If it had touched my bare skin, my flesh would have melted.

The Xargek extends its head, its mandible working overtime. I see my reflection mirrored in its strange, triangular eyes.

With a grunt, I launch both of my swords, plunging them upwards through its head.

For a moment, the creature keeps moving, and I use all my strength to resist it. A low gurgling sound starts to emanate from its throat. I pull out my swords and roll away as it collapses to the floor.

It shudders and jerks and then goes still. A pool of foul-smelling yellowish liquid forms around its head.

That's how they bleed. Yellow.

The thing is finally dead.

I realize that it's gone quiet. The wailing alarm of the station has stopped, and the entire transparent roof of the dome is now covered with some kind of metal emergency shutter.

The air is still. The vacuum created by outer space has been sealed.

I get to my feet, breathing heavily as a faint whimper draws my attention. I swear heavily in Kordolian.

The Human is injured, but she's alive. I rush to her side. She's lying on her back with her legs twisted at an uncomfortable angle. Her face is covered in cuts and grazes. I gently pull the safety goggles away from her face.

She grimaces in pain, but somehow, she manages a smile. "Is that you, General?"

I will my helm to retract and her smile grows. She's lying here battered and bruised with her legs twisted underneath her and she still manages to have that expression on her face. "You killed that awful thing?"

"I killed it."

"Good." Her expression turns fierce, but then she grimaces in pain. "I can't move my legs. They hurt like a bitch. I guess in this case pain is a good thing?"

I take her hands into mine. Human skin is surprisingly soft, and her hand appears tiny against my own. Her fingers are warm.

If only I'd been here sooner, this mess could have been avoided. But now, because of me, this has happened.

She tries to move, but that only increases her pain. I put a hand on her shoulder. "Stop," I say gently. "Don't move."

Her composure in this situation amazes me. I've seen battle-hardened soldiers with lesser injuries wailing like children in the field. Her Human body may be weak, but her will is strong. If she hadn't jumped, she would be dead right now.

I should leave her to the Humans now. She's injured beyond measure, and her recovery will be long and painful. If she survives, her life will never be the same.

Behind her, the Xargek lies in a lifeless heap, its soulless eyes staring at me with seeming hatred, even in death. The Xargek are predators, nothing more. Organized. Efficient. Deadly. They have their own incomprehensible hive intelligence. They are without empathy or remorse. We have tried to understand their motivations, and failed, time and time again.

So instead, we try to eliminate them.

"What was that thing, General?" Her voice cracks. Underneath her brave face is fear. She's never seen a Xargek before.

"Do not worry about such details now, Human."

"It's Abbey," she whispers. "I have a name, General."

"Ah." I watch the rise and fall of her chest as she lets out an involuntary cry of pain. I should call the Human medics, but Humans have not mastered technology on our level.

There's only one thing that can restore her to normal functioning.

She needs a nanograft.

My people will not like it, but I will insist. This is my responsibility.

"Rykal," I snap, activating my comm. "Get Zyara. Tell her I've got a full emergency. She needs to come now. We're in the vegetation dome. If you don't know the way get the Human soldier to lead you. Bring a stretcher."

"What happened, boss?"

"Questions later," I bark. "Just get your asses over here now."

A small hand squeezes my own. "We have medics too, you know. Maybe you should call them. They're more familiar with treating Humans. I get the feeling our biology's a little different to yours."

I look down at her legs. A fragment of bone protrudes from her torn flesh.

"Human medicine can't do what we can," I whisper.

A tortured expression crosses her face. Her breathing is becoming faster, shallower. Crimson blood is pooling around her legs.

"Rykal," I shout into the comm. "Where the fuck are you?"

"On our way, Sir." He sounds breathless.

The female's eyes flutter. Right now, they're pale and brown, almost golden. "The skydome is cracked," she murmurs. "There's no sunlight for the oxygen filters. We need to get it fixed, otherwise we're all going to choke to death."

In the midst of her suffering, she's still worrying about the fate of this Station, making sure the Humans have air to breathe.

Unbelievable.

"You talk too much," I scold, but there's no sting in my voice. She blinks, as if staring at me for the first time, her eyes big in her pale, heart-shaped face. I reach down and wipe away a trickle of blood that's about to enter her eye. Her skin feels clammy, a light sheen of sweat making her features glisten.

Her eyes become unfocused, and her grip becomes weaker.

She's drifting away.

The thought of her dying bothers me. A lot. I shouldn't care about an inferior Human this much, but in the short time I've spent with this female, she has somehow earned my respect.

Some of her traits are so very Kordolian.

And the Xargek are here because of us. I failed to protect her, despite my assurances.

This situation has come about because of me.

It would be a shame if her life slipped away now.

I'm a filthy cur, tainted by war. I have played my part in destroying civilizations and spreading Kordolian rule across the Nine Galaxies, and I have done it well. Under the old regime, I was feared and hated.

I am still feared and hated, but I am not without honor.

And I am not leaving this female to die needlessly, because of my negligence. An instinct stirs in me, stronger than ever before. She's under my protection now. Mine.

I will do everything in my power to cure her, even if it means dragging her back to Kythia and forcing the High Council to grant her the healing privileges given to the Kordolian elite.

They have the ability to restore her body to its original state.

I just need to convince them. And I can be *very* persuasive when I want to be.

CHAPTER FOUR

Abbey

It hurts. I can't move my legs and I'm looking up at the skydome. It's covered over by the emergency shutters, the sunlight shut out. I'm surrounded by something sticky and warm. Is that my own blood?

It's gone dark. I can barely see, but something large and warm squeezes my hand.

It's the General. I can't believe he's bending over me like this, all his hardness and arrogance gone. I suppose there's something about falling off a hundred foot ladder that invokes sympathy.

His palm is rough and callused, and it completely engulfs my hand, but it's warm.

At least these Kordolians aren't cold-blooded.

I try to move, but he puts a firm hand on my shoulder. Something's seriously wrong. The pain is so bad it's almost not painful anymore, if that's even possible. At least my legs actually hurt. I read somewhere that if you're really paralyzed you don't feel pain anymore. I don't know if that's true, but right now, the pain is strangely reassuring, even though it feels as if my legs are broken in a hundred places.

"Don't move." The General's deep voice reaches me through a

fog of agony. I bite my lower lip and nod, trying to reassure him that I'm fine, but my vision's starting to go blurry, and his pale, alien features are becoming distorted. Even when he's trying to be nice, he's still bossy.

He *is* a General, though. Bossy is in the job description.

What a stupid thought to be having right now. I might actually not survive this.

Did I just think that? No way. I can't afford to not survive. I refuse to die, especially because of an oversized cockroach. I am *not* having 'killed by a cockroach' on my obituary.

I can't believe this has happened. In such a short time, my boring, normal life has turned into something out of a ridiculous action movie. I guess they're right when they say anything can happen in deep space.

The General's saying something, but I can't quite make out the words. I close my eyes. Everything's going black.

It's so tempting to drift away into sleep's seductive embrace.

There are lots of voices now. I can't move. I'm floating on a cloud of pain. This really sucks. This morning I was having coffee above the dock. Now, I'm lying here with my legs smashed to bits, after being attacked by a terrifying alien insect.

And another alien is holding my hand. His hand is warm. Rough and warm.

I force my eyes open again. It's an effort to stay awake. His face swims into view. I see deep red eyes. He's staring at me with a strange expression. I can't concentrate. I can't understand anything.

Lots of voices swarm around me. They're speaking another language. Kordolian? I don't understand anything. The General sounds really fired up now, barking orders at them.

Gloved hands are pressing something cool and sticky onto my injuries. There's a momentary stab of pain as something is inserted into a vein in my hand. Then there's no pain anymore.

I try to speak. I try to open my mouth, but nothing's happening.

Hands are all over me, sliding me onto what I think is a hover-stretcher. It floats upwards, and then we're moving. I twist and try to see what's happening. My eyes flutter open and closed, revealing glimpses of the brightly-lit service corridor. We're moving fast.

Others have joined the General now. Kordolians? I'm hooked up to something, and whatever they've put on my legs seems to have stopped the bleeding.

The pain's becoming less, too.

The lights are too bright. I'm floating in and out of consciousness.

Everything's dark now, and there's nothing I can do except let these strange aliens take me away as everything fades to black.

Tarak

AS ZYARA RAISES the hover stretcher with the help of the yellow-haired Human female, Abbey floats in and out of consciousness. With her small body connected to various lines and monitors, she appears so fragile. I glance at her, noting the paleness of her skin. The pink flush to her cheeks is gone, and the delicate skin around her eyes appears grey.

A flicker of movement at the edge of my vision catches my attention, and I turn.

It's the Xargek. It's round abdomen writhes and pulsates, and I curse in frustration. I pull out a plasma gun and run over to it, firing at its mangled body.

"Rykal," I yell, my voice hoarse. "Burn it! It's about to spill its larvae."

"On it, boss." He leaves Zyara's side and pulls a plasma cannon, setting it to incinerate. I step out of the way as a great blue flare of energy engulfs the Xargek's corpse.

The smell of burning chitin rises from it as a swarm of tiny, skittering creatures scatters across the floor. I fire at them, but they disperse like a cloud, disappearing into the vegetation.

"Fuck," I growl. The Xargek, in a final irritating act of defiance, has released its offspring. They're going to be almost impossible to find until they've grown larger.

I will not abandon this station until we've found and killed each and every one of them. It's not for the Humans that I'm doing it. It's for the entire Nine Galaxies. For the Kordolian Empire. We cannot allow the Xargek to gain a foothold in any sector.

And the Humans can't defend against them on their own. They're weak.

I activate my comm. "First Division," I snap, "be aware that our little Xargek problem has now increased by a factor of a hundred. Be alert and exterminate. I want all of them destroyed before we leave this station. As usual, eliminate at all costs. But try not to kill too many Humans in the process. I don't want to deal with another fucking inquiry from the Universal Inter-species Relations Committee." The UIRC is more symbolic than anything else; they have no real power over us, but their endless requests for information can become a real pain-in-the-ass.

Several Kordolian voices filter through my receiver, answering in the affirmative. Satisfied, I turn to Zyara and the Human, who are maneuvering the hover-stretcher away from the scene of destruction. Behind us, the Xargek's foul-smelling yellow blood seeps across the floor, vapor rising it as it burns the surface.

We brought the creatures here. Now we have to take care of the problem.

"Our medical bay is this way." The Human soldier takes the lead, but I hold up a hand.

"No. She comes with us."

"General?" Zyara's orange eyes grow wide. "To the ship? But she's Human."

Ignoring her, I turn to the female soldier. "Look at her," I order, "and answer truthfully. Will your Human medicine be able to restore her?"

A look of intense discomfort crosses the Human's face as she looks down at Abbey's injuries. "I'm no doctor, General, but I've seen injuries like that before. They'll patch her up here, but she needs to go back to Earth. The trip will take its toll. If she's lucky, she'll hold out. If not..." She shrugged, unable to conceal the shadow of worry that crossed her features.

"Not good enough." I try to keep the disdain from creeping into my voice. Are these Humans so primitive that they can only provide basic medical care on their outposts? "She comes with us."

Zyara shoots me a questioning look but keeps her mouth shut. She knows my word is absolute.

I leave Rykal hunting Xargek larvae in the bushes as we escort Abbey towards the docking bay. Zyara's given her a painkiller, and she's drifted off to sleep. She must have been in agony, but never once did she complain.

She may have a weak body, but inside she's tough. What a shame she wasn't born Kordolian. She would have made a worthy mate.

As we reach *Silence*, one of the Human mechanics breaks ranks and rushes over to us. I hold the small dark-haired female back with one hand, and she flails about desperately. "Stand down," I tell her. "What do you think you're doing?"

"She's my friend," the Human gasps. "What the fuck have you done to her? Oh my God, Abbey!"

Abbey's unresponsiveness seems to work her friend into more of a frenzy. "Let go of me, you asshole!" She says something in some Human language that sounds suspiciously like curse-words. I hold her back with ease, her movements ineffective. She tries to scratch me, but her blows glance off my armor as if they were water.

"Calm down, female." I grab both of her arms. She stills immediately, and I sense her fear. "Or I'll have you restrained." I try to soften my tone. "We aren't going to hurt her. She's injured and I can help her."

"Why would *you* want to help her?"

It's a good question. Why am I going out of my way to help this insignificant creature? I should leave her to her fate, but her plight stirs something deep within me. She's a victim of the

Empire, just like so many before her. We Kordolians leave a trail of death and destruction in our wake

"You ask too many questions, Human. Get out of the way." I hold her back as Zyara passes with Abbey on the stretcher. Still the small woman struggles, even though she knows she's no match for me.

I've come to the conclusion that all Human females are crazy.

"Don't you tell me to get out of the way," she snarls. "That's my friend. You at least owe me an explanation."

"No, I don't." I glance at her uniform, which is stained with grease. "You're a mechanic?"

"What's it to you?" Her dark eyes are full of hostility.

"How long until the hull repairs are complete?"

She shakes her head in disbelief. "I'm not telling you anything until you tell me what you're planning to do with Abbey."

"I'm taking her to my planet for treatment."

"Why can't you just take her to Earth?"

"We will be traveling on emergency oxygen, through a wormhole. There isn't enough to sustain a detour to Earth and get us back in a single trip." Not to mention there's no way I'm landing on a planet full of potential hostiles without the Kordolian Fleet to back me up. I release the mechanic's wrists once she stops resisting. She makes a face and rubs them. "Again, I'll ask. How long until the hull is serviceable?"

"You're really taking her to your planet? Won't she be in danger? From what I've heard, your people aren't the most welcoming bunch."

I glare at her. "They won't try anything. Not if she's with me."

"How can I trust you?"

I start to grow impatient. "Human, the longer you waste time here, the longer it will take for your friend to receive treatment. Answer my question, or get out of the way."

She looks at me for a moment, as if weighing up whether she can trust me. I don't really care. If she won't give me the information I need, I'll find another Human. One with sense.

Eventually, she pushes her hands into her pockets and sighs. "We've got one more patch to do, then she'll be serviceable.

Obviously, you'll want to do permanent repairs when you get her back to your planet. But she'll be good for at least a week." She narrows her eyes. "You better take care of her, General, or I'll be coming after you."

It's an idle threat, but I have to admire her loyalty to her friend. "She's my responsibility now, mechanic, and I don't take my responsibilities lightly."

Abbey

I MUST HAVE BEEN out for some time. Stuff must have happened. Because when I come to, I'm floating.

"What the?" I try to yell, but my voice comes out as a hollow echo. I can instantly see why. I squirm, my arms flailing about in the water.

I'm floating. I'm in a tank of sorts, with lines and monitors hooked up to me. It's cold. That's the first thing I notice. It's freezing, and the chill seeps right through me. I'm suspended and trussed up like an experimental guinea pig in a lab.

Over my face is a sleek, clear helmet, supplying fresh air and allowing me to see.

"Ahh." I let out a strangled whimper; a sound of shock. What the hell have these Kordolians done to me?

My legs are all wrapped up in some kind of clear flexible outer coating. The pain's gone, and I can move them very slightly, but I don't dare try and kick them. If my memory's correct, they're smashed to bits.

Is this the part where the doctor comes and tells me I won't walk unless I get prosthetic legs? The waiting list for a pair of decent cybernetic legs is years, unless one can find a very generous donor.

The icy liquid surrounding me isn't water, like I first thought. It's a bit more viscous, and it has a bluish tinge to it. I'm suspended vertically, staring out at the world through a blue filter.

I look beyond the tank, taking in my surroundings. We're not in the station medical bay, that's for sure. This has to be the Kordolian ship. I've never seen anything like this before. The walls are black, and the space is dimly lit, with hundreds of tiny luminous blue lights casting a gentle glow. Shadows gather in the corners, and the room is oddly shaped. Instead of straight lines and corners, it's kind of curved, the walls following some organic pattern.

I feel as if I'm floating in a tank that's inside an earthy cave, cocooned in layers of darkness.

The size of the tank I'm suspended in reminds me this thing is designed for much larger beings. Kordolians. I'm a Human, and they're trying to treat me with their Kordolian medicine. Do they even know what works on Humans? I can't imagine what they'd do to fix my legs.

And do they know that I'm fucking freezing right now?

But despite the cold being so unpleasant, I'm not shivering. That's strange. I usually break out in goosebumps and shivers at the first trace of cold.

"General," I yell, my voice muffled by the helmet. My breath mists up the transparent faceplate. "What the hell have you done to me?"

Nothing. An uneasy feeling starts to work its way into my gut. I'm totally helpless, and I have no idea what's going on. I'm at the mercy of these aliens.

The hundreds of little blue lights blink, and all is silent, save for the low hum of machinery in the background.

I can't even swim in this viscous blue liquid, because my legs won't move properly. And I don't want to try, because I know I have broken bones. I'm surprised I'm even able to flail about a little, considering I've jumped off a hundred foot high ladder.

Right now, I'm cold and alone and feeling a little bit afraid.

"General," I yell again. I realize I don't even know his name. I think I told him mine. I can barely remember.

Shadowy movement at the edge of my vision tells me there's someone else in the room. "General Tarak is busy right now. You need to calm down."

It's a female voice. She speaks perfect, barely accented Universal. Her calm voice reaches me through what appear to be little speakers in my underwater helmet.

I blink as she steps into the glow of the tank. She's definitely Kordolian. Like the others, she's tall and lean. Her long lilac hair is tied up in a sleek ponytail. She's got the same pointed ears and razor sharp cheekbones and silvery skin, but instead of that freaky living armor, she wears flowing white robes.

Her eyes glow orange, reminding me of a cat's.

"Be calm, Abbey. You need to stop trying to move about. Otherwise you'll undo all of my hard work."

"What is all this? Who are you?"

"I am Zyara al Sirian, healer for the First Division. I've stabilized your wounds and put you inside a stasis tank. The bleeding has stopped, but both your legs are broken in several places. I've applied fibrogel to the cuts on your body. You also have several broken ribs and a collapsed lung."

"Oh." That all sounds rather serious. "Damn."

"Right now I'm putting some Human blood back into your body. We were able to obtain some from the station medics. You're lucky that Human and Kordolian biology seem to share some similarities. I think I can work with that."

I look down and see that one of the lines going into my arms is red. That must be the blood. I shudder, and I'm not sure if it's the cold or what's happened in the last few hours that's affecting me the most.

My memories are a little hazy right now, but I have a vague recollection of the skydome caving in, punctured by the claws of that gigantic, disgusting *thing*. That cockroach on growth hormones.

A feeling of disgust ripples through me, making my skin crawl. That was the grossest thing I have ever seen in my life. My horror turns to alarm as I remember the emergency shutters coming over the dome, shutting out the light.

"We have no sunlight in the dome," I gasp. "If the oxygen filters stop working and the biomeric plant stops producing, we're screwed."

A blank look crosses Zyara's face. "I don't know anything about that. I'm sorry. I'm going to put you back under now. The stasis tank can be unpleasant. I went light on the first dose of sedative, because I wasn't sure how you'd metabolize it."

"Wait!" The last thing I want is to be sedated. I need to know what's happening. "You can't just knock me out. I don't even know what's going to happen to me. When are you going to get me out of this guinea pig tank?"

"Guinea pig?" She shrugs. "I don't know what that is."

"I want to be transferred to the station medical bay," I demand. "Let's just say I'd like a second opinion. I appreciate you hooking me up to this thing, but I'm Human. I need a Human doctor."

"I'm afraid that's not possible."

"Why the hell not?"

A look of frustration crosses Zyara's face. "I'm sorry." She sounds genuinely apologetic. "But General Tarak has told me not to discuss that with you."

Urgh. That insensitive prick. Just because he got all sentimental and guilty back there when I was lying on the floor of the biomeric facility, doesn't mean he's changed.

"Zyara," I growl, anger darkening my voice. "You tell that big musclehead to get his silver ass over here right now. Don't you dare sedate me." I've forgotten about the cold. I'm way too livid to think about anything else.

How dare he wire me up like this and stick me in some oversized goldfish bowl? I'm going to demand he hand me over to the Human side. He can't just keep me here like this.

Zyara clasps her hands together in alarm. She looks shocked. Maybe it's because I've insulted her almighty boss. I don't care. I just want to get off this ship.

"Musclehead?" General Tarak's familiar deep voice resonates through the little speakers in my helmet, causing me to shudder. And maybe it's just the drugs Zyara's pumped into me, but a weird sensation courses through me, settling in my lower belly.

He emerges from the shadows, the faint blue light reflecting off his hard features. I swear a little vein is pulsating on the side of his head. And his ears do a rapid little twitch.

I'm starting to figure out what that means. He's annoyed.

"Take me to the station medical bay," I demand. "I want a Human doctor."

He scrutinizes me with those unsettling dark red eyes of his, his expression giving nothing away. The fear I felt before comes back, stronger than ever. I'm helpless and I absolutely hate it.

I don't want to end up as some Kordolian scientist's dissection project.

I open my mouth to speak, but he holds up a hand in that irritating, arrogant way of his. "Zyara, some privacy."

"But Sir, I need to monitor—"

"I need to speak to her alone."

The medic nods and gives him a deferent little bow before disappearing into the shadows.

Tarak steps forward, peering at me through the transparent glass of the tank. A sudden, horrific thought occurs to me and I try to look down.

Am I even wearing anything? Oh, no. They wouldn't dare. Even aliens have some scruples, right?

Thankfully, I seem to be dressed in a garment that at least hides my naughty bits. It clings to my body in all the right places, kind of like a swimsuit, although my arms, shoulders and midriff are left bare. And of course, both my legs are wrapped in that strange, clear membrane.

Well, this is embarrassing. My attire leaves little to the imagination, and the General is staring.

My anger rises again. He put me in this position. And now he has the nerve to look me up and down like I'm a specimen in a zoo?

"Why are you doing this, General? Why not just let my people treat me?"

"You Humans do not possess the technology."

"What does that even mean?"

"I would see you restored to your original state. With the

injuries you've sustained, I don't believe your medicine is capable of achieving that."

"That's not up to you, General. Let me out of here. Please. I need to speak with the other scientists. I need to alert them to the damage in the biomeric facility."

"I'm afraid that won't be possible."

"What do you mean?" A bad feeling settles in the pit of my belly. "Why won't it be possible, General?"

"We are no longer in Sector Nine."

"What the hell are you talking about?" That bad feeling starts to grow.

"While you were sedated, we successfully navigated a wormhole. We are now in Sector Three, heading towards Kythia."

"Please tell me you're joking." I shake my head, ignoring the jolt of pain that shoots through me as I press my hands up against the glass. "You can't do this to me!"

Tarak inclines his head, seemingly unmoved by my distress. "Your injuries are a result of my negligence, so it is my responsibility to see you restored."

"What about my needs in all this, General? With all due respect, I don't *want* to go to Kythia. I'm needed on the Station. So if you'll be so kind to just turn this ship around and get me back to Fortuna Tau, I'll let this slide."

"I'm afraid that's not possible."

"Again with that line. What do you mean?"

"The wormhole we returned through has collapsed, and we only have enough oxygen for the return trip to Kythia. So you are stuck, little Human."

Little human? I consider launching into a diatribe about condescending nicknames, but I decide now's not the time.

"And the people on Fortuna Tau? What about the biomeric plant?"

"I left our main oxygen concentrator on the Station, along with my soldiers, because your oxygen filtering system was damaged, and because our emergency backup would only support three passengers on the return journey. Sacrifices have been made for your sake, Human. An inferior species would not usually receive such treatment. So do not test my patience, Abbey. There is no turning back now."

"Inferior?" Oh, if only I weren't stuck in this tank right now. I try to bang against the glass, but my hand moves painfully slowly through the thick liquid. "If I'm so *inferior*, almighty Kordolian, then why are you even bothering? Is it because you need to feel better for screwing up and turning my life into hell? So you're taking me away from my people, just because it makes you feel good about yourself? You need to do something about that savior complex of yours, General. It will get you into all kinds of trouble."

"Enough!" His low voice cuts through my tirade, deep and menacing. I open my mouth to speak, but the expression on his face is enough to make me re-think the expletives I was about to throw at him. That vein I thought I saw bulging on the side of his temple has grown. His ears twitch again, and his fangs are protruding.

Fangs. Oh, my.

Okay, so maybe it's not a good idea to share my potty-mouth with a Kordolian General. For a moment there, I forgot that this guy comes from one of the most feared races in all of space.

And so far, he's only tried to help me, in his own bullish kind of way.

We Humans don't like to be reminded that there are guys out there who are bigger and badder than us. That's why we keep to ourselves and stay the hell away from the likes of these Kordolians. But if this General is on my side because of some twisted sense of duty, then I'm pretty safe, right?

Still, I get the feeling he's not telling me everything.

I start to shake. The cold's finally gotten to me, and my body breaks out in the worst shivers ever, making my teeth rattle in my skull.

"You're shaking, Human."

"No shit, Sherlock." My voice comes out as a stutter. "This thing is arctic. Why the hell does Zyara have to freeze me half to death? I'll start getting frostbite soon."

"I'm no medic," Tarak shrugs, "but I believe the cold slows

down cellular damage. Still, you Humans seem quite vulnerable to cold. I will ask her to come now and sedate you."

Sedate? My shoulders slump, and I close my eyes. You know things are bad when the only way you can escape your situation is to sleep. I let out a deep sigh, my warm breath misting up the faceplate again. "Dope me up then, General. And please, be a good boy and wake me when we land."

Tarak

SHE'S QUIET NOW, after letting out her anger. Does this tiny female ever run out of energy? Even when finding herself in unfamiliar surroundings, with the wounds she's sustained, she manages to find the strength to challenge me.

I am rarely ever challenged. This feeling is new for me. And she has a point.

Why did I insist on taking her back to Kythia? When I saw her, lying helpless on the floor, injured and broken, a feeling came over me.

I wanted to make things right.

How very un-Kordlian.

A deeper, more primal part of me simply wanted to take her. To protect her. Mine.

I left the rest of the First Division on the mining station. My soldiers didn't question my orders, intent on hunting down every last cursed Xargek larva. They know we'll be back to retrieve them, even if backup has to come the long way. Until their mission is complete, Fortuna Tau is under Kordolian control, and if the station proves to be strategic in our fight against the Xargek, I may even consider keeping it.

They did not question why I was taking this Human female back to Kythia. My soldiers obey me without question, and apart from that crazy female mechanic, the Humans didn't dare stop me. Zyara raised curious eyebrows, but didn't say a thing.

For the rest of this journey, she's my responsibility. Mine.

Her eyes flutter as she stares at me through the clear glass of her respirator. They appear green now, and a blue-green filter has been cast across her face by the liquid in the stasis chamber.

With her fragile body surrounded by various lines and monitors, she looks so small and vulnerable. She's shaking uncontrollably.

I did not realize Humans were so vulnerable to cold. It must be unpleasant for her. Kythia will be unpleasant for her. But we'll worry about that when we get there.

Sedation will be a mercy as we complete the final leg of our journey.

She puts a hand up against the glass, as if to reach out to me.

Her brown hair sways gently in the liquid, forming a soft, moving crown around her pale face. Her body fascinates me. Unlike Kordolian females, who are long-limbed, muscular and lean, there is a softness to her. Although hidden by a fitted garment, I can make out the swell of her breasts. They're full and rounded. Her nipples are erect, two perfect, symmetrical points. I imagine them beneath my fingers, taut with arousal.

Her stomach is exposed, a smooth plane of pale skin leading to rounded hips.

She is small but her body has curves. There is a loveliness to her that is distinctly Human and entirely feminine. And right now, she is completely vulnerable.

I find myself aroused. Her appearance stirs my base instincts. To dominate. To control. To protect. The thought occurs to me that I could keep her on Kythia when she has healed.

But I know she would fight me, each and every step of the way.

That thought stirs my arousal even further. Underneath the exo-suit, I am hard; painfully so. And my headache is starting to return.

I push the insanity from my mind, reminding myself that she's hurt.

There is something desperately sad about seeing her like this, broken and trapped, shivering and alone.

I will ask Zyara to sedate her.

But I cannot tear my gaze from her.

"What are you waiting for, General?" Even though her voice cracks, she manages to inject a hint of mockery into the question. "Knock me out already." Her teeth are chattering. She brings her arms up, hugging herself around the chest, trembling.

Alone.

A strong impulse overtakes me there and then. I need to touch her. To be by her side. To stop this infernal shivering of hers. I walk over to the side of the tank, mentally commanding my exo-suit to retract. Billions of microscopic nanites dissolve, entering the pores of my skin, making their way back into my bloodstream. I haul myself up at the side of the tank.

"Wh-what the hell are you doing, General?" Her sometimes-brown, sometimes-green eyes have gone wide.

"Making you warm," I answer. I pause for a moment, suspended at the edge of the tank, surprised by my own actions. I did not think. It was an instinctive reaction. "If you wish."

She doesn't protest at first, her lips parted in surprise. And for the first time, I see hunger in her gaze.

I don't wait any longer. I plunge into the tank, allowing the blue liquid to engulf me.

CHAPTER FIVE

Abbey

My jaw drops as Tarak does something and his nano-armor just melts away, dissolving back into his skin. What the hell? The nanites can go *inside* him?

But that freakiness isn't what astounds me the most.

Underneath the armor, he's completely butt naked. And he's walking around as if it doesn't bother him in the least.

Oh, sweet Jupiter. I should look away. But I can't. The General is a sight to behold.

He's totally ripped. Defined. Chiseled. His broad chest tapers down to a perfectly formed six-pack. His arms ripple and bulge as he moves. And as I look down, catching sight of what's between his legs, oh mercy, I can't go on. Kordolians are so similar in appearance to Humans, and yet so different.

This is unfair.

I'm injured. This is totally inappropriate. This shouldn't be happening.

He comes up to the side of the giant fishbowl, getting up onto a raised platform. Then he hauls himself up to the top. His muscles bunch up as he suspends himself effortlessly at the side of the tank.

Holy hell. It's a magnificent sight. And it affects me in the most primal of ways.

"Wh-what the hell are you doing?" I gasp. He's not going to get in with me, is he?

"Making you warm," he replies. "If you wish."

My mouth forms a silent 'O', but I can't bring myself to protest. The sheer sight of him has caught me off-guard. I should be telling him to get the hell out of here. This is impossible. There's a naked, aroused male jumping into the fishbowl with me, and he's acting as if nothing's wrong with it. He's not bothered at all by his lack of clothes. But of course, the arrogant bastard *would* be like that, wouldn't he?

Tell him to get the fuck out of here, Abbey.

But even though my brain is thinking it, the signal that goes to my mouth isn't working. I'm too busy staring at his incredible physique, at the way his smooth, silver skin is marred by scars, some of them vicious looking.

He's fought some battles, this one. His body has a story to tell.

It's the body of a warrior. It's magnificent.

And then he's in, dropping into the tank, and of course, I can't move because my legs are wrapped up in that weird alien stuff. Not to mention they're broken in a hundred places.

The truth is, I can't say shit because I'm aroused as hell just looking at him. Warmth pools in my lower belly, spreading to my core, right down into my pussy.

I stare at him through my clear visor, afraid and at the same time aroused.

The lack of air to breathe doesn't seem to bother him. He comes up behind me, his movements fluid and graceful. Strong arms surround me, and all of a sudden the cold is gone.

I take a deep breath, shuddering as my bare skin comes into contact with his. Unable to help myself, I lean into him, savoring his warmth.

What the hell am I thinking? I should tell him to get out.

But I can't. It feels too good.

A monitor starts flashing. I'll bet it's from my heart rate

going through the roof. Moments later Zyara rushes in, takes one look at us and promptly runs out, not saying a word. In other circumstances, I might have called the expression on her face 'hilarious'. I might have laughed out loud.

In *other* circumstances.

My body doesn't lie. The monitors don't lie.

As if this couldn't get any more embarrassing, even though it's amazing.

Why does it feel so good? Damn it.

Tarak isn't moving. He simply holds on to me, the warmth from his body seeping into me, taking away the terrible chill. Being totally submerged doesn't seem to bother him. The lack of air doesn't bother him. How long can he hold his breath?

His large hands are curled around my upper arms, his fingers tracing my skin.

Seriously, if it's going to be like this, maybe I don't need the sedation. I could stay floating in a stasis tank with a big, warm, muscular alien for weeks.

This one just happens to be a General, a hardened fighter, a warrior from a fearsome alien empire. I don't even know that much about him or his culture.

This is madness.

He pulls me into him, and the hard length of his cock brushes against my ass. Sweet Jupiter, it's as impressive as the rest of him. No disappointment there. And there are some interesting, er, variations down there.

Despite his arousal, he's incredibly careful, skillfully avoiding the various lines and objects attached to my body. He's gentle, making sure he doesn't hurt me in my injured state.

He doesn't do anything else. He simply holds me in his arms.

Talk about surreal. "This is unfair, General," I protest, not sure whether he can actually hear me while he's submerged. But the truth is, I'm enjoying the feeling of his hard body against me. I bask in the heat radiating from him.

My teeth have stopped chattering. That terrible, bone-deep sensation of coldness is gone.

And I'm worlds away from Earth, speeding towards a foreign

planet, my fate taken out of my hands. Has a Human even set foot on Kythia before?

What if they fix me up, only to sell me into slavery? Or what if they're going to dissect me like a lab specimen?

I don't really know what the General's true motivations are. What if he's just toying with me?

Yes, he's attractive, in an exotic, alien way. But I can't afford to let that turn my brain to mush.

I start to push him away, resisting his embrace. At first, he's immovable, but after a while, he responds to my movement by disengaging, swimming slowly up to the edge of the tank, pulling himself out in a single, powerful movement.

I turn away, on purpose. I don't want to look at him.

I'm unnerved by the effect he has on me. Maybe it's better to be sedated.

"You play dirty, General," I complain as the liquid's temperature drops again. He's taken all the warmth with him. "The odds aren't even."

"Odds?" He's returned to the front of the tank, and he raises an eyebrow. He's still naked, as if it's the most natural thing in the universe. Well, I guess it is.

He's standing there in all of his infuriating, unselfconscious glory, his dripping wet body glistening under the muted glow of tiny blue lights. I'd call him arrogant, narcissistic, a show-off, except he's not trying to impress anybody. He just *is*.

Are all Kordolians like this? Or is it just *him*?

"I'm at a bit of an unfair disadvantage right now, don't you think?" I glance down at my mangled legs. The pain has left me again, courtesy of whatever drug Zyara is pumping into me through those twisted cables. My body looks as if it's been through hell.

"Then I shall wait until the 'odds' have balanced out."

"I have no idea what you're talking about. And will you please put some pants on? Do you even *have* pants, or do you just wear that freaky nano armor all the time?"

Tarak looks at me in genuine surprise. "Does my current state somehow offend you? Does it not please you?"

"It's indecent."

"You weren't thinking such things when I was in there with you."

"You didn't give me much of a choice." I let out an incredulous snort. "And you were trying to lecture *me* about decorum?"

"There is nothing unbecoming about my state of undress."

I shake my head in exasperation. This must be a Kordolian thing, because I really don't get it.

He's still aroused. I'm stuck in a giant fish tank while a very attractive, very naked alien debates with me over his lack of attire. Said alien was only recently wrapping his warm arms around me.

What was he thinking?

What was I thinking?

"Zyara," I yell, hoping she can hear me. "I need drugs. Can you please tell this big silver jerk to leave me alone?"

This situation is spiraling out of control, and it's starting to freak me out. I get the feeling nothing good will come from whatever is happening between us. A sudden thought occurs to me.

"General," I say, "you're not going to, uh, try anything while I'm under, are you?"

He stiffens. "You think I'm capable of something so dishonorable?"

I answer with a pointed stare. "You tell me."

He seems genuinely offended. After what he just did, I'm surprised it's such a big deal. I sigh. Kordolians. I don't understand them at all.

At least he seems to actually be offended by the alien equivalent of date rape. That's reassuring, I guess.

"I cannot take pleasure if the other is unwilling." He leans close to the tank, and all of a sudden, his seamless black attire is back, the nanites or whatever they are forming millions of tiny black dots on his skin that seem to mesh together in an instant. The armor stretches along his arms, extending down his torso and legs. Once again, he's fully clothed.

And the liquid that was on him sluices to the floor, forming a blue puddle around him.

"Neat trick." I try not to gape like an idiot. I really need to find out how he does that. It looks like the nanites have been implanted into his body. He appears to control them at will. It's unthinkable technology, light years beyond what Humans are capable of.

I shudder. What else are these Kordolians capable of?

And what the hell are they going to do to me?

I've never been this helpless before. "General," I whisper, feeling lost. "You're going to make sure I get fixed, aren't you?"

He stands rigidly, his jaw set in a hard line. "I don't go back on my word." Then his voice softens. "Get some rest, Abbey. I'll get Zyara to attend to you."

I nod in thanks, still disbelieving of the whole situation. He leaves me alone, merging with the shadows of this strange alien ship.

Tarak

I ENCOUNTER Zyara in the corridor. She regards me with a silent look, her purple eyebrows raised.

"Not a word," I snap, annoyed that she witnessed my moment of weakness.

Her incredulous expression doesn't change. "What's gotten into you, Tarak?" She breaks the formality by using my first name, something she rarely ever does.

She's one of the few who would dare, but then again, she's been with the First Division since the beginning. She's witnessed everything we've done in the name of the Empire, both good and bad.

"What I do with the Human is none of your business, medic."

"It is when she's my patient." Zyara steps forward, her orange eyes glowing in the dimly lit passageway. "The only reason I let it slide was because I knew you wouldn't harm her." She averts her eyes for a moment, in embarrassment.

"It's heartwarming to see that you have such faith in me."

"What are your plans for the Human, General?"

"I will see her fully restored," I reply. "It's my responsibility." Behind Zyara's intelligent gaze, a thousand questions burn, but she doesn't ask me anything further. I owe her half an explanation, at least. "We'll be in communication range with Kythia soon. I will be sending backup to Fortuna Tau." I know what she's worried about. I've left the entire First Division on the Human station to deal with the Xargek.

She should know better.

"It will take much longer to reach the Station now that the wormhole's collapsed, but I've calculated that the main concentrator we left on Fortuna Tau has plenty of reserve. The Humans should have fixed their supply by then. I've changed my mind, Zyara. I have plans for that little outpost."

"Cryptic as always, General."

"You should know by now that I will never abandon my troops."

"Yes, and of the thousands you command, the First Division holds special meaning for you, doesn't it?"

I choose not to answer, turning my gaze towards the entrance of the medical bay. "Your patient needs your attention, medic."

Again she tries to pin me with that questioning stare. "The authorities on Kythia aren't going to accept her, you know. Without your protection, she'll be in danger."

"You let me worry about that." On Kythia, lesser species do not have rights. They're assigned to the servant classes. The High Council will challenge me, and I will fight back. These days, I've come to relish my battles with the ruling class. I have nothing but disdain for those pampered, self-indulgent fools.

"From what I've seen, she's not going to be happy about it when she realizes how things are."

"Again, let me worry about that." She's right. Abbey won't be pleased at all. She's stubborn. Obstinate. She will argue and complain and fight. She has no filter and speaks her mind at will. Without fear.

I find it strangely refreshing.

The very thought causes my erection to return.

She won't be happy at all. But if that's the price to pay for her to be healed, then so be it.

I will deal with the aftermath when it comes.

Abbey

DRIFTING in and out of sleep, I hear faint voices outside. It sounds like the General's debriefing Zyara on the little situation she just walked in on.

It all feels very awkward right about now.

My heart's still racing even though I'm dead tired. The injuries and events of the past few hours are taking their toll, and a bone-deep weariness creeps through me.

I might not need that sedative after all. I could drop off to sleep right about now.

But movement catches my attention, and I realize that Zyara's back, looking at me through the thick glass.

This feeling of being stared at like an exotic creature is quickly becoming old. I remember going to an orbit-zoo with my dad when I was a kid. They had aliens there, strange looking creatures with oddly shaped limbs and wild coloring. They were put in glass-walled pens, and we gaped at them and took pictures, watching as they shuffled around with a resigned sort of apathy.

I wonder of any of them were intelligent lifeforms.

Now I get an idea of how they would have felt. Thank Mars the orbit-zoos were shut down a few years ago.

"Forget you saw that just now," I blurt, fighting my rising embarrassment. Why should I feel embarrassed? It wasn't my fault that a certain oversized, grey musclehead just happened to drop in beside me.

But deep down, I know why I feel this way. It's because I liked it. His body felt good against mine, sending a gooey warm feeling all though me.

I hope I'm not blushing right now.

Zyara shrugs, trying to hide her curiosity. If she's anything like a Human chick, she'll be burning with questions and dying to get gossip out of me. But she looks like the cool, composed, collected type and we don't really know each other all that well yet. So of course, she's not going to ask.

"Your relationship with the General is none of my business," she says stiffly, and I wonder if she's got a secret thing for the big guy.

"There's no relationship," I respond without thinking. "He just, uh," I shake my head, "never mind. You seem to have worked pretty closely with him. Can I ask you one thing?"

"What's that?"

"Can I trust him?"

"Of course," she snaps, in an instant. "General Tarak is well respected on Kythia. He's served the Empire with honor."

It's an automatic, almost scripted response. Interesting. Who is this Tarak guy, really, that he can inspire such loyalty in his subordinates?

And there's no way I can blindly trust him. Not when I'm Human, and he's Kordolian. He said it himself. Apparently, I'm *inferior*.

And now, for reasons I don't yet fully understand, I'm the subject of my own crazy space-opera fantasy, hurtling towards an unknown planet that's too far away for Humans to have ever set foot on.

Our space cruisers just don't travel that far.

I'm out of reach of my people, unable to run, and stuck with aliens I don't trust.

Why would he bring me so many millions of light years just to patch me up? *Me?* I'm not a valuable asset. I'm just a simple scientist, trying to get a promotion so I can get back to Earth.

And now I'm impossibly far away from Earth, with no way of getting back on my own.

Suddenly, the liquid in the cryo-tank feels super cold, and I feel very, very small.

I try not to think about what might greet me when we reach Kythia, the Kordolian home planet. I don't want to know. For now, it might just be better to escape to the only place I can go.

"Zyara," I say, as she fiddles with various machines and monitors, "what are you waiting for? Knock me out. This cold is killing me. Can't you make it warmer?"

"That's not possible, I'm afraid. The low temperature slows cellular damage. If you're not tolerating it well, I'll sedate you."

I nod, closing my eyes, resigned to my temporary state.

I'm not looking forward to what happens when we get to Kythia. With my jittery nerves threatening to take over and cause a minor meltdown, I'd rather just sleep.

Tarak had better be as good as his word and get me fixed. And once I can walk again, I'm figuring out how to return to Earth, even if I have to hijack a Kordolian battle cruiser to get there.

Sounds preposterous, huh? But in these outrageous, terrifying circumstances, a girl needs to cling onto hope—even if hope is just a thought.

CHAPTER SIX

Tarak

The familiar outline of Kythia comes into view as we approach. From this distance, the Dark Planet is nothing more than a giant shadow, forbidding and mysterious.

It's been this way for millions of orbits, ever since the nearest star began to die.

The surface of the planet is imprinted with a network of glittering lights, the only sign of life on its cold exterior.

As a species, we have adapted to suit the environment. We see well in the dark and tolerate below-freezing temperatures. And we have mined the precious metal Callidum from the planet's core, using it to fashion weapons that have no match in the Nine Galaxies.

But our race is dying, much like Ithra, the faded star.

As I guide *Silence* towards our destination, the comm screen lights up.

"This is Fleet Station One, flight control. Requesting identification." The Kordolian voice that reaches me over the connection is young and eager.

"Fleet Station One," I reply, slightly amused at the flight

controller's enthusiasm, "since when do you not recognize your own?"

"We do not have any entries scheduled over the next cycle." The controller's response comes back terse and mechanical. He's sticking to the book. "State your identification code."

"Fleet Station, this is General Akkadian, and I am not requesting but *ordering* you to prepare the dock for landing. And have a medical team on standby. I have one injured on board."

There's a pause, and I catch frantic murmuring in the background.

"Right away, Sir. And, uh, apologies for not recognizing you."

"Identification is part of your job, controller. You're technically correct in not relying on the visual alone, so a verbal ID is appropriate."

His relief seems to filter through the comm. "Understood, Sir."

I guide *Silence* between a dense array of orbiting defense posts, past stationed freighters and towards the giant Fleet Station. It's a huge floating mass, suspended in permanent orbit around Kythia, and it's part of my command.

As we approach, the docking station opens, revealing the outer airlock.

A red warning signal flashes, telling me our oxygen supply is about to run out. Ignoring it, I guide *Silence* into the dock. It lists to one side slightly as I land, unbalanced as a result of the hasty Human repairs that were done on Fortuna Tau. Because of the damage sustained, she's going to need a major overhaul.

I thank the Goddess that the Human repairs held long enough to get us back to Kythia, especially after we navigated the disintegrating wormhole.

As the airlock depressurizes, I make my way to the medical bay, where Zyara is staring intently at a series of monitors.

"How is our patient doing?"

Zyara spins, a startled expression crossing her face. She obviously hadn't noticed me behind her. But as ever, she regains her composure quickly. "Vitals are stable, although I had to increase the dose of Sylerian to keep her asleep. For some reason, her Human physiology means she metabolizes it faster."

I watch Abbey as she bobs gently up and down, suspended in the stasis chamber. The cold liquid of the chamber was proving to be uncomfortable for her, so she opted for sedation for the rest of the journey.

One thing I've learnt about Humans is that they don't like the cold.

In sleep, her delicate face is peaceful. Humans are an interesting species. The intel we have on them isn't much, but from what I've read, they're still a young race. Primitive in their technology, self-destructive in their ideology. Soft-bodied, able to survive only in gentle climates.

The Kordolian Empire has always dismissed them under the label of 'non-threatening.'

I stare at Abbey, taking in her pale, damaged skin, which is marred by hundreds of tiny cuts. Her lower body has suffered the most; her legs have been deformed and crushed by the impact of falling from a dizzying height. Purple bruises have spread across her legs and stomach.

The only things keeping her alive right now are the stasis chamber and the lines Zyara's stuck into her, providing her with vital liquids.

Engulfed in blue liquid, she looks so small, so fragile. How do these humans cling so stubbornly to life when they can be crushed so easily?

She's vulnerable and imperfect, and yet I find myself drawn to her in a way I can't explain.

Maybe it's this so-called 'Mating Fever' Zyara has diagnosed me with. Perhaps I'm conditioned to react to the presence of a suitable female.

But a *Human*, of all creatures?

I'm now questioning why I was so intent on saving her from that poorly resourced Human mining station in the first place. I didn't trust the Human medics to save her and restore her back to normal. Their technology is still primitive. And she'd been hurt because of me; because of *us*.

In ordinary circumstances, I would have left her to her own kind. But my only instinct had been to bring her back. She was, and is, *my* responsibility.

At the height of her helplessness, I'd been compelled to touch her, to be near her. To take her in my arms. She'd looked so alone, so afraid. I'd jumped in the tank with her.

I'd been aroused. Hard. Filled with almost uncontrollable lust. The only thing stopping me from taking her then and there was the fact that she was injured.

Never before have I given in to emotion like this. Control is a virtue I live by.

Perhaps I took this 'Mating Fever' business too lightly. Zyara warned me I would need to do something about it. Otherwise, the effects will become stronger. The headaches are already close to unbearable.

I need to be rational and clear-headed. I can't afford this sort of shit on the battlefield.

Perhaps this Human is the answer to this sickness. Maybe I am no better than Rykal after all, unable to control my attraction to this so-called 'exotic fruit'.

But first, she needs treatment.

A soft voice snaps me out of my thoughts. "General?" Zyara is standing by, awaiting orders. She tries to keep the emotion from her features, but one slightly raised lilac eyebrow gives her away.

"Is there a problem, Zyara?" I can't help the menace that creeps into my voice. I'm not in the mood for questions, and Zyara knows me too well.

She holds up a placating hand. "I need to prepare her for transfer to the military hospital, but I don't know how to explain the situation to the Chief Surgeon. They're not expecting a Human."

"I'll talk to Mirkel." I glance at the Human again, observing the way her body sways, gently buffered by the stasis liquid. "Apart from the obvious resemblance, you say they share some biological similarities with us?"

"I've done a DNA analysis," Zyara replies, returning to her

businesslike tone. "Our genetic code is remarkably similar. In fact, I'd say Humans resemble the Early Kordolians most closely. Before the death of our planet's star billions of years ago, our environments were probably similar. And as you know, the basic building blocks of life are the same, all across the universe."

I study Abbey closely, noting the similarities, and the differences. "They resemble our ancestors, before we evolved?"

"You could say that."

"Hm." I allow the silence to stretch between us. We're both very aware of the potential implications of Zyara's discovery. "Will she tolerate a nanograft?" I ask finally.

"Well, theoretically, yes, but medical nanites have been in short supply lately. I doubt they'd authorize their use on a Human."

"*They*? This is *my* Fleet Station, Zyara. When have you ever known me to blindly follow protocol?" A flare of anger courses through me, fury at the thought that anyone would question my authority. Of course, there will be questions, rumors, perhaps even reports to the Kaiin-cursed High Council. But I would like to think that after loyally serving the Empire for so long, I might be granted a little autonomy on the Fleet Station that is under my fucking command.

Zyara looks at me for a moment, her expression unreadable. Then, she sighs. "A nanograft is the best way to restore her to her original state. She's entirely compatible. Physiologically, she'll probably be even stronger after the graft. But you need to talk to Chief Surgeon Mirkel. He won't listen to me, but he's scared shitless of you."

"Hm." Mirkel will never, ever forget the day I almost killed him. I was a young recruit then, and he was a junior medic. Of course, the experiments they carried out on me in those days were obscene.

Mirkel nearly killed me, and I simply returned the favor.

He still does his best to avoid me after all this time, sending the necessary communications through subordinates. I have no issue with that. As long as he follows my orders and remains loyal to the military, I couldn't give a shit if he thinks I'm Kaiin, the lord of the Netherworld, himself.

But now, I decide it's time for Mirkel's avoidance to end. It's about time I paid the Chief Surgeon a visit.

Zyara stares at her holoscreen. "The medical team's here," she announces.

"Then organize the transfer," I snap. "And let it be known that she's *my* property. If anything happens to her, whoever's responsible will answer to me directly. I'll deal with Mirkel."

"I'd love to be a witness to *that* conversation," Zyara remarks dryly as I take one last look at Abbey. In sleep, she reminds me of a delicate sculpture; a mythical creature. Even with her injuries, she's ethereally beautiful.

Otherworldly. So similar to us, and yet so different.

I've developed an unhealthy, irrational obsession with this female. I let out a derisive snort. A Human, of all beings.

Perhaps this so-called 'Mating Fever' is affecting me more than I thought.

Abbey

WHEN I WAKE UP, all I see is dim light and shadows. The first thing I notice is that it's warm. The liquid's gone, and to my intense relief, the horrible, freezing cold is gone too.

Wait. That means I'm not in that awful stasis tank anymore. I sit up, startled, then I lie back down again as the memories return.

Both of my legs were broken, right? I shouldn't be moving.

But there's no pain.

Tentatively, I try to move one foot. Yep, it seems to be fine, and it doesn't hurt at all. I wiggle the toes on my other foot, and then, slowly, gingerly, I move my legs.

They don't hurt either. Everything's intact. Am I dreaming?

I glance around and see that I'm in a small spartan room. I'm in a bed, or at least I think it's a bed. It's a person-shaped pod, made out of a dark, organic looking substance. It's not wood or metal or anything I recognize. It's warm inside, and it's covered in soft black sheets.

I sit up, my bare feet touching the floor. I've been dressed in dark flowing robes that are about five sizes too big for me. The fabric is softer than silk, impossibly luxurious and voluminous.

I'm drowning in mysterious fabric that carries a faint spicy scent. Like cinnamon, but different.

I know that smell. It tickles the back of my foggy memory. It reminds me of *him*.

I shudder, remembering the feel of his warm skin against mine and the sensation of his big rough hands on my body.

Idiot. I should stop thinking about that. I was probably affected by all the drugs they were pumping through me.

I glance around, trying to get my bearings. Where the hell am I? The last thing I remember was being stuck in a freezing cold stasis tank against my will. The General was so damn blasé about taking me away from Fortuna Tau, but when it came to everything else, he seemed deadly serious.

Doesn't he get that you don't just *take* people away from their home planets? That you don't just separate people from their own species?

Obviously, he doesn't. It's something to do with that weird sense of honor he has. Something about keeping his word. About being responsible for everything.

Stubborn, domineering, irritating male.

He's got control freak written all over him.

It must come with the territory.

But if the current state of my legs is anything to go by, he's been true to his word and had them healed.

Amazing. I flex them experimentally, watching as they peek out underneath swathes of black fabric. There's not a single break in the skin or trace of a healing wound to be seen.

It's as if the accident and my encounter with that disgusting vomit-inducing creature never happened.

I drop to my feet, allowing my legs to take my full weight. There's no pain at all.

I take a few experimental steps. Everything seems to be working fine.

What the hell did they do to me? And at what cost?

I pad across the dark floor. It's like ice underneath my bare feet. There's a closed door to one side. It's made of that same black wood-but-not-wood material that the whole room is constructed of. I push on it, but nothing happens.

A shot of panic rips through me. Am I locked in? Trapped like a prisoner?

I'm a bit claustrophobic. I don't like tiny, confined spaces. The thought of being stuck in this dim, warm, creepy little room makes me go a bit funny. My pulse goes up, and I start to feel nauseous. I'm trapped in the confines of some dark, organic *thing*, and it's all rather embryonic, as if I've been placed back inside the womb.

I push again, harder this time. Still, the stupid thing won't budge. I look around for a control panel of some sort, but the way the door joins the wall is seamless.

I'm breaking out in a cold sweat now, and starting to feel short of breath. My arms are tingling. I can't think straight.

I'm having a panic attack. I can't believe it. I haven't had one of these in years.

Calm down, Abbey!

I start pounding at the door, and when that doesn't work, I run my fingers along the edges, looking for a gap, a seam, anything, hopping to find a weakness I can use to wrench it apart.

Nothing.

Damn these Kordolians and their weird technology. I step back, forcing myself to breathe more slowly, trying to calm my racing pulse. I study the door in more detail. It's made of hundreds of horizontal interlocking dark strands, like a woven basket.

Does it swing, or slide, or retract?

I need to get out of here. I need to escape from this dark, windowless, tiny room. I take a few steps back, thinking I'll give the stupid thing one last solid kick. Even if it doesn't open, it will feel good just to kick something.

To vent some of my fear and frustration.

So I take two big strides forward, hiking up my ridiculous, tent-like garment. Going with the momentum, I execute a solid high kick, just like I've seen them do in those ridiculous twentieth-century action flicks.

It's true, I have a secret obsession with everything twentieth-century. There has never been an era of Human creativity quite like it.

Van Damme, eat your heart out.

There's a dull thud as my foot connects, and I'm surprised that it doesn't hurt one bit. And is it just me, or is there a little indent right there, where I've kicked it?

Still, the door doesn't open. I take a deep breath, trying to calm my racing thoughts. But just as I'm about to step back, the weird little fibers come apart, disappearing into a cavity in the wall.

I stumble forward in shock, losing my balance.

"What the?" I yelp, as I crash into something hard and solid and warm. I look up to find the General staring down at me, a frown creasing his hard features. He raises an eyebrow as he grabs me by the shoulders, steadying me. An electric tingle courses through me. Through the thin fabric of my oversized robes, his fingers feel oh-so warm.

"You should be resting," he growls. "Not trying to damage my sleeping pod."

"Your what?" I look around wildly, taking in my surroundings. We're in what looks like a living space. It has the same cold dark floors and oddly curved walls as the rest of this craft, reminding me of the Kordolian medical bay I was stuck in when I was injured. To my left, soaring windows provide a view of the endless starry sky. But amongst the glittering backdrop, there's a giant black planet swallowing up most of the view. It's dotted with millions of glowing blue lights, reminding me of Earth at night.

Whoa. That's Kythia?

In front of the window is a low seating area made of dark cushions. The rest of the space is quite boring and uncluttered. There's a desk surrounded by an array of complex looking holo-screens, but not much else. There's no kitchen, no eating area. There's nothing to identify the owner of the place, no pictures on the walls or trinkets or cozy rugs on the floor.

This place could really use a woven rug or two. Some colorful vases and maybe a terrarium would spruce the place up. Right now, it's a total man-cave. Quite fitting for a dour, humorless military General.

"Where the hell am I, General?" I ask, backpedalling out of his grasp. Oh, no. I'm not ready for that quite yet. I need to get my bearings first, *without* being distracted by his warm, roving hands. "Wh- what have you done to me?"

"You're in my quarters," he replies, looking me up and down. "And it appears you have responded quite well to the treatment."

"What treatment?" Suspicion clouds my tone as I glance down at my bare legs, which peek out of the loose robes. Surely miracles don't come without a hefty price. There has to be a catch.

"A nanograft," he shrugs. "You will understand the implications with time."

As usual, he's not the most forthcoming character. My gaze returns to rest on him. Something's different. He's no longer decked out in his crazy nano-armor. Instead, he wears dark robes similar to mine, which are loosely belted at the waist. Whereas the ones I wear are huge on me, swamping my small frame, his fit perfectly, hanging off his large body and revealing his smooth, sculpted chest.

He notices the direction of my gaze and for just a split-second, something like a smug look crosses his face. I grit my teeth, annoyed that he's just caught me checking him out. But then, he's back to his usual form, glaring at me with a serious expression.

"You need to eat," he growls, as he walks over to a panel in the wall that I hadn't noticed before. "Tissue healing requires energy." The General taps a code on some kind of sleek silver device that's set into the wall. It lights up and emits a low hum. After a brief wait, it opens, and he fishes out a dark rectangular object.

He offers it to me. "Eat."

"Huh?" I eye the lump in his hand with confusion. "What's that?"

"Food. Eat." He thrusts it in front of my face. Okay, so we're down to one-word commands. Why does this all suddenly feel a bit neolithic? Gingerly, I take the, er, thing.

It looks like an energy bar of some sort. I hope it's chocolate? Ha. What are the chances? Looking at its dark, semi-transparent color and slightly gooey consistency, like hard, compacted gelatin, I'm not convinced. I sniff it cautiously. It smells like a combination of dried seaweed and beef jerky.

Not unpleasant, but not mind-blowing either.

"It's not to your taste?" He's watching me closely, curiously.

"I could murder a bowl of nachos right about now," I reply. "You guys don't do nachos? Or fries with chicken salt? Is ramen off the menu?"

Tarak glares at me, irritation making his lips curve downwards in a disapproving frown. My sarcasm is totally lost on him. "We don't have Human food here."

"I figured." A sly smile tugs at the corners of my mouth. "You have no idea what you're missing out on." I take an experimental bite of the bar. It melts in my mouth, all salty and meaty and thick. I chew a bit more, realizing that I'm actually starving.

Okay, so I'll admit, it's edible. I munch down on the rest of the bar as the General watches me. It's all slightly awkward. I feel like a kid who's being forced by their parents to eat their brussels sprouts, or else.

When I'm done, the stuff settles in my belly like a lead weight, making me feel instantly full. "So, General," I begin tentatively, not really sure how to bring this up, especially when he's gone and had my body magically fixed. "When do we set off for Fortuna Tau?"

He responds with a cryptic look. There's something in his

eyes that tells me this isn't going to be straightforward. "In time," he says.

I'm about to demand that he organize for me to go back straight away, but our attention is diverted as one of the holo-screens lights up, and a stone-faced Kordolian guy appears. He rattles something off in rapid-fire Kordolian. Tarak stiffens, his jaw set in a rigid line. He doesn't like whatever the guy is telling him.

The General snaps back at him and ends the communication. He mutters something under his breath that sounds a lot like swearing. That little bulging vein at the side of his head is back. I'm starting to figure out his little tells. Right now, he's irritated.

"I have to go," he announces. "Do not leave my quarters. The troops will not tolerate a Human roaming about on this station."

"Wait," I protest. "You can't just leave me. What am I supposed to do here?"

"Rest." He disappears into his dark sleeping chamber and returns a moment later, decked out in a uniform of sorts. It's all black, of course. There's a high-necked jacket with long tails and a pair of sleek trousers. There's some sort of insignia embroidered at the neck in red, the first hint of color I've seen on any of his attire.

I try not to gape. It's a severe, intimidating uniform, but it compliments his broad frame, and it all looks quite dapper in an Evil Empire sort of way.

"Stay here," he growls threateningly, before disappearing through his front door, the thing sliding shut with the same interlocking mechanism, effectively trapping me inside.

Great. I'm stuck in an alien General's personal quarters on a floating station in an entirely different sector of the universe.

What's a girl to do? For starters, I guess I could try to figure out this body of mine, and see exactly what's changed.

And then? Plot an escape plan? Yeah. That sounds like a rather good way to pass the time.

Tarak

I LEAVE Abbey in my quarters, the Qualum door fusing shut behind me. The entrance is keyed to my biological signature, and no-one else can enter or exit. Even on this orbiting fortress, where my word is absolute, I spare no precaution when it comes to security.

The fucking dress uniform I'm wearing is stiff and uncomfortable. I find it ridiculous, but when one is summoned to stand before the High Council, this is the customary attire.

More formality and nonsense. It's an annoyance. A complete waste of my time.

I'd rather be mobilizing a retrieval team for my First Division. Without the wormhole, it will take at least six cycles for *Silence* to reach the Human mining station. First Division won't be happy with the wait, but they'll adapt. In the meantime, I can send a backup crew from one of the outer sectors.

And then there's the matter of my exotic female guest. She doesn't know that I watched her when she was asleep. I sat on the floor of my sleeping chamber, cross-legged, observing her pale face and her soft, fragile body. For the most part, she appeared peaceful, except for when she tossed and turned. Every now and then a flicker of pain would cross her features. Her skin would become moist, and I would lay a hand on her forehead, waiting for her to fall back into a deep sleep.

I only left her side once I was certain the nanograft had taken, once I was sure that she was in the clear. I hadn't trusted any of the medics to watch her, not even Zyara.

I hadn't trusted them to take care of a Human. That idiot Mirkel had been hesitant to treat her at first, but he had quickly changed his mind after our little 'discussion.'

As I stride down the corridor, an officer comes up beside me, anxiously taking in my appearance. Dress uniform means only one thing. That I've been summoned. "Shall I arrange an escort for you, General?"

"Not necessary," I snap, glancing at the soldier. The face is familiar. "Keron, isn't it?" His face lights up as I mention his name. So this one isn't worn and jaded yet. I doubt Officer Keron has seen much off-planet action. "I'll be using my own transport. A guard isn't necessary. I'm only going landside, for fuck's sake."

"Understood, Sir." He starts to carry out that irritating formal bow, but I cut him off with a slice of my hand. "There's none of that onboard my Fleet Station, Officer. Keep your formalities for the landside folk." That infernal bow was introduced by the Empress after Emperor Ilhan died. It never fails to get under my skin. In contrast, the High Council live for such things.

Bunch of ostentatious pricks.

Keron blinks in surprise, but wisely decides not to argue.

"While you're here, Keron, you can arrange something for me."

"Sir?"

"Get an order of Veronian food from landside. Those sweet things they make. Have it sent to my quarters by internal delivery."

"Veronian food. Got it." Curiosity burns in Keron's eyes, but he doesn't dare probe the issue. For all he knows, I've just developed a craving for sweet things.

We reach a docking station reserved for smaller craft. Keron starts to bow reflexively, but as I narrow my eyes he catches himself, straightening to his full height.

"Dismissed, Officer," I say, a trace of irony creeping into my voice. As he disappears, I enter one of the solo transports, a sleek, unarmed cruiser designed for speed and little else. A dull throb begins at the back of my eyes, and I resist the urge to groan.

The headaches are coming back.

Strangely, when I'm with *her*, there are no symptoms at all. No headaches. No stabbing pain behind my eyes. No burning irritability that threatens to explode into anger at any given moment.

Just her scent is enough to calm me. It reminds me of that Human garden, all green stems and fruits and wildflowers.

Things that are entirely alien to Kythia. Our planet does not support that kind of life.

I activate the flyer and ease it out of the dock, navigating it through the airlock. Once I've passed the outer lock, I communicate with flight control.

"Cleared for departure, General."

I gun the thrusters and speed towards Kythia, wondering what in Kaiin's name the High Council want with me this time. Whatever it is, it won't be anything good. It never is.

CHAPTER SEVEN

Abbey

I explore the General's quarters for a while, looking around, running my hand over things, and pressing various panels on the walls. Everything is so alien looking. It's all quite fascinating.

My legs are holding up just fine, and I'm actually feeling really good, better than I've felt in a long time. Whatever the Kordolians have pumped into me seems to have worked.

I return to his sleeping chamber—that dark, cocoon-like place—and search around. There must be a wardrobe in here, because otherwise how could he get changed into that sexy dress uniform so quickly?

Oh, my. Did I just think that?

Let me rephrase that. Not sexy. *Distinguished* is more like it.

Hell, Abbey, you thought he was sexy. Just admit it.

There's a little triangular arrangement of blue lights in the wall that I hadn't noticed before. I touch my palm to it and bingo, the dark wall magically comes apart, revealing a walk-in wardrobe. Apart from the muted glow of the little blue lights, it's dim inside. Why do Kordolians prefer everything to be hidden in shadow? It's as if they've got something to hide.

There are only a few garments hanging on the racks. I

suppose he doesn't need much clothing because he's wearing armor most of the time. And underneath the freaky nano-armor, he's very naked, *all* the time. I shudder, goosebumps rippling on my skin as I remember the way he stood before me when I was in the stasis tank.

Unashamed, in all of his naked glory.

I couldn't take my eyes off him.

The wardrobe contains a duplicate of the fancy uniform he was wearing, another robe, and some plain looking trousers. All black, of course.

The guy needs some color. I'm thinking a dark red, like wine, might suit him. It would match his eyes.

I grab the trousers and try them on, discarding the billowing robe. I need something a bit less cumbersome to go around in. I can't be tripping over swathes of fabric at every turn.

The trousers are big and long, but I manage to roll them up and fashion the belt-like thing so that it cinches nicely at my waist.

I grab a soft, sleeveless tunic and slip it over my head. It falls to about mid-thigh, like a short dress.

Too bad there's no mirror. At least I feel a lot more presentable now. It's not the most fashionable getup, but at least I can move around freely.

I go back into the living space and do a few experimental squats. Easy. No pain, no stiffness. I hop on one leg, and then the other. I'm as good as new. There's no deformity and no scarring, thank Jupiter. I bend over and touch my toes. I've always been flexible, and it seems nothing's changed. I'm able to reach over and touch both palms to the floor.

What the hell did these Kordolians do to me?

A nanograft? I don't like the sound of that.

But I seem to be healthy and whole, and so far, there's no sign that they've taken my organs or tried to experiment on me or stuck a control chip in my brain.

The only problem right now is that I'm locked in the General's chambers and I have no idea when he plans on sending me home.

Does he even plan on returning me? He seemed a little cagey on that point. Perhaps I shouldn't wait around to find out exactly what he has in store for me.

I don't trust Kordolians.

There has to be a way to get out of here. I pace over to the weird looking door that marks the entrance to the quarters. It's made of that same woven looking stuff; those weird black fibers that seem to peel apart when opening. The light in here is so scant that it's hard to make out the fine detail, but at least there's some starlight to go by.

Seriously, Kordolians? What's with the darkness and gloom? I'm starting to miss the sunshine already.

From what I've seen, they don't have an equivalent to the Sun. Just a dim, dying star; a fading memory of what once was there. How many hundreds, or thousands, or *millions* of years has it been like that?

There's a thin fissure in the centre of the door, where I've seen the fibre-like things slide apart. They're like tiny interlocking fingers, sealed impossibly tight. Yet when the General walked up to the door, it just opened.

I dig my fingers into the grooves of the fissure, trying to pry it open.

It's a bit stupid of me. Why would a futuristic alien door have a weakness where I could just pull it open? But I'm desperate to get out of here, so still I tug, hoping for a bit of give.

"Ow!" I wince as one of my fingernails rips, revealing a small patch of raw nailbed. A tiny droplet of blood beads there, smearing on the door's surface as I pull my finger away to suck on it.

There's a rushing sound, and a whoosh of air, and suddenly the interlocking, black fibers are gone, revealing a shadowy corridor.

Uh, did I do that? What the hell did I just do?

I blink, looking left and right, startled by my sudden, unexpected freedom. The corridor curves around in each direction, disappearing into the darkness.

Which way do I go? I turn left, guided by a hunch, keeping an eye out for any sign of movement. The General told me not to go out of his quarters, but there's no way I can just sit around and wait for him to come back.

That would be placing my fate in *his* hands, and I'm not about to allow that when I know *nothing* about the man or his motivations. I need to figure out an escape plan. I need to get the lay of the place.

Some might call me reckless. I'll admit, I'm an *act now, think later* kind of girl. It's calculated recklessness, though. I figure that if the Big Bad *wanted* me harmed or dead, I'd already be harmed or dead.

I try to be stealthy, making my footfalls light, watching for a change in the shadows, listening for any sound that might indicate an approaching Kordolian. The problem is that there's nowhere to hide.

The passageway leads to an open area which must be some kind of communal space, judging by the soft seating and array of tables. The huge vaulted windows look out onto the dark planet below. A river of blue lights creeps across its surface, winking against the inky blackness. The place is empty right now, much to my relief.

The entire scene below me is eerie and intimidating and darkly beautiful.

Just like the Dark Planet's inhabitants.

I pass through the quiet room, alert for any signs of movement. But there's not a Kordolian to be seen. I move through a series of wide arches into another cavernous space, stopping dead in my tracks.

I've come to a lookout, and there's a lake below me.

Incredible. As I stare down at the giant expanse of water, I realize it's not a lake but a swimming pool. Like all things Kordolian, it doesn't have straight edges, but smooth, curved corners. There are lines marked for lap swimming.

But what's most astonishing about the pool is that it's completely transparent at the bottom, looking out onto the stars and the ominous shadow of the Dark Planet below.

Magnified by water, the stars and lights are surreal.

Talk about an infinity pool.

I stiffen as the sound of voices drifts towards me through the stillness. It's difficult to figure out which direction they're coming from. The voices become louder, turning into a raucous exchange of Kordolian banter.

Shit. They're heading this way.

I look around in panic, but there's nowhere to hide. If I go down to the pool area below, I'll be easy to spot. My pale skin will surely stand out in the darkness. If I go back the way I've come, I'll run straight into them.

The voices are louder now, and two Kordolian males appear. They see me as soon as I see them, and for a moment, we all freeze. If I weren't freaking out, the situation might almost be comical.

They start babbling at me in Kordolian. I can't understand a word they're saying.

I hold up a hand. "Do you guys speak Universal?"

At the sound of my voice, they hesitate. They're both military, by the looks of things; fit, lean, and clean-cut. We stare at each other, having a real first-contact sort of moment. I doubt they've ever seen a real live Human before.

"H- Human!" One of the guys raises a hand and points at me. "What are you doing here?" His Universal is heavily accented, but I can understand him well enough.

I decide to bluff it out. "I'm a guest of General Tarak's." Even though they tower above me, I straighten to my full height, trying to appear confident and intimidating.

At the mention of the General's name, both of them have a rapid-fire exchange in Kordolian. The first guy turns back to me. "You are not authorized to be in this area. We must detain you while we confirm the correct clearances."

"Uh, I don't think the General would be very happy to hear I've been detained over something so trivial." I wave my hand imperiously, stepping forward to glare at the guy. He has light amber eyes, which go wide as I poke him in the chest. "Soldier, would you like to answer to General Tarak over this? He's gone to the effort of bringing me here all the way from Sector Nine.

Do you really think I would have free run of this area if he hadn't allowed it? This is your *General* we're talking about here. Are you accusing him of being negligent?"

Uncertainty plays across the soldier's face as his buddy whispers something to him in Kordolian. He shies away from my touch, nervously wiping his hands down the front of his uniform.

It seems the threat of facing the General is a very scary one indeed.

Huh. I file away that useful bit of information. It seems even regular Kordolians are scared of my Big Bad.

Oops. Did I just think of him as *my* Tarak?

The soldiers stare at me for a moment, then both execute an odd little bow, backing away. "No offense was intended, Human. Please do not mention this incident to General Akkadian."

"I won't if you won't." I wink, and that seems to send them into further confusion. They back away as if I'm some kind of venomous creature. "Oh, you guys. Relax." I wave them away. "Go and enjoy your swim." That pool, with its amazing clear bottom, looks incredibly inviting.

The Kordolians retreat, stepping onto a hoverlift, which takes them to the lower level.

You'd almost think they were afraid of females, or Humans. Or both.

Except that they're now both stripping off, in full view of me.

And of course, they're not wearing anything underneath. Totally in their birthday suits. I shake my head, fighting the embarrassment that rises. My ears feel hot. I'm reminded of Tarak and his perfectly sculpted body, the impressive length of him, and the feel of his deft, sure hands on my skin.

I clutch the metal railing of the balcony with moist palms. The thought of the General sends a warm feeling through my core, right down to my most sensitive area.

And here I was supposed to be looking for an escape route. I try to banish the sensual thoughts from my mind. I need a clear head for this. Perhaps a swim in that inviting pool below will help. *After* the young, naked Kordolians have finished, of course.

Anything to get these thoughts out of my head.

———————

Tarak

I STAND before the twelve heads of the High Council with my teeth clenched in irritation. My fangs break the skin of my lower lip, and I taste blood in my mouth.

But as always, the tiny wound heals as quickly as it was made.

The representatives of the High Council look down upon me from their elevated seats. There are six females and six males, all born of one of Kythia's twelve Noble Houses. Several of the males are wearing elaborate robes which I recognize as Veronian in origin, with their fine, colorful embroidery. Thin fingers are decked out with intricate rings bearing cumbersome, glittering jewels. Some of the males have grown their hair long, in a style that seems to be fashionable on Kythia at the moment.

The females, on the other hand, are dressed in the plain black robes of their office.

In these times, Kordolian females do not have to try hard to impress anyone. There are so few of them left that they can have their pick of any male on the planet.

"General Akkadian." One of the representatives, a tall, severe female with long hair that is darkening with age, addresses me, her low voice echoing throughout the small chamber. I recognize her as Councillor Sivian, the elected head. "It has come to our attention that you have a Human onboard the Fleet Station." Her cold, amber gaze locks with mine, and she arches one eyebrow. "When were you going to inform us of that particular detail?"

The Council know about Abbey. Fuck. How in Kaiin's hells did they find out?

I resist the urge to leap up to the pedestal and grab her by the throat. Instead, I fight to keep my tone even. "I am not required to inform the Council of every little thing that goes on aboard the Fleet Station. I'd hardly think the presence of a Human would be of any concern to you."

"When we are told that this Human, a *female* at that, is repro-ductively compatible with our species, then it most certainly becomes the business of the High Council, General."

I hide my shock behind a carefully blank expression. Repro-ductively compatible? Zyara said our species had some similari-ties, but the ability to mate?

And who would have informed the landside authorities of such a thing?

My suspicions lie with Mirkel. If he's gone to the Council on this, I'll tear his fucking head off.

"I am requesting you to hand over custody of the Human to the Genetic Research Unit. Such a discovery cannot be kept quiet because of personal desires, General."

I fight to keep still, but underneath my skin, the black nanites are seething. They've escaped my bloodstream in response to my anger, and they're ready to emerge and equip me for combat at any moment.

"The Human is mine," I say quietly, calmly. "There will be no handover."

"Are you sure about that, General? Withholding any resource that might help the future survival of our race is akin to trea-son." The eleven other Councillors nod in agreement, their cold gazes fixed on me.

That look. Derision. Scorn. Judgement. It's a look I've received my entire life. I am, and always will be, an outsider. Like many Kordolians who haven't been born into a Noble House, I'm still considered a second-class citizen, regardless of my rank.

Inferior, even though I now hold half of their military in the palm of my hand. The nobles are blinded by their own arrogance.

"Councillor Sivian," I say mildly, disguising my rage. "Are you accusing me of treason?"

She responds with a deceptively gentle smile. "Of course not, General. We are all aware of your exploits in the expansion efforts and the fight against our eternal enemy, the Xargek. I was merely suggesting a course of action. Surely you're not so attached to this feeble Human that you'd put her welfare above the needs of your own race?"

"And if I am?"

"Then this becomes an insurmountable dispute. One that needs to be resolved at all costs."

I shake my head slowly. "No, Councillor. There is no dispute here. The human is mine, and you and your scientists will not touch as much as a single hair on her head. If you wish to carry out experiments, find another subject at your own expense."

"General Akkadian!" An outraged male voice rings across the chamber as one of the Councillors stands. Luron Alerak. An idiot with yellow robes and metal piercings bristling from both ears. "You will not address the High Councillor with such disrespect. Or do you forget that you survive here by the grace of the Empress alone?"

A harsh laugh escapes me. "Do you forget that I have half of the Kordolian military under my command, Luron? The Empress acts graciously because I agreed to peace."

"Outrageous! You go too far, General!"

"The Human is mine," I repeat. "There will be consequences if any harm comes to her." I turn to leave, a cold fury rising inside me. The thought of handing Abbey over to be experimented on makes me want to hurt someone. And the headache behind my eyes has become a thousand times worse.

If I don't leave now, I may very well do something violent.

Shocked murmurs break out as I turn my back on the Council. But as I start to walk out, a familiar voice rings through the chamber. "General Akkadian, I don't recall you being dismissed."

I turn slowly and find myself face to face with the arguably the most dangerous being on Kythia.

"Empress Vionn." I look up towards the gallery, where she is standing at the railing. The Empress smiles, baring her fangs. But there is no warmth in her crimson eyes.

I stiffen, refusing to stoop to the ridiculous customary bow that she loves. I receive twelve disapproving stares from the Council, but I hold my ground.

I'm no longer afraid of the High Council. There's nothing they can do to me now. They hadn't realized how much my influence in the military had grown until it was too late. Being a war hero has its perks. My soldiers are loyal to me only. And Kythia needs us. The Kordolian race is nothing without its army.

The Empress waves a slender hand, her sharpened obsidian fingernails glinting under the overly bright lights. "The rest of you, get out. I will have words with the General alone."

"But Infinite Mother," Luron whines, the trinkets in his pierced ear clinking as he shakes his head, "Akkadian is a savage. You cannot—"

Vionn stalks over to the Councilor and slaps him in the face, her sharp nails drawing blood. A trickle of black seeps down Luron's pale cheek. "Do not presume, child. *Never* presume on my behalf."

I close my eyes and take a deep breath as the stabbing pain behind my eyes intensifies. Luron spews forth a stream of groveling apologies, bowing repeatedly as he backs away. The other Councilors follow him in haste.

We all know who holds the true power on Kythia. Ever since Emperor Ilhan died, Vionn has been spreading her influence. Her power multiplies like billions of unstoppable Xargek larvae.

Detestable female.

With the chamber empty, the Empress grabs the railing and leaps to the lower floor, landing in front of me, her loose robes billowing around her. Her wild untamed hair is darkening with age, and as she moves closer, I see faint lines at the corners of her eyes and mouth.

No matter how powerful she is, the Infinte Empress cannot defeat time.

"I'm disappointed in you, Tarak. I never thought that you, of all Kordolians, would become attached to a lesser species. And to show your weakness in front of the entire High Council? Are you becoming soft, General?"

"What do you want, Vionn?" I freeze as she stops just in front of me. She's so close I can feel her warm breath on my face.

"I want to understand what's going on inside that hard head of yours, General. You know our species is dying out. That there haven't been any females born in the most recent reproductive season. And yet you withhold an important clue that could lead to our survival. A reproductively compatible female. Is celibacy your problem, boy? Is abstinence clouding your judgement? You know, I can help you with that." She draws her fingers down the side of my face, her long nails grazing my skin. "Why is it that of all the males I've desired, only you have been immune to me? Are you defective, General?"

I clench my teeth as her chemical scent surrounds me. It's harsh and cloying, a pale imitation of Abbey's sweet perfume. The Empress leans close and draws her pointed black tongue across my cheek. "I haven't been able to feel true pleasure since Ilhan died. You know as well as I do that this generation of males isn't the same. With such a brutal military to protect us, ordinary civilians have become soft." She places her hand at the opening of my trousers, her claw-like fingers resting on my cock. "You, on the other hand, would make me a most suitable mate."

She strokes my dick through the thin fabric of my pants, before snorting in disgust. "Disappointing. Not even a twitch. Are you perhaps fond of the other sex, boy? Or maybe you desire the Human female. Would you willingly dilute the Kordolian gene pool with that filth? Why, oh, why, do all the males with a shred of promise act like raving lunatics? Even that uncivilized son of mine has gone insane."

Unable to take it any more, I grasp her wrist, pulling her hand away. "My sexual preferences are none of your business, Vionn." My headache is excruciating now, threatening to bring me to my knees. My vision starts to blur a little. I squeeze Vionn's wrist and she smiles, showing her fangs.

"Oh, I like a male who isn't afraid to hurt me. None have had the balls to try, aside from you. They forget that pain can be a great aphrodisiac."

Her words cause me to release her in disgust. She laughs. "It's too bad about your Human pet. I can see you're quite attached to it. But we're arranging to have it brought here as I speak. You'll just have to replace it with another Human. Perhaps you can catch another the next time you're passing by Sector Nine."

Something inside me snaps, and the next thing I know, I have her pinned to the floor, my hand around her neck. The black nanites respond to my will, forming an armored glove around my hand. The hard, impenetrable material of the exo-suit bites into her pale skin.

White-hot rage erupts at the thought of Abbey being at the mercy of this bitch. I could so easily squeeze my hand right now and drain the life from Vionn.

For a sliver of a moment, I catch a flicker of fear in her gaze. It's so fleeting I almost miss it.

But then she's laughing. It's more of a faint, noiseless wheeze, but she's laughing. Her dark red eyes shine with a mixture of desire and amusement. She's enjoying this. Revulsion creeps through me. "You can't bring yourself to do it, General. Go on, kill me and invite war. Our species will not survive another civil war *or* the loss of another female. You can bring about our downfall, right here, right now, if you wish."

I wrench my hand away in disgust, stepping up off her.

The Infinite Empress, ruler of Kythia and the declining Kordolian race, is insane.

I leave her lying on the black floor of the Council chambers, her long hair strewn around her head like a wild crown. A mad laugh echoes through the room as I escape, my skin crawling with disgust. The agony behind my eyes pounds incessantly, sharp and insistent.

"Go, Tarak. Try and save her. You're already too late."

And all I can think is that I need to get to my Human before they do. They will dissect her and destroy her, because they don't value any other form of life besides their own.

I know it all too well, because I was the same, once.

Abbey

AS I TURN AWAY from the pool hall, the sound of splashing water echoes through the huge space and two more Kordolians appear. Unlike the military guys, they're both wearing white robes similar to those I've seen on Zyara.

And these two males don't look so friendly.

They don't seem surprised to see me, either. Uh, oh. I'm getting a bad feeling about these guys.

I look around for somewhere to go, but they're blocking the only exit, and the pool area is a dead end. There's nowhere to hide.

"Can I help you?" I blurt, trying to edge around them. They stare back at me, stone-faced, not saying a word.

Okay, so they're definitely not friendly.

The lead guy has something in his hand. It looks like a needle of some sort. I try to weigh up my options. They're advancing on me and muttering to each other in Kordolian. I decide I don't want to be a part of anything they've got planned.

I feint to the left then dash to the right, evading them and making for the exit.

Run!

They shout in their strange tongue, rushing after me, but I'm faster, and I pump my arms and legs, racing across the common area. These new legs are working a treat. Somehow, I can run really, really fast.

What the hell did they do to me?

But I don't have time to contemplate my newfound speed right now, because two other white-robed Kordolians have appeared, blocking off the way to the General's quarters.

Cutting me off. Shit.

I look around, but there's nowhere to go. The two males who were in the pool have appeared behind the robed guys, still naked and dripping wet, yelling and adding to all the confusion.

If I weren't so terrified right now, I'd roll my eyes. What is it with Kordolian males and nudity?

Everyone's started screaming, and I can't understand a word

of it. The unfriendly guys advance on me, tall and intimidating, marching forward like robots.

There's nowhere for me to run, nowhere to hide.

Where the hell is Tarak when I need him? As I try to evade the Kordolians, one of them catches me by the wrist, his grip like steel. Like the General, these guys are insanely strong. I flail about, trying to wrench away from his iron grasp.

His buddy comes up behind me, and the other two guys also close in. I'm outnumbered four-to-one.

The soldiers are staring at the scene before them in shock, still engaged in a rapid-fire back-and-forth with the white robe guys. "A little help here," I gasp, appealing to them with a desperate glance.

They stare at me in confusion, but just as I sense I'm getting through to them, something sharp pokes me in the back of the neck.

It feels like a needle.

Oh, shit.

My last thought, before I black out, is that I really need to stop letting these Kordolians sedate me all the time. Then my vision goes hazy, and everything fades away.

Abbey

WHEN I OPEN my eyes again, the world slowly blurs back into focus. Kordolian voices murmur all around me. My head is spinning.

I try to move, but something is pinning down my arms and legs. Something hard and inflexible is clamped around my wrists and feet. The restraints have sharp edges. I think I'm bleeding a little bit.

And it's bloody freezing cold. There's no warmth in this Kordolian world. Everything is dark and cold and inhuman. They've lived without the warmth of a star for so long they've turned into creatures of darkness and ice.

I'm strapped down on some kind of table, and I'm totally naked.

Oh sweet Earth, how I miss you right now. I preferred life when it was simple, when I could just retreat into my room and watch silly twentieth-century movies on Netcom in my pajamas, with a bowl of ramen in front of me.

Oh, for the good old days.

I shudder, closing my eyes again as a white-robed figure passes close to me. I feign unconsciousness.

This is beyond bad.

Drugged and strapped to a table on an alien space station? That only means one thing. They're about to turn me into a giant lab rat.

The hard, frigid surface of the table is brutal against the bare skin of my back and ass, My body trembles slightly, threatening to erupt into full-blown shivering.

I am so sick and tired of this damn cold. If I ever make it back to Earth, I'm having a month-long warm bubble bath.

What would be better than a long, hot soak right about now? A long, hot soak with a grumpy, bossy, silver alien? There would be something so oddly satisfying about seeing General Tarak covered in fluffy bubble bath suds.

A robotic machine-sound brings me back to reality and I mentally kick myself for thinking such stupid things at a time like this. I'm about to be dissected by aliens and I'm thinking about that muscle-headed jerk, naked? The word delirious comes to mind. Maybe it's the drugs they shot into me.

Speaking of the jerk, where the hell is he, anyway? My anger rises, mingling with a growing sense of helplessness. He's the one who got me into this situation, and now he's letting these robe-wearing assholes turn me into a human guinea pig?

I hope this isn't what he intended all along. I really hope he hasn't sold me out.

Because that would be rather disappointing.

I almost thought we had a little connection going on there.

I freeze as a pair of cold, gloved hands touches the bare skin at my neck. I fight with every ounce of my self-control to keep from moving. Some instinct tells me I shouldn't let them know that I'm awake right now. The hands trace down my chest, resting at my breasts, before examining my stomach. They poke and prod and feel around, and I fight to keep from wincing in pain.

Seriously dude, I'm not a fucking beanbag.

The creepy alien hands descend to my pelvis, moving over the prominent bones of my hips, tracing down to my pussy, running over the soft, sensitive flesh. I bite down on my lower lip, drawing blood. It's the only thing that's stopping me from screaming as revulsion courses through me. This is like every bad twentieth-century alien movie coming true all at once.

But all of a sudden, the hand freezes.

"*Zhyl sarba ak Human regeliss.*" Or something like that. The sharp voice pierces my misery. I recognize it all too well. Zyara.

The hand stops, then it's gone. Oh, thank sweet Jupiter.

Zyara and the pervert examiner, a male Kordolian with a deep voice, exchange heated words as I keep my eyes closed. I'm dying to see what's going on, and yet I'm desperate to seem asleep. I don't want to draw his attention again.

Then a distant alarm sounds, and Mr Creepyhands curses in Kordolian before leaving in a huff.

It's only when he's gone that I dare open my eyes again.

Zyara's standing over me, her orange gaze brimming with pity.

"Oh don't give me that look," I growl as she rests a cool hand on my cheek. "I was going to kick him in the nuts as soon as I got the chance."

"Strange Human," Zyara murmurs, shaking her head. "The Sylerian has become so much less effective on you since I first dosed you. You've developed remarkable tolerance in such a short time."

"I've been told I have an efficient liver. Always did well in drinking contests. So are you going to help me get out of here, or are you one of the bad guys too?" I try to look up, but even my head is strapped down, a thick, metal band resting against my forehead. I'm naked all over. They didn't even leave me a scrap for modesty. Bastards.

I should be blushing all over, but Zyara's the one who stuck me in the stasis tank to begin with, and I'm sure she's seen all my naughty bits before. So to hell with 'decorum', as the General calls it.

"Quiet, Abbey." Zyara fiddles with something on the side of the table and the restraints are suddenly gone, retracting into the metal surface. "We don't have much time. I've created a diversion, but the scientists will soon de-activate the alarm. You need to run. And just so you know, I'm loyal to the General."

"So all this bizarro test-subject stuff isn't his doing?"

That little shake of her head in response is the sweetest thing I've seen all day. I breathe a sigh of relief as I sit up, stretching my stiff limbs. "You've got impeccable timing, Zyara."

She stares at me blankly before turning and ripping a curtain-thing from a nearby cubicle, making it look effortless. I guess lady Kordolians must also be ridiculously strong.

She hands me the silvery fabric. "I'm afraid I have no garments for you. Cover yourself and run. The General's quarters are on the lowest level. Keep going down until you reach the windows with the view of the Dark Planet. I'll distract the scientists." She punches a machine beside the table, causing sparks to fly everywhere. A holoscreen starts to flicker, a rapid sequence of images flitting across it. She rips her own white robes a little and messes her hair. "Now it looks as if you've overpowered me."

"Ha," I grin as I wrap the silvery material around my body. It's like liquid silk, all slippery and fine, but I manage to fashion it into an awkward sort of toga, securing a knot over one shoulder. "Like Frankenstein, the big, bad Human escapes."

Zyara gives me an odd look, before rolling her eyes in exasperation. "Human, go," she sighs. "I will hold them off until the General gets here."

"He's uh, on his way?"

"Oh, he'll be here," she says darkly. "And he's *not* going to be pleased."

CHAPTER EIGHT

Tarak

I run to the medical bay, pushing startled troops out of the way. I need to get there before they do anything irreversible to Abbey. The return trip to the Fleet Station took long enough, and time is running out. I can't afford to let the High Council get their hands on her.

I pump my legs, taking long strides down the sloping corridor. Bloodlust sharpens my vision and makes my heart pound. I'm ready to kill the one who dared to touch *my* Human.

The pain behind my eyes is still there, but I channel it into aggression.

A distant voice at the back of my mind tells me I'm acting irrationally.

I don't care. How dare the Council take what's mine from right under my nose? On *my* Fleet Station?

Unacceptable.

As I round a corner, I see a group of medics running out of the medical bay, heading towards the lower levels. "She's headed towards the rec hall," one of them shouts. I catch up to them easily, overtaking them. They don't hear me until I'm just behind them.

"Do you want to die?" I snarl, coming up beside the medics. Three Kordolian males. Their eyes widen in recognition and they stop in the centre of the corridor. They're young, barely old enough to have finished their training.

The problem these days is that all the experienced military medics get stationed off-planet.

Fleet Station, where no action ever happens, gets stuck with fucking recruits.

"Sir?" The male in the lead blinks as slow realization creeps across his face.

"Under whose orders are you acting, recruit?" My question comes out low and menacing. The junior medic unconsciously steps back, fear making his movements stiff.

"I thought these were your orders, General," he replies, in growing horror. "Y-you mean you didn't want her captured and restrained?"

"Restrained?" I clench my fist to keep from punching something. The nanites that usually flow in my bloodstream have come to the surface, rippling just beneath my skin. It's slightly painful and I embrace it. Pain is a gift. It keeps me alert. Sharpens my senses. It's been a familiar companion for most of my life. "I have not given you permission to *restrain* anyone."

"But the Chief Surgeon said—"

"The Chief Surgeon does not speak for me, Medic. Once you've spent a bit of time on Fleet Station, you'll understand that. Now, who are you going to believe?"

"Y-you, of course, General."

"Good. Now where is the Human?"

Ashen-faced, they all point in the direction of the communal area. I give them a dark look, baring my fangs. "Get the fuck out of here. The Human is my property. You will abandon your pursuit."

"Understood, Sir!"

As they disappear in the opposite direction, I speed down the hallway, following its slope as it leads me down to the lower levels. I pass by the communal area and find it empty. Several seats are cast aside, and a table is overturned, telling me the pursuit must have passed this way.

She's heading for my quarters. Smart female.

By now, she will start to discover that her body isn't the one she was born with. That she's stronger than before. As a Human, she needed strengthening. They're such fragile creatures.

Ordinary Humans would not survive Kythia's harsh climate.

A familiar tendril of scent reaches my nose. It's unmistakably hers, wild and taunting. But now it's laced with fear.

And that makes me angry.

There's something else mixed in with it. Metallic. Sweet and yet pungent. I remember it from the surgery. Human blood. She's injured again.

This has happened to her because of my species. I should have known that even on *my* Fleet Station, she wouldn't be safe from Kordolians. A Human has never been brought to this side of the Nine Galaxies before. To some, she'd be considered a prize.

But never in my wildest dreams had I expected her to be so genetically similar.

It makes her valuable. Her very existence here has become dangerous.

I follow the alluring scent. It sings to me, stirring my most primal instincts. That's been happening a lot since I found her.

The scent of female, mingled with blood and fear. It has a strange effect on me, awakening something dark and predatory.

I follow my nose as the scent becomes stronger. It's not leading me to my quarters, but to the entrance of the swimming facility.

As I reach the platform overlooking the pool, I hear a splash, accompanied by an angry yell. "Get away from me, you creepy bastards!"

Mirkel is standing between two assistants, a sedation needle in hand. He's at the edge of the pool, peering down into the dark waters. "Keep shooting. Aim for the far end. Once the dart hits her, she will be immobilized," he says, his emotionless voice echoing throughout the chamber.

I'm driven by a sudden urge to kill. As one of his assistants raises a long projectile firing device, I launch myself over the railing, bringing my foot down on the assistant's skull as I land. The male crashes to the hard floor, unconscious. The weapon falls out of his grasp, rolling into the cold water.

I see a pale human face rise out of the water briefly, before disappearing again. Abbey. She's submerged, hiding on the other side of the pool.

Mirkel whirls around, his thin face contorted with rage. "Akkadian, the Human is no longer your possession. She has been marked as an official asset of the Empire. You will cease and desist from this madness!"

His white robes are tainted with small crimson stains. Human blood.

"Did you touch her, Medic?" I take a deep breath. "I can smell her on you."

"Get away from me, Akkadian." Mirkel's voice rises a notch. "This is the Empire's jurisdiction. Interfere and face the consequences."

I laugh, a harsh, bitter sound. "Is that supposed to scare me? Unlike you, I'm no longer a slave of the Empire." I stalk forward until Mirkel is teetering at the edge of the pool. My dominant hand twitches, seeking the familiar weight of my sword. But I'm still wearing the ridiculous, stiff dress uniform, and weapons aren't a part of this attire.

Doesn't matter. I don't need weapons to finish off this idiot.

He must see death in my eyes, because he yells at his accomplice. "Get the tranquilizer. Shoot him!"

I glare at the kid. "Try it," I snarl. "See what happens." The medic freezes, glancing nervously back and forth.

"Do it, Jerik! This is an order from your superior!"

The kid fumbles around, retrieving the gun from where it floats in the pool. He raises the weapon with trembling hands. I turn back to Mirkel, ignoring his assistant. "You of all people should know that tranq won't work on me, Chief Surgeon." I take a step forward. He falls backwards into the water, his long white robes swirling around him. I grab him by the collar and haul him out again. Water streams off him, plastering his pale hair to his face. Mirkel flails against me, but he knows he's no match for me.

"You wouldn't dare kill me," he hisses. "I'm the son of a Noble House. The Empress would have your head, freak."

"Freak? You made me this way," I shrug, dumping him on his feet. Water pools beneath him and makes his light robes stick to his thin frame. "And now you want to undo all the good work you've done for my Human?"

A faint splash makes me look up and I see her pale face rising out of the water. She's at the far end of the pool, closest to the windows. She's staring at me.

I cannot allow a transgression like this to go unpunished. On *my* Fleet Station? Mirkel has overstepped his bounds. After this incident I'm kicking him off the fleet. Talented surgeon or not, disloyalty has no place here. I've only tolerated his presence here for the sake of keeping peace with the High Council.

"You're right. I wish I could kill you, but I don't want to deal with the aftermath." I grab his wrist. He hits me with his free hand, but the blow glances off my cheek without a scratch. No matter how hard he tries, he can't break out of my grasp.

"Freak," he hisses. "Savage."

"*Your* experiments made me into this, Mirkel." I twist, and the sharp crack of bones is accompanied by Mirkel's high-pitched scream. I squeeze his hand, and the fine bones give way under my grasp. He cries out in agony.

"The Empress will hear of this," he shrieks. "Your days in this ill-advised role are numbered. Ilhan was crazy to appoint you!"

"Shut up." I twist again, crushing the flesh of his hand to a pulp. Black blood starts to seep from a protruding bone, and Mirkel falls to his knees in agony. "Or I'll crush your other hand as well. But you know very well it's nothing a nanograft won't fix. *If* you can get the nanites in the critical period. I hear there's been a shortage lately. Too many wars, you see. I won't be donating any of mine."

"Yet you would give them to a *Human*?"

I throw him to the floor, black blood spraying everywhere. His right hand is mangled and twisted.

"Go back to Kythia and get it fixed. Otherwise your days as a surgeon are finished."

Mirkel scrambles backwards, glaring at his subordinate. The kid is gaping, but he doesn't move. He can't. He's frozen with fear. I tend to have that effect on people.

"Touch my property again and I'll cut off your hands," I snarl. "Harm her, and you're dead."

Mirkel glares at me with hatred in his yellow eyes. He's as poisonous as ever. I shouldn't have left him on the Fleet Station for so long. He's never accepted the fact that I, the only subject to survive that particular project of his, am no longer under his control.

The High Council aren't going to be happy. But then again, our race as a whole hasn't been happy with anything for thousands of orbits. All is not well on dark, frigid Kythia.

Perhaps it's finally time for change.

I turn my attention to the ripple at the far end of the pool.

Abbey.

She's disappeared beneath the surface again, hidden from view.

I have the feeling she may not be entirely pleased to see me.

No matter. I will simply need to convince her otherwise.

Abbey

I GO BACK under the water, and all I can see underneath me are blurry stars. I hate to say it, but this pool is freaking amazing. Gotta hand it to those Kordolians, they've built a bad-ass aquatic facility. It's as if you're actually swimming in space; floating above the stars. Incredible.

Too bad I'm stuck in the middle of a hostile situation.

And the problem with being underwater is that it's like the cold vacuum of space. You can't breathe.

Above me, some guy is getting his hand crushed to smithereens by a very scary, very angry General.

Good. I recognized the voice. The thin guy with the creepy glasses and cold stare is the same pervert who tried to feel me up earlier when I was strapped down to the metal table.

That's probably why I'm not feeling as sorry for him as I should, even though his piercing shrieks are painful to listen to.

I pull the remnants of the silvery fabric around me, and the diaphanous material swirls around in the water like rolling clouds. I sink down to the bottom of the pool, peering through the clear barrier at the stars below.

With the water obscuring my view, the planet Kythia just looks like a big, black blob; an empty hole in the tapestry of space.

Mysterious and hidden.

Underwater, busting my lungs out, for just a moment, I can only pretend that I'm not here. That someone isn't getting his bones cracked upstairs by the very alien who saved me.

That I don't find myself attracted to a wild, violent creature, who just happens to be a big, bad Kordolian.

I shiver, because the water is cold, and because I'm not sure what happens next.

I hold my breath for a little longer, distracting myself from the burning in my chest as my body runs out of air.

It's a bit absurd that I jumped in the pool to escape. But those assholes had cut off the way to Tarak's quarters, and I'd had no other option. When I'd dived into the water, Mr Creepyhands and his buddies had flailed about at the edge, trying to shoot tranq darts at me.

Does that mean they can't swim?

For a supposedly superior alien species, they'd ended up looking a bit silly standing at the edge of the pool. While they were arguing with each other, I swam underwater to the far end of the pool, out of reach of their tranq gun. And they just stood at the edge, gaping at me, feebly trying to hit me with their little darts.

They're totally different to the scary black-armored Kordolians who stormed Fortuna Tau. Tarak's men are like the freaking Kordolian elite Special Forces or something. I got the feeling early on that the General was in a different class to these medical guys. It seems not all Kordolians are born fighters.

What I know about their society so far only scratches the surface. I haven't even touched foot on their planet yet. I don't know whether I even want to. It looks so cold and forbidding.

I close my eyes and try to remember the feeling of sunshine on my face. I miss the sun's warmth so much, but that memory can only distract me for so long.

My lungs feel like they're about to burst. I surface again, sucking in air like a gaping fish. This time, everything's gone quiet.

Creepyhands McPervert and his assistants are gone.

Tarak's gone.

Where the hell is he? He was here just minutes ago. I look around in panic, wondering if the medics did something to him. But there's no way they could have. He seems damn near invincible. I don't think even a tranq dart could put him down.

I kick my legs, the gentle motion keeping me afloat as I peer into the shadows, looking for Tarak. At least the guys chasing me are gone. He came at the right time.

He's getting better at this rescuing business. Last time, I ended up breaking nearly every bone in my body. This time, I only sustained grazes where the restraints held me down. Did't break anything, didn't die.

His timing's getting better, and I'm *extremely* lucky.

Thank Jupiter for that.

I start to swim slowly towards the other side of the pool, my strokes awkward and clumsy with the ballooning silver fabric swirling around me. I drag it with me in a half-hearted attempt at modesty.

As I reach the edge, something warm wraps around my waist, sliding beneath the silky material.

"Oh no you don't," I gasp, trying to squirm away. But the warm thing tightens, and I find myself pressed against a hard, muscular body.

Uh, oh. I remember the feel of that body. It couldn't be anyone else. It's *him*.

Now how did he get into this dark, shimmering pool without me noticing? Without even a splash?

He's full of sneak tactics, this one. Always playing dirty.

I've just been chased around a giant floating alien space station, doped up, strapped to a dissection table, and shot at. And somehow, I find myself wrapped up in half a curtain and embraced by a whole lot of Kordolian male.

He surfaces behind me, his arms encircling my waist. "I thought I told you to stay in my quarters," he whispers, his warm breath tickling my ear. I shiver, and not just because of the cold. "See what happens when you don't follow my orders?"

"I'm claustrophobic," I reply, going still. There's no point in squirming half-heartedly when his warmth feels so good. "I don't do well in confined spaces."

"Clearly."

"You need to take me home. To Earth. Your people want to do bad things to me." I close my eyes as he pulls me against him, holding me tight. "And what's this business about me being your 'property'? I mean, that's very sweet of you and all, in an overly possessive alpha-male sort of way, but I don't belong to anyone, General."

"Hm."

"And what's with you sneaking up on me in the water all the time? You're like a shark." A big, warm, sexy shark. It kinda fits. He *is* silver, and he's got sharp teeth.

"Shark?"

"It's an Earth creature. Extinct now, except for in aquariums." I shake my head. "Never mind." We're getting sidetracked.

"You talk a lot, female." His hands are devious; large and callused, yet gentle. A study in contrasts. They slide upwards, his fingers caressing the underside of my breasts.

I try again, feebly, to push him away. But the truth is, I'm enjoying the feel of his touch, his warmth, of the smooth, sculpted planes of his chest pressed against my back.

"Why do you fight, Human?" He traces the swell of my

breasts, his fingers moving over my nipples. They're sensitive as hell. I arc my back a little as he plays with them, teasing them. They grow taut under his touch, and I curl my legs up in front of me, weightless in the cool water as desire floods through me.

"Hang on," I protest weakly. He lets out a low growl of approval in response to my body's reaction. "I thought you were super pissed off just now. What happened to all the anger?"

"I'm not angry at you," he murmurs. "Forget all that now."

"I want to get out now." I draw the floating folds of fabric around us, foolishly trying to cover myself. From what, exactly? In the dark water, against a backdrop of millions of distant, glittering stars, the scrap of curtain from a medical cubicle is transformed into ethereal, floating gossamer. It becomes something otherworldly, swirling around us like a slow-motion dream.

Tarak lets go of my breasts and tears the material away with an irritated growl. "Stop fussing with that, Abbey." Even with his annoyed voice, my name sounds good coming from his lips. It's spoken in deep, resonating tones and rounded by his exotic accent.

The sound of his voice sends a ripple of warmth through me, right down into my core.

The scrap of fabric floats away like a lost spirit, disappearing into the starry depths. Water laps gently around us, stirred by our movements.

Without the fabric, I'm naked, and of course, so is he.

Why am I not surprised?

When Tarak's hands come back to me, they're cupping my bare ass, curving over the swell of my hips, gently prising my legs apart. He slides his hands down the insides of my thighs with a satisfied grunt.

Straightening my body, I lower my legs, coming into line with him. He's standing. My feet don't touch the bottom. The swell of his cock presses against my skin, hard and insistent, like its owner.

I'm suspended vertically in the water, and he uses my weightlessness to his advantage, exploring the curves of my body.

"I should go now," I whisper.

"Go where?" He's tracing the soft skin at the entrance to my pussy.

"Away. From you." My voice trembles as he caresses me there, sending ripples of pleasure through me.

"Your body is telling me otherwise." He spins me around slowly, grabbing both my thighs, gently wrapping my legs around his torso. His warmth radiates through me, and suddenly, the water no longer feels cold.

"In terms of anatomy, it seems Humans and Kordolians aren't so different." His devilish hands are back, parting the lips of my pussy, and he slides a finger deep inside me, stroking up and down.

"Aah," I let out a slow, shuddering sigh and look up, taking him in. He's so different in appearance. I still can't get over it. His skin shimmers slightly in the faint starlight, and his grey lips are parted, revealing the points of his fangs.

So alien. He's intimidating; hard-looking. Impossible. It's as if he'd only exist in one of my wild fantasy novels.

His is a savage kind of beauty.

His deep, red eyes burn with lust. Despite my misgivings, I find him irresistible.

Uh, oh.

I'm at a crossroads right now.

I don't know what's going to happen to me after all this, but I might as well enjoy myself, right? Ever since this infuriating male set foot on Fortuna Tau, my life has spiraled out of control, turning into one crazy event after another.

He's been the source of the chaos, but he's also been the only constant, and he's stuck to his word at every step.

Can I trust him to return me?

When it's like this, with what he's doing to me right now, I don't know anything anymore. I can't even think straight. He's running his finger over the tender nub of my clit now, fondling it with a satisfied growl. "Even *this* is the same." He strokes back and forth, bringing my pleasure up a notch.

A delicious tightness builds in my core; an intense, erotic kind of pressure.

"Oh," I whimper, wrapping my legs tighter around him as he increases the pressure.

Should you be doing this, Abbey?

An irritating, insistent voice lingers at the back of my thoughts; a shadow of doubt, almost drowned out by these sensations of pleasure. I close my eyes and decide to ignore it.

Fuck it.

I'm billions of light years away in a part of the universe Humans don't even go to. I'm floating in the water with just a thin barrier separating us from the very fabric of space itself. We're suspended above the stars. I'm weightless, directionless, without any ties.

The rulebook has been thrown out the window.

And nobody knows me here. Nobody cares about me here. Except for this male, who is bringing me closer and closer to the edge of climax. With just his damn finger.

Urgh. He just happens to be good at both fighting *and* foreplay.

Not usually my type. But then again, I've never encountered a being quite like him before.

I yelp as he disappears soundlessly under the water, leaving me breathless, staring up into the darkness. I'm a bit disappointed when he withdraws his fingers, leaving my clit throbbing with unfulfilled promises. He brings his hands down around my hips, anchoring my weightless body. The surface of the water has gone still, and all around me is silence, save for the sound of my own rapid breathing.

My heart pounds.

The tension in me becomes almost unbearable. I'm desperate for release.

He's kept me hanging.

He's taken complete control, and I can't do a thing.

Something warm slides between the folds of my pussy and I shudder. I reach down and realize he's down there kissing me, licking me, his tongue deft and sure. And long. It's longer than a Human tongue.

His lips press against my tender skin, his tongue circling my clit. The vicious fangs I've seen do not graze me, do not touch me, even once.

I cry out, glad that he's underwater so he can't hear how much I'm enjoying this. I run my fingers through his short hair, tracing the points of his ears, stroking his temples.

There's something at the edge of his temples. Two raised points. Small, hard bumps. When my fingers come into contact with them, he stiffens a little.

I withdraw my hands as he sucks my sensitive flesh, and the pressure inside me starts to build.

It's like nothing I've ever felt before.

I hook my legs over his shoulders, and he grips my ass with his rough hands, flicking his tongue back and forth along my pussy, my clit, faster, harder, until I can do nothing but close my eyes and see stars.

And with each and every caress, he drags me closer to the edge of pure bliss.

The water swirls around me as I move gently back and forth, my breathing rough and uneven, my soft grunts of pleasure echoing in the giant, black space.

We're floating in infinity.

I'm quivering, a powerful sensation coiled tight within me, and as he sucks, just a little bit more, that feeling starts to unfurl, like a blossoming flower.

Slowly, at first. He goes again, back and forth.

Then again.

Then, like a torrent of water bursting from a dam, that feeling of insane pleasure spills over and I'm coming, hard, fast, clenching my legs around him, crying out, my voice echoing in the empty space.

We're fucking in an ocean, suspended above the universe.

And I'm swept up in a powerful orgasm, wrapped around an impossible male who mystifies and infuriates me. Pleasure surges through me; intense, fierce, and I cry out in release.

The water, cold and serene, laps a soft rhythm around us.

I open my eyes, looking down into the depths below. He's

coming up now, rising slowly, unable to keep his hands off my body. I slide down off him, feeling utterly satisfied.

As he breaks the surface, I move back out of his grasp, watching as he regards me with a molten red gaze. He's gone still, and he's not saying a word.

I'd expected him to be smug, but he's looking at me expectantly.

Several glib remarks come to mind, but I stay quiet for once, not wanting to ruin the moment. I'm wondering if I've bitten off more than I can chew.

Too late now.

"Your turn," I whisper, making languid strokes as I come in close. I bring my hands up to his face, watching his expression closely as I trace those strange bumps I felt at the edge of his temples. He exhales as I circle them with my fingers. They're definitely there; two slight swellings just beneath his hairline.

They seem to be quite sensitive.

We lock gazes, and I'm drawn into the wine-dark depths of his eyes. There's a kind of relief there, his hard features becoming somehow peaceful.

Strange, inscrutable male.

I trace my fingers down his sharp cheekbones, down past his lips, which are parted. In contrast with the hard elegance of his features, they're soft and sensuous. Unable to resist, I kiss him. At first, his lips are cool, but as I part them with my tongue, they become warm. His tongue meets mine, and I taste a hint of myself and the fresh water of the pool.

Warmth rushes through me all over again.

I run my hands over his bare back, feeling rippling muscle and the soft irregularity of the occasional scar. Again I bring my legs up around him, grinding my hips, enjoying the feel of our bodies connecting, buffeted by the water's embrace.

I kiss him, enjoying the sensation, running my tongue over the sharp points of his fangs.

I don't know what purpose they serve, but that little detail turns me on.

His erection presses against me, and I bring my hand down, my fingers curling around his cock.

Oh, my.

He's nothing short of impressive.

I run my hand along its length. There are small, raised ridges along the top of his shaft. A sigh escapes me as I wonder what it would feel like inside me.

I close my fingers around his erection and move my hand back and forth, drawing a satisfied growl from him. He pulls me close, his strong arms curling around my waist. Slowly, he guides himself inside me, thrusting deep as I let out a satisfied groan.

The ridges at the top of his shaft rub against me, against my clit, feeling so good, and as I rock my hips back and forth, that sweet sensation builds again.

He lets me fuck him for a while, running his strong fingers through my hair, grunting in pleasure. I lose myself in the rhythm, enjoying the feeling of having him deep inside me. I let my body take over, going deeper, faster.

Then all of a sudden, he takes over, reversing our roles, bringing his feet off the floor, our bodies buoyed in the water. He dips below the surface, taking me with him, pulling me close.

I lose air and I lose sound.

Submerged.

He fucks me with his hands wrapped around my ass, thrusting his hips and pounding harder as I find myself in a breathless, quiet wonderland, surrounded by the galaxy.

The cold water wraps around us, but he's warm.

Our bodies move together. I can't breathe, but I don't care. It feels amazing.

He fucks me underwater, fucks me hard, fucks me deep until I'm coming again, and he's coming, holding me close. We're hidden together in darkness, wrapped in a cold, depthless cocoon. We shudder together as release comes, and I cry out, my voice distorted by the water, pale bubbles of air rising sinuously to the surface.

He holds me there for a moment afterwards, and everything

is silent and still, but I can feel the pounding of his heart beneath my fingers, telling me that he's real, and he's alive.

He may not be Human, but he's definitely a living, breathing male who has needs.

I savor the sensation of the afterglow, holding him against me until I can't take it anymore. Deprived of oxygen, my lungs are about to explode.

I shoot for the surface, pulling him with me, drawing in sweet air. I'm breathless.

For a moment, we just stare at each other, and it's as if something unexpected has happened between us.

Then, he turns, and without a word, hauls himself up out of the water, liquid sluicing off his magnificent body, highlighting the ripples and contours of his muscular physique.

I half expect him to leave me here, but he's standing at the edge, holding out a hand. I place my small hand into his large one, and he pulls me up out of the water in a single effortless movement.

He's too strong for his own good.

Goosebumps instantly appear on my bare skin, drawn out by the cold air.

I look around in panic for the curtain thing, but it's floated off somewhere and probably sunk down into the depths. It's nowhere to be seen.

Tarak bends down and picks something up from the floor.

It's his dress jacket, neatly folded.

With all that drama, when did he have time to fold his suit up into a neat little pile?

"You Humans seem to tolerate low temperatures poorly," he remarks, draping the jacket around my shoulders. The fabric is thick and soft, and it smells of him. It feels good after being in the pool. I've been in the water for so long my fingers have become wrinkled, like little prunes. He fastens the gleaming black buttons at the front. The sleeves are too long, covering my hands entirely, and the entire thing falls to about mid-thigh. At the back, the long tails of the coat cover the backs of my knees.

It looks ridiculous, but it feels so good. Warm. Familiar.

Meanwhile, the General is still stark naked. "Uh, thanks." I wrap my arms around my chest, comfortable in my little cocoon, not caring that it's an oversized Imperial Military dress uniform.

He picks up his pants, throwing them over his shoulder and gestures to me to follow. "Come. Now we can return to my quarters." He shoots me a pointed look. "Where you were supposed to remain in the first place. All of this could have been avoided."

"Even that last part?" I tease him, but he simply stares back at me, stone-faced. I roll my eyes. "You could have warned me about the mad scientists. Maybe if you'd explained things a bit better, I wouldn't have gone out," I'm unable to take my eyes off his gleaming, naked body. It's far too distracting. "And General?"

He raises a pale eyebrow.

I point at his pants. "Aren't you going to, uh, wear those?"

"What for?" He really doesn't seem to get it. "Does my body offend you somehow? Even after we've mated?"

"No," I begin, shaking my head. Quite the opposite, actually. "Never mind," I sigh. "If you ever decide to visit Earth, remind me to go through a few cultural things with you first."

At least I've got a fine view of his taut, toned ass as I follow him back to his quarters, wondering what the hell I've gotten myself into.

Tarak

SHE'S quiet on the way back, this small female. She follows me soundlessly and I wonder if I've upset her somehow. We pass through the common area where several of my soldiers are now seated, eating or playing games or watching the Imperial Broadcast on the large holoscreen.

Some of them glance at us in surprise, but they quickly turn away when they see me.

Of course, they will talk with one another, but they know

better than to invade my privacy. The High Council already knows of my transgression, anyway. Mirkel will go running back to them like a pathetic wounded Xargek larvae returning to its queen, but my soldiers will never sell me out to the Nobility.

There's nothing unusual about taking a female on the sly in one's leisure time, even though it's frowned upon. Males have needs. A Human is unexpected, though. Some of my soldiers probably don't even know what a Human is.

As their leader, I should be setting an example and following the High Council's edict discouraging inter-species mating, but I decide I don't care anymore.

With so few Kordolian females left, we have little choice but to look outside their race for pleasure and companionship.

However, I had never thought it was possible to have offspring with another species. This Human female is truly a revelation. And her body is a source of deep, unfettered pleasure.

So responsive. She seemed to enjoy the mating as much as I did.

But I have no idea of Human mating rituals. I don't know what she expects. Did I please her enough? Was I adequate?

We enter my quarters, the Qualum door unfusing as I stand before it. A thought occurs to me and I turn to her. "How did you manage to open this door?"

She blinks, not seeming to understand. "I don't really know. I was stupidly trying to pull it open, then I tore a nail," she shows me her finger, where part of the fingernail is torn, revealing raw pink flesh underneath. "Then somehow it came apart."

"Did you bleed?"

"A little, I think. Just a drop."

"Ah." The traces of my biological signature in her blood must have been enough to activate it.

"What do you mean, 'ah'? Care to explain a little more? You have to be one of the most secretive guys I've ever met."

I keep quiet, and she does that funny thing where her eyes roll up into her head. It seems to be a Human expression of frustration. I don't want her to know, just yet, that the nanograft she was given came from me. She's received my blood, and under ancient Kordolian Law, that constitutes a blood-bond. But after what that idiot Mirkel put her through , I don't think she'd process the concept very well.

The door fuses behind us and she closes her eyes, letting out a deep, shuddering sigh.

There are dark circles underneath her eyes, marring her pale, otherwise flawless skin. She seems drained; tired. Of course she's tired. She's just survived a nanograft and an abduction attempt.

"Did they harm you?" I ask darkly, pushing the sleeves of the jacket back to reveal her delicate wrists. There are bruises there, and the skin is broken in several places. At some point, she's bled. Her ankles are also marked, and there's a faint line along her forehead. They're marks from restraints. I know them all too well.

"Not really," she replies. "Don't worry. You've made that creepy doctor suffer enough."

"Did he touch you?" I'm going to break Mirkel's neck. Fuck the High Council and the Twelve Noble Houses. If they provoke me, I'll set into motion the plan the Prince and I have been assembling for so long and I will raze their Empire to the ground.

"Tarak." She pulls herself from my grasp, placing a hand on my bare chest. "Enough. I'm fine, thanks to you. But you need to tell me what you want. You look like you still want to kill that guy. You look as if you want to kill a whole bunch of guys. But why does it bother you so much that I was captured and almost experimented on? I'm not your property, General, no matter what you think. And according to you, I'm *inferior*."

I open my mouth to argue. Under Kordolian Law, she *is* my property. But seeing the expression on her face, I remain silent. Telling her that would only anger her.

"So I'm asking for the truth now, General. Do you plan on keeping me here? Or are you going to be as good as your word and take me back to Fortuna Tau?"

"You want to go back so badly?"

"It's my home, General. And they need me in the biomeric plant. As much as I appreciate your efforts to have me healed, I get the feeling your species aren't really going to accept me. And frankly, that scares the shit out of me. Kordolians in general scare the shit out of me. I've actually enjoyed our short time together, and believe it or not, I don't think you're really all that bad, but I don't think I'll survive here."

She's right, of course. On Kythia, she would never be accepted as my mate. I'd have to register her as a slave and keep her in an authorized household.

And she, as free and fearless as she is, would be utterly miserable.

But some indisputable facts remain. She's biologically compatible with our species, and I've blood-bonded her *and* mated her. We could possibly have offspring together.

And for the first time, with her, I reached ecstasy. I'm calm now, more at peace than I've been in longer than I can remember. The headache has dissipated completely.

Mating with her felt incredible. It was everything I'd been told about, and more.

Perhaps she didn't feel the same way.

"Did you not enjoy it?" I ask, watching her closely.

"What?" She blinks, seemingly confused. "What are you talking about?"

"The mating." I'm starting to feel, more strongly than ever, that I can't let her go. "Was it not as good for you?"

"The sex?" The way she looks up at me, with her pink lips slightly parted, makes me want to do it all over again. "Oh the sex was amazing and you know it. Stop trying to distract from the issue. I mean, you're obviously experienced when it comes to, uh, pleasuring women, but that's not going to convince me to stick around. I'm not going to be your concubine, General."

Experienced? Concubine? What nonsense is she babbling now? I narrow my eyes in annoyance. "What are you talking about, Human? I have not been with another female."

"I mean, what do you expect me to do, hang around in your

quarters all—" She stops mid-sentence, looking at me with wide, disbelieving eyes. "What did you just say?"

"I have not been with another." I shrug, turning to retrieve food from the internal delivery chute. There's protein mix and the Veronian food I ordered earlier. I detest the over-sweetened, cloying desserts those strange Veronians make, but I have the feeling they might be to Abbey's taste.

When I turn, she's staring at me with a shocked expression.

"Why does that surprise you so?" I summon a table from the side wall, tapping a command on the small holo-panel. It slides out, and I place the food upon it. A pair of seats slides out after it, and I gesture for her to sit. "Eat." I nod towards the woven Veronian package. It's brightly colored, just like its makers.

She looks at me, then at the package, her eyes green and wide. Underneath our dim blue lights, her eyes appear green. In the light of that star called the Sun, they're brown. I've never heard of eyes that can change color before.

She's still wearing that shocked expression.

"What?" I growl, taking a bite of my protein mix.

"Pants," she snaps, gesturing to the garment beside me. "Put them on."

I shrug and pull on the trousers. If it makes her feel at ease, then fine. I could as easily draw out my exo-armor, but it doesn't seem appropriate in this situation.

So my appearance offends her, and she's surprised I haven't been with a female before. I'm confused. What's her problem? They say on Kythia that Kordolian females are complex creatures, but this Human would certainly be a match for them.

Females. I suspect I will never fully understand what goes on inside their heads.

Abbey

THANK SATURN he's put his pants back on. I mean, I was enjoying the view and all, but it was becoming too damn overwhelming. And we're about to eat. And he still doesn't have a shirt on. I'm sitting opposite a shirtless General with magnificent abs. He's chomping on one of those uninspiring meaty seaweed bars, and I've got a colorful package sitting in front of me.

I stare at it for a moment, trying to process what I've just learnt.

So let me get this straight. Before we made love in the pool, he was a virgin? And the admission doesn't seem to have bothered him at all. Most Human guys would be getting a bit awkward right about now.

It doesn't add up.

He takes another bite of his food, looking at me with a calm, scrutinizing gaze. It's as if he wants to gauge my reaction to this strange little package.

"So I'm your first?" I still don't quite get it. He seemed to know his way around the female body all too well. He was confident as hell; he knew exactly what he was doing.

"Yes."

"Oh." I blink, trying to look for any clue that he's messing with me. "So how did you know what to do, if you don't mind me asking?" I run my fingers over the package. It's covered in a wrapper made up of thousands of tiny, interwoven hexagons. The pattern is all kinds of colors; pinks, purples, blues, greens.

It's exquisitely beautiful.

Tarak frowns. "Know what to do? Of course I know. We learn when we reach maturity. It's a rite of passage for all males."

"You get lessons?" My jaw drops. "Like an initiation of sorts?"

"There is a *Sendar*, a scholar of female pleasure. All males who reach maturity see the *Sendar* for training." He takes another bite of the gelatinous brick, looking at me quizzically. "You Humans do not have something similar on Earth?"

"Not at all," I reply. "So you're telling me all Kordolian males have to learn this stuff? How to, uh, please a woman?"

"Of course. If the skill is not acquired, one has no hope of gaining a mate."

"That bad, is it?" I fiddle with the multicolored package,

trying to get it to open. "So I imagine the women also go through some sort of training." I suddenly feel a little insecure. How would I compare to a Kordolian female?

Tarak laughs then, and it's a surprisingly warm, rich sound. I've never heard him laugh before, let alone seen him smile. For a moment, he looks kind of adorable, his white fangs flashing in his dark mouth. "Why would a female need such lessons? They can take their pick of the males. Most end up with multiple mates."

I try to digest that information. "Sounds like there's an imbalance."

"Only one in a hundred Kordolian males ever has hope of being selected as a mate."

I dig my nails into the hexagon-patterned wrapper, trying to tear it open. But really, I'm trying to process what the General's telling me. "That's quite a serious shortage of ladies."

Imagine women on Earth with that kind of power. With their own personal harem. I think we'd all go a little bit drunk with sexual power. What kind of life do these Kordolian females lead?

Shit. I've just been transported to a planet of horny, silver-skinned alien males who happen to be tutored in the art of pleasure.

What's a girl not to like?

Apart from the fact that some of them seem to want to take my organs. For *science*.

Fuck that. Hands off the ovaries, bitches.

Tarak takes the package from me, a flicker of annoyance crossing his elegant features. "If you do not know how to do it, just ask." He presses something on the side, and the little hexagons all seem to fold into themselves, sliding off the package and forming a tight little ball.

Before I can protest, he tosses the thing into a little garbage chute. I would have kept it. It seemed too beautiful to throw away.

He slides the package across to me. It's a box with a transparent lid.

"There have been no females born on our planet for the last hundred orbits. And it's common knowledge that a female cannot become pregnant if she does not climax. So we try our best to make conditions right, but there hasn't been any success yet." He shrugs. "Maybe it's just the way of things. Perhaps it's a sign from the Goddess that we are not meant to survive another era."

"That's a bit fatalistic, isn't it, General?"

"Eat your food, Abbey." He ignores the question, gesturing towards the box.

I look down and see neat rows of little squares.

Sweets of some sort? They're like little chocolates or something, but each square is different, covered in some kind of design.

I look more closely and realize some of the squares are transparent. There are tiny glittering specks inside. The specks look like stars, and they're interspersed with colorful nebulas. The other squares are solid, etched with pictures of distant planets.

They're miniature works of art. "Is this really food?"

"Try one."

I pick up one of the squares, take a deep breath, and pop it in my mouth. I'm starving again. I don't know what this stuff is, or whether it's even good for Humans, but I don't really have any choice. I can't afford to waste away here. Especially if I'm going to have to figure out how to escape.

An explosion happens. It's a burst of pure flavor, complex and sweet.

It's like nothing I've ever tasted before. I can't equate it to anything I've had on Earth.

It's fruity, I guess. A bit like a combination of lychee and mango and pineapple. But those things don't even compare. It's as if those crazy minuscule nebulas I saw inside it are blossoming on my tongue.

Surely something that tastes this good can't be bad for me. I hate to say it, but it's as good as chocolate. Maybe even better. No way. That last thought makes me feel like a traitor to my own species.

Tarak's watching my reaction carefully. He seems rather pleased with himself.

"What is this stuff?" I ask in wonder.

"Veronian food." As if that explains everything. He finishes the last of his protein bar thing and taps a panel on the wall. Moments later, two steaming cups of some sort of drink appear in the hatch. He passes one across to me. "Drink."

I sniff the stuff cautiously. Smells okay, if a little bitter. I sip. It's pungent and herbal, but the distinct flavor contrasts nicely with the sweetness of the cubes.

I'm contemplating these culinary wonders and pondering the nature of a race that's overwhelmingly male and generally unfriendly towards every other species in the universe when a sharp beeping sound fills the room. Tarak's on his feet in an instant and he's armoring up, the black nanites appearing all over his skin like tiny liquid droplets. They coalesce and form the hardened outer exo-suit I'm familiar with.

The dress trousers he's so graciously put on start to tear at the seams.

"Into the sleeping pod with you," he snaps, taking my food and the cup of bitter tea. "I have visitors. Do not come out."

I open my mouth to protest, but he holds up a hand. That little vein on the side of his temple is twitching again. "Do not argue this time, female. You have had enough danger already."

"Fine," I sigh, not looking forward to being locked up in that little room again, but feeling as if I have no choice. I don't want to be at the centre of a shitfight in the General's quarters.

I follow him through, and he places my food on a little table beside the bed-pod thing.

"Eat and rest," he says, his voice unexpectedly gentle. "And do not worry. You are always safe with me."

"I don't doubt that," I reply, eyeing the rest of the Veronian sweets. At least I can munch on those while I try not to get claustrophobic, wondering how the hell I'm going to get out of here. Am I ever going to see Earth again? Am I going to feel the sunshine on my face again?

There has to be a way. And maybe it involves convincing this stubborn musclehead to come with me.

Because I don't know if I can fight through hordes of hostile Kordolians on my own.

And underneath the scary armor and bossy attitude, he's not all that bad, really.

CHAPTER NINE

Tarak

I peer at the holoscreen and recognize a familiar face. Pale eyes blink back at me. The door opens, and a slender male dressed in a maintenance worker's suit steps through.

"What are you doing here, Syrak? You're not supposed to be on the lower decks."

Syrak bows. The dark scales on his face gleam, contrasting with the pale blue of his eyes. Syrak is a Soldar, a member of an alien race occupying a large humid planet in the next sector. His body is covered in dark grey scales, and he has a series of ridges, like fins, running down his back. The Soldar are hairless, and they have long arms and legs that are capable of great flexibility. Their feet are like hands, giving them the ability to grasp things and do manual work with all four limbs. That's why many Soldar are used as maintenance workers. They have an uncanny ability with all things mechanical.

And they obey orders without question. They've been conditioned to.

Kordolians took over their planet in the days of Emperor Ilhan, and the Soldar have been under our rule ever since.

I should know. I was there.

"I apologize, General Akkadian." He bows again, speaking perfect Kordolian. I wave off the gesture in irritation, indicating for him to sit. I order another cup of hot elixir and present it to him. He mumbles profuse words of thanks.

"So what brings you to my chambers, Syrak? Urgent news, I expect."

"The Prince asked me to send word. The High Council are unhappy with your recent defiance, and they're uncomfortable with the direction you're taking. They want to regain control of the military. Rumors are a secret Kill Order has been placed on you. They won't announce it publicly, of course. You're too much of a talisman for the people."

I shrug. The news is of no real surprise to me. I've always made the Nobles uncomfortable, even more so ever since Emperor Ilhan promoted me to the rank of General. I suspect they've been plotting my downfall for years. "And where is Xalikian now?" The Wild Prince, unpredictable and unconventional, had always been a great disappointment to his parents. Of late, he's been absent from the civilized zones of Kythia.

Very few actually know where he's been hiding.

"Prince Xalikian has gone deep into the Vaal," Syrak replies, sipping his elixir. "He urges you to be mindful of your own safety. They may send an assassin after you and the Human." Syrak pauses, staring into his drink. His hand is trembling slightly. He shouldn't stay here for too long. "Prince Xalikian also wishes to arrange a meeting in a secure place of your choosing."

"I'm not so easy to kill, Syrak." I turn and walk over to the internal delivery chute. "And as for the Prince, I will find him." I punch the panel beside the delivery chute. It crumples, sending out a shower of blue sparks. It startles Syrak, and he almost spills his beverage.

"My delivery chute malfunctioned," I say nonchalantly, as he gets to his feet. "I've put in a maintenance request. You've been sent to fix it, haven't you?"

"O-of course, General."

"Well, you've done a preliminary inspection. Go fetch your repairbots and sort it out."

"Uh, yes Sir." It's as if a light goes on in his pale blue eyes. Now that he's been given a legitimate excuse to be here, he scurries off, leaving the half-finished cup of elixir.

The Soldar may act subservient, but they've become an invaluable network of intelligence for Prince Xalikian. In exchange, he's promised them their freedom when he succeeds the throne.

Most Kordolians would think that an outrageous deal.

But like me, the Prince isn't a typical Kordolian.

Kythian society considers many of his ideas extreme. He's been ridiculed and discredited for most of his mature life. Ilhan is to blame. He raised Xalikian a certain way, and it's backfired. Or turned out for the best, depending on one's perspective.

As Syrak leaves, I open the comm holoscreen. A familiar face fills the screen. It's Keron, the young recruit I encountered earlier. "General!" He looks around nervously, as if to locate his superior.

"Keron," I snap, not wanting to waste time. "Send a message to all the Commanders on the Fleet Station. They are to assemble in the Command Room in one half-phase."

"Uh, yes Sir. Anything else for me to do?"

"That's all for now, Keron." I flick the screen off.

Whether by design or not, the inevitable has just been set in motion. The High Council will try to kill me and replace me. The appearance of the Human and my actions before them have become the catalyst for treachery.

But they will have a hard time removing me.

When they sanctioned those experiments on me so many orbits ago, they never foresaw that I would become a monster they were unable to control. They nearly killed me then. But I've exceeded all expectations. I have the First Division and half of the Kordolian fleet under my command. And I have virulent black nanites fused to my genome. They will not kill me so easily, especially once I go to ground.

I also have a female in my possession. She's perplexing and fearless. She's far from stupid.

She's an odd blessing. She cures me of the rage, the pent-up frustration, and the unbearable headaches.

Humans certainly have their own way of going about things. I'm starting to appreciate her bluntness, that odd blend of cynicism and innocence that only she can bring to a situation.

They will not have her. I've decided I need her. For my sanity.

Regardless of what she believes, she is mine.

Abbey

I DITCH the dress uniform because it's starting to become a little stiff and itchy. And it's adding to the feeling of being restricted and cooped up in a small, dark space.

Seriously, what the hell am I doing?

The biomeric plant on Fortuna Tau is broken, and the station is possibly being overrun by giant, presumably flesh-eating insectoid monsters. At least Tarak left the rest of the Kordolian soldiers behind to take care of things.

I should be figuring out how to steal a Kordolian cruiser so I can get back to Earth or at least make it to a friendly sector.

But a few things have become clear.

One, the General doesn't want me to go anywhere.

Two, these Kordolians are scary motherfuckers.

Three, I'm not a fighter. The nanograft thing has made me into a fast runner, but I don't know my way around a weapon to save my life. I don't know if I can even kill someone, even if that someone is an evil alien.

And I seem to be under the protection of the one Kordolian who can keep the wolves at bay. The General is one tough bastard.

I grab the sheets from the bed-pod thing and move over to the door, pressing my ear against it. But the stupid thing is soundproof. I can't hear what's going on out there. And even if I could, they'd probably be speaking Kordolian, so what's the point?

I sigh, trying not to let the dark walls and dim lights of the windowless pod bother me. Instead, I grab the box of delectable Veronian treats. I pop another into my mouth and get a different flavor. Like the other one, it's complex and fragrant. The closest thing I can think of is rosewater and spice.

These Veronians, whoever they are, sure know what's up. It kind of makes me want to go there, wherever their planet is.

If I ever get back to Earth, I'll sure have a story to tell. I could go to one of those celebrity gossip networks and get a big payout. I can just see the headlines now:

My Forbidden Adventure: Encounter with a Kordolian Sex God.

I snort. It sounds like a good title for a smut novel. But I'm still coming to grips with the fact that Tarak was a virgin before he made love to me. And there he was answering all my questions as if it were the most natural thing in the world.

There's one little detail I didn't reveal to him. I'm no saint. I've been with guys before. I've had my share of flings, pyrrhic break-ups and one-night stands. At one point or another, they all said the same thing about me. Apparently, I'm a commitment-phobe, whatever that means.

So I've had sex before. Lots of it. But he's the first one to ever make me come.

He had me dancing at his fingertips, playing me like an instrument. And boy did I orgasm. It felt so fucking good.

There's no way I'm going to tell him that. I don't want him to get all big-headed over it.

He's arrogant enough as it is.

Urgh. What am I going to do? I pop another bliss-cube in my mouth and settle into the bed, my head full of conflicting thoughts as a riot of flavors blossoms in my mouth.

My limbs grow heavy, and the food settles in my belly, making me feel relaxed. Those bite-sized sweets are deceptive. They're surprisingly filling.

I close my eyes, just for a moment, and enjoy the feeling of being warm and safe in this sealed little room. It's strangely reas-suring, knowing that he's just outside the door.

I must have fallen asleep for a while, because I open my eyes to the sound of faint rustling.

Tarak is standing before me, watching me.

"Hey." I stretch, luxuriating in the soft, warm sheets that carry his scent. How long was I out for?

"You slept," he remarks, going into his little wardrobe. He's carrying some large packages. Curious, I let the bedsheets slip and follow him, deciding to do the Kordolian thing and walk around in my birthday suit.

His gaze roams over my body appreciatively as I approach, his crimson eyes darkening with hunger. That look sends a funny little thrill through me. Big Bad can't take his eyes off me. It's strangely empowering.

He's pulling something out of one of the packages. It's a big white, furry, er, thing.

He thrusts it at me. "Try it."

"This?" I take the thing into my arms and realize it's a coat. A huge furry coat. It's impossibly soft and warm. It's like those ridiculous old-fashioned fur coats we Humans used to wear back in the twentieth century.

Of course, using animal fur for clothing is unheard of these days.

I slip my arms into the sleeves, pulling it around me. It fits perfectly, even down to the length, sitting at about mid-calf. It's more decadent than any garment I've ever owned. It has a hood attached. Tarak lifts the hood over my short hair.

It flops over my face. I'm sure it conceals my features.

I push it back, astonished. "What's this?"

"*Szkazajik* fur. I had it altered for your height."

"O-okay." I don't know what the hell a Skaz-whatever is, but this coat sure feels nice to wear. It's impossibly cosy and warm. "Are we going somewhere?"

"I have business on Kythia." He passes me a few other things. There are stretchy black garments that seem to be made of some kind of thermal fabric. There's a pair of long boots that go up to my knees. They're made from some leathery or synthetic type of material. They look flexible but durable at the same time. "These are custom made," he growls. "It's hard to find anything in your size."

There's a pair of goggles and a scarf-like thing for my face. "These will help you see in the dark."

A little pile of stuff is forming in my arms. I stare at it for a moment, bemused. It's enough for an Antarctic expedition.

"Kythia is cold," Tarak continues, "and Humans are vulnerable to cold."

"So I take it I'm going with you?"

"Of course. After what happened, I'm not letting you out of my sight."

"Oh." I'm dismayed yet at the same time thrilled. There's been no mention of returning to Earth yet. Instead we're traveling to the surface of a harsh, hostile planet where they don't even have the equivalent of a sun. I have no idea what lies in store for me there. Great. Talk about getting sidetracked from the goal.

But as dark and scary as Kythia looks, I'm curious. As long as Tarak sticks to his word and keeps the other nasty Kordolians away, I should be safe, right?

"Promise you'll keep the mad scientists away?"

"Any who dares touch you is dead," he growls, with a flash of his fangs.

Ooh.

I guess we're going to Kythia, then.

CHAPTER TEN

Abbey

I squirm in my seat, becoming restless. We've been waiting here for what seems like hours, suspended in orbit just above Kythia.

The river-like network of blue lights stretching across the surface of the Dark Planet winks back at us, mysterious and seductive.

I still don't really understand what the General's objective is. Since we left the Fleet Station, we've done nothing except sit in this small two-person sized transport, watching a stream of traffic through the navigation window. It's been fascinating, actually. I feel as if the entire universe wants to get to Kythia. There are all kinds of craft drifting past; space vehicles of the like I've never seen before are heading for the planet. There are large cargo freighters and small, private transports. Some of the craft look sleek and modern, while others look as if they're barely holding together. Some are oddly shaped and don't even look like spacecraft at all.

They're all entering Kythia's atmosphere, heading for the blue lights below.

"So let me get this straight." I turn to face him, swiveling my seat around. "You don't want to enter Kythia using a military vessel because this is some sort of unofficial business, and you don't want to be noticed."

Tarak wears his usual expression of mild irritation. "We are waiting for the right moment," he says slowly, as if explaining to a child. I roll my eyes. As if that tells me anything.

All he's told me is that he needs to go to Kythia for something important. And because I'm a rare being in these parts—the only Human this side of the galaxy—every Kordolian wants a piece of me. Literally. So Tarak is refusing to let me out of his sight.

Hence why I'm stuck here in this tiny cruiser, watching the Kordolian version of rush hour.

Still, I could think of worse places to be.

Say, strapped to a dissection table, or imprisoned somewhere.

Tarak's reclining in the pilot's seat, sharpening a small blade of some sort. It's black, like just about everything he owns. The obsidian blade gleams wickedly in the pale starlight. He's sharpening it on a small metal object with slow, methodical strokes.

The way he does it is almost reverent, as if the blade is somehow sacred.

He inspects it for imperfections, then pops it back in its sheath. It's all a little bit obsessive-compulsive.

Tarak turns to me, holding out the blade, hilt first. "Take it," he says.

"You want me to have this?" I stare at the sheathed weapon. It's compact and deadly looking. Ooh, a strange, alien dagger. Just what I've always wanted. How sweet of him.

"One should always carry a weapon. What happened to you on the Fleet Station was unacceptable. You need to be able to defend yourself. When we reach Kythia, I will teach you how to use a plasma gun."

My first instinct is to wave the knife away. I'm not a fighter. I'm good at running away from things, and climbing, and jumping, and perhaps kicking a guy in the nuts if he steps out of line, but I've never seriously hurt anyone in my life.

I don't know if I could stab someone.

But I've landed in the midst of an evil alien Empire, and I'm surrounded by potential enemies. Common sense prevails. I take the knife. Even though I've got the General backing me up, you just never know when such a thing might come in handy.

It's surprisingly light. I wrap my fingers around the hilt, testing its weight. It feels good in my hand.

Tarak grunts in approval, reaching over to adjust my fingers. "Hold it like this." His large, rough hand wraps around mine, moving my hand so I hold the knife in a more solid grip. "When you use it, move your arm like this, and twist."

He goes through the motion with me, gripping my forearm. His touch is firm but gentle. It feels good. Familiar. A warm little shiver courses through me, and I let out a small sigh.

Only Tarak could make the act of teaching a person how to stab someone seem romantic.

When I think about it, the intent behind the move is quite chilling. I don't know whether I could twist the knife once it's in.

"Now try it on your own."

"Like this?" I copy the movement half-heartedly.

"Put some force behind it," he urges.

I do it again, with a bit more effort. I try to imagine there's a bad guy in front of me, visualizing that creepy Kordolian scientist who had me strapped to a table. I'll bet he was going to harvest my organs. He seemed the type. He had that psycho-stalker look about him.

Asshole.

"Good," Tarak murmurs. "That is the correct way." Despite myself, I feel a little rush of satisfaction at his nod of approval.

I stash the sheathed knife away in a little pocket at my thigh. I'm wearing the clothes Tarak got for me; warm, black, stretchy garments that seem to fit perfectly, moulding to my curves. They've got pockets hidden at strategic spots all over them. There's also a light silver jacket that goes over the top. It's got a strange closure at the front; when I put it together the whole thing just magically zips up and becomes seamless.

The decadent, white Skaz-whatever fur coat he got me is draped over the back of my seat.

It's a lot of layers. I feel warm and toasty for once, in contrast to the bone-chilling cold I've had to deal with ever since Tarak and Zyara stuck me in that horrible stasis tank.

Looking down at the impenetrable, dark mass of Kythia, I get the feeling it will be even colder once we reach the surface. That's one of the consequences of not having a sun. I can't imagine what's in store for me down there. Funny, the cold never seems to bother the Kordolians. Especially the General, who's more than happy to walk around without a scrap of clothing on his body.

Not that his blatant nudity bothers me. There are worse sights than a completely naked, muscular Kordolian male.

Heat surges between my thighs. The sheer thought of him is turning me on. I try to keep a straight face. I can't let Big Bad know of the effect he has on me, especially when he's right beside me.

Outside the window, the stream of space-traffic continues on, endless and inevitable. Occasionally, a bit of space-junk floats by. There are scraps of metal and bits of machinery and things that look like communication devices, flashing with an array of colorful lights.

And we're just parked here, waiting.

What the hell is he up to?

"So remind me again," I probe, trying to put a lid on my growing arousal. "What exactly are we waiting for?"

Tarak stares back at me with a hooded gaze, his dark red eyes like burning embers. His face is expressionless aside from a tiny quirk at the corners of his lips.

"A way into Kythia. It's coming. But do not worry about that now. There are better ways to pass the time." He turns his chair to face me, and I'm torn between irritation and desire. Tarak's ditched his usual exo-armor in favor of a nondescript outfit that consists of black robes. The clothes are worn; almost tattered looking. They're at complete odds with his hard features and sharp haircut.

They don't suit him at all.

Is this part of the whole staying incognito business?

Is it supposed to be some kind of disguise? It's definitely not his usual style.

Before I can piece it all together, he moves so fast I don't have time to react. The big guy can be lightning quick when he wants. His recent displays of uh, affection have almost made me forget that he's actually a lethal fighter. A predator.

He kneels before me, looking up. I'm sitting in the passenger seat and he's running his hands up my thighs, his fingers warm and insistent through the thin, stretchy fabric of my pants.

I grab his hands, stopping him as he reaches the waistband of my pants, just as he tucks his fingers under it, brushing against my bare skin.

"Oh no you don't," I growl, pushing his hands away. "Not until you tell me what you're up to. What's with all the subterfuge? Where are we going?" I roll my eyes in frustration. "You have to be the most cryptic male I've ever met."

Tarak snorts. Is that amusement flickering across his face? He doesn't resist me when I push his hands away.

"Don't just ignore the question," I snap, but what comes out of my mouth is at odds with what I'm feeling. His touch leaves my skin tingling; leaves me wanting more.

He moves then, all fluid, sinuous grace, and before I know it, I'm lifted up and moved around and I'm not even really sure what happened just now, but I somehow end up in his lap while he reclines on the passenger seat.

He's got an arm around my waist.

"No, no, no," I protest, but I'm secretly enjoying the feel of his hard body pressed against mine. "You're not distracting me with *that*." I can feel his erection through the thin material of our garments.

"Oh?" He leans in close, so that his lips brush against my ear. "Abbey of Earth, why are you saying such things when the scent of your arousal is driving me crazy?"

Be strong, Abbey.

"I'm not going to be distracted by your dirty tricks." I'm only half serious. Part of me wants him to rip my clothes off and just get on with it. But no. He has to know that I'm not just going to stop asking questions because he's seduced me.

This overconfident jerk. Who does he think he is?

"Tricks?" Tarak raises an eyebrow as I untangle myself from his arms. "I do not play at tricks, female. When it comes to you, I am deadly serious."

The way he says it, with a rumble in his deep voice, melts my theoretical panties. Theoretical, because I'm not wearing any under all this fancy Kordolian thermo-wear.

Dammit. Why does he say these things that get under my skin, that make me go all jelly inside?

This silver-skinned alien is dangerous. I need to disengage now, otherwise I won't be able to stop myself. I pull away, leaving him with half-disbelieving look on his face.

"You do not want me to give you pleasure?"

I frown. "I do like it, very much. But not when you're doing it to distract me from your shady little mission."

"Shady?" His eyebrow twitches, just a little. "You think I would act dishonorably?"

"I don't know. You haven't told me anything. Therefore, one can only assume." I step back, bumping into the control panel. As I make contact, a shrill beep goes off, and the holoscreen starts talking in a robot-voice. It's all in Kordolian; I don't understand any of it. A warning, maybe?

"What did I do?" I back away nervously. Tarak mutters softly to himself in Kordolian. It sounds like swearing. I really need to learn me some Kordolian curse-words. He gets to his feet, grabs me at the waist and gently directs me back to my seat.

"The timing is not ideal," he growls, sounding decidedly grumpy, probably because his little attempt at getting into my pants has been interrupted. "But you wanted to know what we are doing here? You are about to find out." He jumps back into the pilot's seat and feeds some power to the thrusters.

The stream of space-traffic outside has slowed. A huge, slow-moving red craft comes into sight. It's impossibly long, and as it drifts across, it fills our entire view. Hundreds of tiny brightly lit windows wink along its body. As it gets closer, I realize it's not in perfect condition. There are cracks in the hull here and there, and various stains and scratches mark the gleaming red body.

Has it been through a few asteroid storms, perhaps?

"What the hell is that?"

"Veronian freighter." Our little space cruiser starts to move. Tarak guides it between passing traffic as it joins the slipstream, and we come up alongside the hulking freighter. "It's our ticket onto Kythia, so prepare yourself. We will be boarding shortly."

As usual, he's not big on the detail. I'll have to work on that annoying trait of his. When you're a badass General who's used to being obeyed without question, explaining things probably isn't a big priority.

So it looks as if we're going to get onto this big red behemoth of a freighter. Veronian, he says? Well, they make those amazing sweets, so they can't be all that bad, right?

There's no way the makers of the bliss-cubes could be evil, right?

I guess I have no choice but to stick with the big guy here and find out.

Tarak

ABBEY GIVES ME A STRANGE LOOK. I don't know what it means, so I ignore it. But I can't help the soft dissatisfied growl that escapes me.

I hate being interrupted, especially when presented with such an interesting challenge. I hadn't expected her to refuse my advances, not with the scent of her arousal wrapping around me, drawing me in so powerfully. She's full of questions, this Human, wishing to know the reason for our method of entry to Kythia.

What am I supposed to tell her? That the High Council has placed a Kill Order on my head? That I am going to visit an exiled Prince who has hidden deep in the icy wastelands of the

Vaal? That she should stay vigilant, in case a dread Silent One, the most deadly of all assassins, appears on our trail?

She would not react well to such news. My intention is to keep her safe and keep her satisfied. She does not need to know the details of Kythian politics.

And no matter how skilled they are, even a Silent One could not take me.

Such things are too complicated to explain. I see little point in it, because we will soon be finished with this business, and I will be able to check on my First Division. They have a difficult task to complete, but I am not concerned about them in the slightest. They are all highly competent and resourceful soldiers, which is why I was able to leave them there in the first place.

I watch Abbey out of the corner of my vision as I navigate our cruiser past a lumbering, ancient looking Soldaran freighter, cutting in front of it. She's watching everything with bright, curious eyes.

The Soldaran freighter is diminutive in size compared to the Veronian ship. It's probably bringing workers landside.

I come alongside the massive Veronian freighter. I plan for us to hitch a ride on it. Traveling in on such a large craft, we are more likely to pass unnoticed. Abbey cranes her neck, looking up in wonder at the giant ship. She's probably never seen one of the characteristic red freighters before. They transport exotic goods from Veronia to Kythia in huge volumes to satisfy the demand of the Nobles.

On Kythia, we do not create anything. All we do is consume. Kordolians exist as parasites in the universe. Only Callidum is produced, mined from great scars in the planet's surface, and that is kept for making the tools of war.

We hold on so tightly to this barren, frozen wasteland of ours only because of its mineral wealth. Callidum is the key to conquering the universe, and the Nobles, obsessed with history and tradition, refuse to leave this place in search of gentler climates.

There are hundreds of planets Kordolians could have settled on.

As my female stares at the scene unfolding outside, I steal a moment to watch her, unnoticed.

She's wearing the outfit I ordered for her. She doesn't know it, but I could have chosen looser fitting garments. Even though they're tight, the thermoprotective clothes I chose for her fit her perfectly. They hug her curves, emphasizing her rounded posterior. Seeing her walk makes me hard. The way her body moves is perfection.

A trace of pink coloring has spread across her cheeks. Humans, I've realized, tend to change color a lot. It's fascinating. It happens when she's aroused.

Why does she not just give in and let me pleasure her?

Stubborn female.

I turn away from her, concentrating on the comm. The holo-screen lights up as I make contact with the freighter. "Lyria 4," I address the bridge, speaking in Universal. "Get Captain Resha on the comm."

A young Veronian female appears, wearing a typical grey Empire-issued uniform. She blinks, startled by my sudden appearance. She clears her throat nervously. "Ah, eternal greetings, distinguished Sir. I do regret to inform you that your craft is straying too close to our markers. I humbly request that you maintain a safe distance." She's speaking in that Kaiin-cursed formal manner. On Kythia, it's the way that servants address their Kordolian masters. It's another bit of indulgent nonsense perpetuated by the Noble Houses. I'm thankful that she obviously doesn't recognize me, dressed as I am in simple civilian robes. Otherwise, she'd probably be bowing. Fucking Vionn and her ridiculous formalities. How can she derive satisfaction from such behavior?

"I will speak to Captain Resha only," I reply, not wanting to waste time. "Tell him to engage, or there will be consequences."

She turns to seek advice from some unseen source in the background. She turns to me again, the bright lighting of the bridge adding a sheen to her brightly colored skin. Like Humans, Veronians don't see too well in darkness. They need the light. "Certainly, Sir."

There's movement in the background, then a familiar face appears on screen.

"Y-you!" Resha's expression is one of shock and dismay. The reality of who he's speaking with hits him, and his golden eyes widen. He tries to gather his composure, doing that stupid, Imperial bow. "Gen—"

"Resha." I cut him off before he has the chance to announce my presence to his whole fucking bridge. "Clear your navigation center, now."

Resha issues orders to his subordinates in his soft native tongue. The other Veronians disappear in a blur of movement.

"There is no-one left?"

He nods.

"Show me the bridge."

He enters a command and the viewpoint shifts to show me a top-down of the entire bridge. There's not a single Veronian in sight.

"Good. You may remember me from a previous encounter, but your comrades don't. Be aware that my presence here is off the record."

"Uh, no problem, Sir." The Veronian's distinctive purple markings start to glow, betraying his anxiety. "But I'm afraid I need you to state your business, official or not. This cargo belongs to the House of Krel, and my Masters have expressly forbidden me from accepting any other goods on this shipment." He pauses. "Or passengers."

"Resha," I say mildly, "who are you more worried about upsetting? The House of Krel, or me?"

His long tail flicks back and forth, a pink blur in the background. Veronians tend to do that whey they're unsettled. They are the worst at hiding inner emotions. He opens his mouth, but no words come out.

"You *will* allow us passage on board Lyria 4. It's not an argument, Captain."

"Yes, Master." Resha's pointed ears droop. He's unhappy, but he has no choice. The last time I caught Resha, he was smuggling in an illegal shipment of Sylerian. Aside from its medical uses, some Kordolian Nobles take it to get high. After a rather pointed conversation and confiscation of his cargo, I let him go.

The Veronian owes me a favor and he knows it.

"Unidentified craft," he sighs, "the lateral bay will open to admit you. Prepare for transfer and docking."

At least Resha has enough sense not to argue with me. I wait until the docking bay opens, guiding our craft into the giant airlock.

Abbey is looking at me with narrowed eyes.

"What?" I raise an eyebrow, not liking that look. It shouldn't bother me, but it does.

"As if that wasn't just the most suspicious conversation I've ever witnessed." She rolls her eyes, an action I've come to understand is the Human female sign of irritation. "Do you always get your way by threatening others into submission?"

"It's effective." I shrug. How else am I supposed to make the slippery Veronian Captain cooperate? And how is it suspicious? For all the other Veronians know, I could be from the House of Krel, coming to inspect my cargo.

I alternate the thrusters, reducing power and balancing the small craft as it descends. The landing gear engages, and the airlock depressurizes.

Veronians start to scurry across the shiny floor of the dock. The place is lit up brightly, and I squint as my eyes adjust to the conditions.

Abbey is looking out across the floor, her eyes, now a soft brown color, going wide. "Who are those little pink and purple guys?"

"Veronians." I get to my feet, holding out a hand. "Come."

"The guys that make those amazing, melt-in-your-mouth delicacies?" She sounds almost reverent. I have no idea what's so fascinating. The thought of eating Veronian food makes me queasy. It's too rich; too sweet. How does she enjoy the stuff?

Humans are strange.

She looks at my hand, shakes her head and stands on her own.

Strange, indeed.

I pick up the Szkazajik coat and offer it to her. She gives me that look again, before reluctantly taking it.

"You will need it," I warn, although I'd much prefer her without the extra layer concealing her delicious body. "Once we reach Kythia, we're on foot. I don't have to remind you that your kind do not do well in the cold. Put it on now and conceal your features. I don't want the Veronians to realize there's a human on board." They will assume she's a servant of mine. Such garments are popular amongst many of the alien species that live on Kythia. Most habitable planets in the universe are warmer than Kythia, and most of the servant classes despise the cold.

A fine Szkazajik coat is considered a status symbol amongst servants. Kordolians have no use for the things.

She takes the coat with a raise of her eyebrow, wearing an expression that's equal parts irritation and desire.

Her eyes are full of defiance and unspoken challenges. Her heady, female scent surrounds me.

Oh Goddess, how she turns me on.

Abbey

AS WE DISEMBARK from the cruiser, one of the Veronians scampers forward to greet us. I recognize the guy from the holo-link. He's called Resha, and he's the Captain of this red monstrosity.

In real life, he's taller than I expected, about the same height as me. But of course, the General towers over both of us.

Now that I've seen a real-live Veronian, the creations Tarak gave me suddenly make sense. How can I forget that box of mysterious, mind-blowing treats, each one a hidden world ready to explore? Not to mention the brightly colored, mystifying packaging; thousands of tiny hexagons that disappeared into each other. I get it.

A race that looks like these guys *would* make incredible things like that.

Resha does a weird little bow as he approaches Tarak, his ears twitching. His furry, pointed ears emerge from his head through a thicket of gleaming caramel colored hair. They remind me of a cat's ears.

I stare at him unashamedly from underneath the cover of my furry hood, even though the damn thing blocks half my vision.

I can't *stop* staring at him.

Because he's pink.

He's pink all over, with striped purple markings across his cheeks. His eyes are round and golden and huge, and as he takes in Tarak and his grumpy expression, they go a little wider. Me, on the other hand, he barely spares a glance, as if short people in fur coats are a common sight. Tarak's also made me wear the scarf thing, to conceal my face. Yeah, yeah, I know. I'm a Human. On Kordolian turf. Apparently, that makes me a walking trophy in these parts, hence the disguise.

As Resha looks up at the General, the purple markings on his face start to glow.

In all my time spent in space, I have never encountered such an exotic looking creature. What kind of a place does this guy come from? In my mind, he must come from a planet made up of rainbows and stardust where they ride unicorns. I'm totally fascinated by him.

Tarak, on the other hand, is glowering at the poor guy. Resha's tail starts moving faster, his delicate features highlighted by the glowing purple stripes across his face.

"Gen- ah, Master," he says, his voice soft and light. "Welcome aboard Lyria 4."

Universal is such a boring sounding language, but when Resha speaks, it somehow gains a musical quality.

Tarak's oblivious to the cuteness. His jaw is stiff, and that little vein on the side of his head is bulging. How can he be annoyed by this pretty little creature? Poor Resha. "You have a cabin prepared for me, Resha?"

"Of course, Master. Will you and your servant be requiring separate quarters?"

Servant? *Servant?* I clench my teeth, resisting the urge to correct Resha. The General has obviously omitted a few rather important details here. I shoot him a venomous glare. He glances back at me, insolently giving me the slow up-and-down, checking me out even though I'm wearing this ridiculous fur coat.

Is he mentally undressing me right now? It's not as if he can see what's underneath all these layers. The bastard. We are going to have words.

"I don't think separate quarters will be necessary," he says slowly as he looks at me, his dark red eyes full of heat. Damn him! Underneath that facade of military discipline, he's such a devious male. "It's barely a half-phase until we reach Kythia. I assume you'll be docking at the Trader's Market?"

"As always, Master. Let me show you the way."

Tarak turns and starts to walk off, snapping his fingers imperiously. "Come, servant." And just like that, he's expecting me to follow. Urgh. If I didn't know better, I'd swear he was enjoying this. Tarak with a sense of humor? No way.

"You just wait," I mutter darkly under my breath as we pass through the airlock and into a huge storage bay. It's filled with containers of all shapes and sizes. In the background, robotic arms are moving up and down amongst the cargo, sorting, lifting, and scanning.

Some of the containers are open at the top, resembling oversized metal baskets. They hold fruits I've never seen before. There are round blue fruits and pink curved ones. There are oblong stripy ones. Those last ones give off a delicious aroma, causing my stomach to rumble. I resist the urge to pilfer one as I walk further, passing sealed barrels and pallets of brightly colored fabrics. The place smells incredible, a mix of spice and perfume and fresh organic matter.

It reminds me of Earth.

Tarak and Resha have gone ahead of me. Without realizing it, I've slowed down, because I can't help but stare at all the stuff. If this is just one cargo freighter, I can't imagine what this so-called Trader's Market looks like.

As I pass by another crate, I see something I recognize.

My jaw drops.

Pineapples. They have freaking pineapples. Unless there's another planet where they grow pineapples, those have come from Earth.

How did they get pineapples all this way without them ripening?

Oh, how I wish I had access to a bio-lab. I could put those things into a recombinant tissue culture and make a killing over here selling lab-grown pineapples. I snort to myself in amusement. Yeah, right. As if I'm going to hang around this frigid place forever.

I'm going to find a way to get back to Earth, one way or another.

"Are you asleep on your feet, servant?" Tarak's deep voice echoes across the space, jolting me out of my daydreaming. "Hurry up." He motions to me with a wave of his hand, acting every bit the impatient master.

I am not amused. The General had better watch his back. I am so going to get him for this.

What's with the sudden attitude, anyway? Even if it's all an act, it says a lot about Kordolians. Is this whole master-servant thing considered socially acceptable, then?

These bloody Kordolians think they're the center of the universe, and they expect every other alien species to step into line. What a bunch of stuck-up pricks. They have no right, even if Sector One *is* the center of the Universe, and all flight paths lead to Kythia.

With an aggravated sigh, I follow Tarak and Resha. Several Veronian workers wearing nondescript grey uniforms pass us along the way. They dip their heads in a respectful little gesture as Tarak passes. They don't spare me a second glance.

We go through a maze of corridors, some brightly lit, others dim and narrow. We pass offices where Veronians are hard at work under bright lights.

Eventually, we reach a plain looking door. Resha taps a panel and it slides open, revealing a room inside. "Your quarters until we land, Master. There is a separate exit to the outside. You may access it after landing and depressurization." He gestures towards the inside, his tail waving back and forth. The markings on his face have gone back to normal. Tarak looks down at him, his expression unreadable.

Resha's tail starts to move faster, becoming a soft pink blur.

"Resha," Tarak says, after an uncomfortable silence. It's uncomfortable because of the way the General is glaring threateningly at the poor Veronian. "If anyone asks, we are from the House of Krel. You won't under any circumstances reveal that I was on this transport."

"O-of course not, Master."

"And Resha?"

"Y-yes Master?"

"If I hear there was illegal Sylerian on this shipment, I'll have to come back. Do not give me a reason to come back. You would not enjoy it."

"There is none, I promise." Resha's stripes light up again as he steps back without even seeming to realize it. Tarak looms over him like a darkening storm. Resha's furry ears droop. Tarak's in full intimidation mode, his red eyes narrowed menacingly.

What the hell was that all about? Illegal Sylerian? Isn't that the stuff that Zyara dosed me with? That would make Captain Resha a drug smuggler. That can't be. He's too cute to be a criminal.

I'm about to step in and say something when Tarak diverts his attention to me.

He's looking at me and his expression is unreadable. His hard, elegant features are like stone. Only his eyes betray him as they darken with hunger.

Oh, come on. How can he be finding me attractive when I'm wrapped up in this Skaz-thing coat?

"That will be all, Captain." He dismisses Resha with a glare and beckons to me. He pauses, the silence growing heavy between us.

Don't say it, General, I'll freaking kill you.

"Come, Servant." A hint of a smile tugs at the corner of his mouth.

It's official. I'm going to kill him.

Resha's scampering off, his tail between his legs.

Tarak's giving me that damn look, and I've got no choice but to follow him into the room. As the door slides closed behind us, he catches me off-guard, pushing my hood back, pressing me against the wall.

My short brown hair escapes, falling around my face.

His rough hands caress my face, pushing down the scarf that conceals my features. He bends over, pressing his lips to my temple, burying his nose in my hair. He inhales, and a shudder courses through him.

I stiffen, pushing him back. It takes all of my willpower, because my legs have gone weak and wobbly. Pent-up desire spreads through me, causing a delicious, infuriating sensation in my core.

I'm trying to be outraged here, and he's ruining it.

Impossible male.

I give him a dark look. "Since when am I your servant?" My voice is low and frosty. I stand with my hands pressed against his chest, holding him back. He inclines his head, and I have no idea whether he's laughing inside or deadly serious.

Urgh. Someday, I'll figure him out.

Just as I'm about to unleash all hell on him, he does the most unexpected thing. He drops to his knees, his hands slipping inside the folds of my coat, caressing my hips with an appreciative growl. He shakes his head. "You? No. You are not the subservient type." His fingers are tracing little circles on my thighs, sliding over the smooth fabric of my pants, drifting closer towards my pussy. "But that is what Kythian society expects. For me to act any other way would draw suspicion. But in fact, the opposite is true."

"What do you mean?" That feeling of need grows, and warmth spreads between my legs in response to his featherlight touch.

"I am *your* servant, am I not, Abbey of Earth?"

Tarak

I PICK up where I left off before we docked on Lyria 4. Her scent has been driving me crazy ever since. It calls to me, stirring some deep, primal instinct within. I'm guided by my desire.

She thought she could push me away, but what she doesn't understand is that I am a very persistent male.

She looks down at me, perplexed but aroused.

"I don't understand what you're talking about," she whispers, as I bring my fingers against the soft mound of her sex. Our skin is separated only by a thin layer of fabric. Her glistening lips part slightly, revealing perfect white teeth.

She is all female; soft, inviting and impossible to resist.

"You do not need to understand." I stroke her gently and she leans in, unable to help herself, her hips moving forward. "Just give in."

What I told her just now, about being her servant, is partly true. When I offered my blood for her nanograft, it could have been considered a blood-gift, a traditional Kordolian symbol of bonding between a male and his female.

It is not practised anymore. Not since the ratio of males to females became imbalanced beyond proportion. Our females see no reason to bond themselves to only one mate.

My species has no reason to exchange blood anymore.

I had offered my blood for the graft in desperation, because Mirkel, that spineless fuck, had told me medical nanites were in short supply.

Of course, it was irradiated first, to kill the virus that has infected my nanites and given it such unique properties. Her delicate physiology would not survive that horror. Even I barely survived my first graft.

But the fact remains that she has received my blood, as a gift. Under ancient Kordolian Law, that constitutes a traditional bond, and the rule of the bond is that the male protects his female, always.

Therefore, I am her servant.

And she belongs to me.

"You're impossible," she grumbles, her eyes flashing, caught somewhere between brown and green. Her body sways as I slide my hand under the band of her trousers, brushing against her soft skin. I trace my fingers down to the entrance of her pussy and find her wet.

"Impossible," she says again, breathlessly.

My erection strains against my trousers as I take her in, watching her from my unique vantage point. She shrugs off the fur coat, letting it drop to the floor. Her cheeks have turned a soft pink color, and they gleam with a faint sheen of moisture.

I watch the rise and fall of her chest, appreciating the rounded swell of her breasts.

I circle the tender jewel at the entrance to her sex with one finger. That part is so sensitive, and she's so, so responsive.

She lets out a soft, shuddering sigh. I increase the speed of my caress and she runs her fingers through my hair, finding the place where the remnants of my horns are concealed beneath my skin.

They've been cut and sealed, in the modern fashion. In the military, we do it for practical reasons. On Kythia, it's considered barbaric to grow one's horns.

The Nobles disapprove of it.

Abbey runs her fingers over the sensitive points, causing a ripple of intense pleasure. Zyara was right. They've been growing back. Somehow, the chemical seal has failed. Apparently, it's an effect of this so-called *Mating Fever*. At this rate, they will soon break through the skin.

The horns are an extremely erogenous area. Her touch causes a low growl to escape my lips. The sensation becomes more powerful, and I'm overwhelmed with the urge to take her. I need to be inside her.

I rise to my feet, sliding two fingers between her silken folds. She whimpers at my touch.

It's a plea for more; she's begging for release.

The sound pleases me. Oh, I will give her release.

I push her back against the wall, just as a loud, metallic groan reverberates around us. A great tremor shakes the walls and floor of the cabin.

"What's happening?" Her eyes meet mine and I'm drawn into their mesmerizing flecked depths. Her irises are as complex and intricate as a Veronian puzzle.

"Entering the atmosphere," I murmur, as I thrust my fingers deeper.

She squirms in pleasure, her back pressed against the wall.

All around us, the room is shaking.

I tug her pants down, sliding them over the smooth curve of her hips. She fumbles with the clasp of my robes. I help her, tugging the garments free, undoing my trousers. My cock springs free, and she takes it into her hand. I tremble, bringing my lips to her neck, inhaling her essence. The smell of her, earthy and wild, with a hint of something sweet, stokes my lust even further.

I can't hold on any longer.

The giant Veronian freighter creaks and groans, gaining speed as it breaches the skies of my home planet. I withdraw my hand and she moans with need.

I cup my hands around her ripe ass, lifting her. She gets the idea, curling her legs around me as I enter her with a slow, deep thrust.

It is bliss.

She wraps her arms around my neck, her body pressed against mine. I grind my hips, going deeper, pressing her against the wall as need overtakes me. My body is moving of its own accord and she moves with me, her strong legs tightening. We're melded together, moving as one, lost to the rhythm of our fucking. She's deliciously tight, and she lets out a low, throaty groan as I increase the speed of my thrusts.

Humans, I realize now, can be exquisitely sexual creatures.

Her fingers dig into the skin at my neck, her soft Human fingernails threatening to break my skin. It's almost painful, and the sensation adds to my growing pleasure.

Turbulence shakes the freighter, but we're oblivious to whatever is happening outside. I taste the skin at her neck, grazing it with my sharp canines. She's fragrant and salty and distinctly Human; distinctly female.

A rare delicacy.

Mine.

I go harder, faster, swept up in a frenzy of lust and pleasure, enjoying her soft cries and the feel of her body against me as I reach the edge of climax.

I slow for a moment, holding us both there, watching her face.

"Please," she begs. Such a sweet sound. Her eyes are wide, her breathing rapid, her black pupils dilated. The sight of her makes me lose control. I push myself deeper inside her.

I cry out in release as the climax comes, powerful and unstoppable. I'm holding her close to me, consumed by the sensations coursing through me.

Her whole body trembles as she finds her release. And then there's the sound she makes, innocent and pure, a cry of unbridled pleasure.

Sweet female.

As our lovemaking settles into an afterglow, she curls her arms and legs around me, letting out a satisfied sigh.

The turbulence has passed, and once again the freighter is moving smoothly, soundlessly.

From a hidden speaker above, the generic landing announcement sounds.

"It seems we have arrived," I murmur, before sucking on the delicate flesh of her earlobe.

"It seems we have," she replies dryly, her voice a perfect mixture of irony and wonder, making me want to do her all over again.

CHAPTER ELEVEN

Abbey

We disembark from the massive freighter, going on foot. There's some sort of secret passageway leading from our room to the outside. It ends in a long metal ladder attached to the hull.

As the door slides open, the bitter cold hits me in the face like a vicious slap.

"Whoa." We're in some kind of cargo port, where freighters of all sizes and shapes, some as big as the Lyria 4, are parked. Workers, robots, and vehicles swarm around the craft, transporting crates and items.

The place is a hive of activity.

Soft blue lights illuminate the way, and above us the sky is cloudless, the stars bright and distinct.

A chill wind whips past, followed by an eerie howling sound.

So this is Kythia, huh?

The wind tugs at my hair, chilling the exposed skin of my face. I can't feel the tip of my nose anymore, and my fingers have turned to ice.

Standing behind me, Tarak hands me my scarf, pressing it into my palm, his large hand curling around mine.

It's warm.

The cold doesn't seem to bother him at all. He's wearing only his light robes over thin black trousers, surveying the scene below with a hawklike gaze. "Protect your skin," he orders, as I don the scarf, concealing my numb face.

Kythia's as cold as it looks. It has to be well below sub-zero right now. I tuck my hands into the Skaz-thing coat, pressing them against my body, trying to get some warmth. At least the Kordolian thermal wear is keeping the rest of me nice and toasty.

I stare at the ladder with trepidation. "Hey Tarak," I say, eyeing the metal rungs. "We're going down that thing, right?"

"It's the standard exit route."

"I'm not going to have any skin left on my hands by the time we reach the bottom. You got any gloves?"

"Gloves?" He blinks.

"You forgot that little detail, didn't you?" I can't fault him too much, though. The thermals and the boots and the Skaz-coat are just perfect. He got my size exactly right, even down to the footwear.

"You are right." Tarak inclines his head, as if calculating something. Before I can figure out what's happening, he's scooped me up into his arms.

And suddenly, Tarak jumps, and we're in freefall.

I stifle a yelp as he lands on the frosty ground, his knees bending to absorb the impact. He lets me down gently as I stare up at the exit door in amazement. That had to be about a forty-foot drop.

The General really is a freak of nature.

"I will purchase some gloves. I did not think." He sounds almost apologetic. I'm floored. Is such a thing even possible? Big Bad seems like the kind of guy who wouldn't apologize even if he accidentally ran over your pet dog twice. He beckons to me. "Come."

We turn and trudge off into the howling wind, Tarak setting a fast pace, as we cut a straight path through swarms of workers and passengers

He doesn't have to worry about bumping into anyone,

because they all take one look at him and get out of the way. Sometimes it pays to be big, tall, and Kordolian.

I scurry after him, sticking close, because his large frame blocks the wind a little. I pull the hood over my hair, bracing against the chill.

We leave the docking area and enter a large building with high, vaulted ceilings. It's huge, seemingly endless. I can't see where it ends. The roof of the place is completely transparent, revealing the starry sky above. There's a bustle about this place, and what hits me at first is the sound. It's the buzz that comes from thousands of voices in conversation. It's deafening.

This must be the Trader's Market.

The space is awash with faint blue light, and we pass stalls and shops of all kinds, too numerous to count.

It's a galactic mega-mall on steroids. If I had credits to spare, I could eat, sleep, and die happy here.

Even more fascinating than the enticing shops with their exotic wares are the aliens. There are races from all planets here. I spot Veronians, Kordolians, feathered Avein, tentacled Ordoon, and others that I don't recognize. There are scaly grey and black guys with glowing blue eyes and legless guys who go around on small, single-person hover-transports.

This place is blowing my mind.

But there's no time to stop and stare, because Tarak is barreling through the crowds at light-speed, and I'm flat out keeping up with him.

All I can do is follow. I try to keep focused, fixing on his broad shoulders to stop from going into sensory overload. The sights, sounds and smells of the Trader's Market are completely overwhelming.

I don't know where the hell we're going, but all I can do right now is trust him, even if he *is* a devious, sneaky male who deflects all my questions with his damn sexiness.

Seriously, how did he pull off that little move back there on the freighter? Did he learn that at his fancy Kordolian sex academy?

How to distract a female and get into her pants in less than thirty seconds, 101.

He's totally shameless.

I try to get annoyed over it, but I can't help but smile underneath my scarf, because it was so insanely good. Tarak is a dangerous operator, in more ways than one.

But I *am* going to get answers out of him, one way or another.

I have questions he needs to answer. Such as: where are we going? Why the secrecy? And when does he plan on returning me to my home sector?

And there's a bigger dilemma. What in Jupiter's name am I going to do about this male? He's overbearing, obnoxious and he still doesn't want to tell me anything, much to my irritation. But then he goes and says shit like *I am your servant* like some gallant knight from ancient times, making me go all weak at the knees.

Dissipating my anger in an instant.

Damn him!

I hate to say it, but I am officially flustered. And that doesn't happen very often.

Tarak

WE PASS through the Trader's Market, making for the Upper Entrance. Abbey is close behind me. In her fur coat and scarf, she's inconspicuous, just another household servant following her master. She acts sufficiently subservient, just like I've instructed her to.

She doesn't like to be cast in that role, even if it's only for show. Oh, she detests it.

From her, I wouldn't expect anything less.

Perhaps I pushed her a little too far back on the Veronian freighter. But she needs to understand how things are on Kythia. Kordolians are the masters. All other races are servants.

However, the reality is that I would never force her into that role. Subservience is not something I desire in a mate.

As we pass through the large gates of the Upper Entrance, I spot the type of shop I'm looking for. I turn, motioning for her to follow.

The attendant, a Veronian, leaps up as I approach. As I am Kordolian, he probably considers me a walking source of endless credits.

"Eternal greetings, esteemed Master," he begins, but I cut him off by making a slicing motion with my hand. I have no time for flowery pleasantries.

"Five finger gloves," I snap. "Show me your range."

"C-certainly, Master." He presses a button and a drawer opens, revealing a range of gloves. Some sparkle with jeweled embroidery. Others have ridiculous frills around the openings. Who would wear such impractical things? Actually, I can think of a few idiots who might. "Would you desire a certain type of embellishment? We have monogrammed varieties of all the Noble Houses if you—"

"I'll take those." I point to a pair of small black gloves made from flexible material. They look warm, and they will fit her.

The attendant lifts them out of the display case. He stares at my hands, then looks at the gloves. "Are these a gift, or—"

"Too many questions, Veronian." I pass him a credit chip. He bows and starts to mutter an apology, but I'm already exiting the shop. "Keep the change," I tell him as we disappear back into the crowd.

"Are you always this mean to those little guys?" Abbey mutters the question under her breath, but I'm able to hear her just fine, my ears twitching.

Mean? I'm not sure what she means, so I don't say anything. Instead, I pass the gloves to her, holding them out behind me as we cross the threshold of the Trader's Market.

"Thanks," she mumbles, brushing her fingers against my palm as she takes them. They're cold, like ice.

Humans are fragile indeed.

We pass into the pleasure sector, an unsanctioned area the

High Council turns a blind eye to, probably because so many of their Nobles frequent the area. A muffled sound of disbelief escapes my female as a troupe of barely dressed Kordolian males passes by.

Pleasure workers, or pleasure seekers? It's hard to tell these days.

The throughway is lined with all types of establishments, both Kordolian and otherwise. There are brightly colored signs and lights above some, while others are discreet, not even bearing a name. Pulsing music surrounds us, and the intoxicating scent of smoked Khafa leaf lingers in the air. At the front of some of the entrances, gaudily dressed males and females of all species stand, their faces painted with bright colors. They call out to passers by, trying to lure them in.

An Ordoon female sidles up to me, her black tentacles flickering in and out of voluminous skirts. "Ye in the market for some tentacle girls, esteemed Master?" She speaks Kordolian with a rough, lisping accent. I wave her away in irritation as we move past.

In the pleasure sector, all tastes and fetishes are catered for.

"And we have come to this place because why?" Abbey's voice is laced with suspicion. I can almost feel her accusing gaze burning into me from behind. "Don't tell me your 'unofficial business' is to visit a brothel."

"I know it is strange, but be patient." I stop as we come to a storefront with a nondescript black door. Amongst the noise and activity and bright colors of the other establishments, I almost missed it. But it's the place I remember. After pressing my hand to the identification panel, it slides open instantly.

We descend down a steep flight of stairs into darkness. Abbey's footsteps slow behind me, and I glance back to see her tracing one hand along the wall, supporting herself.

I forgot. Humans don't see well in the dark.

Like all Kordolians, I can see perfectly in darkness.

I pull the dark-vision goggles from a hidden pocket in my robe. They're the same ones the Veronians and other light-dwelling species use on Kythia. "These will help you see."

She takes them in her gloved hand. "You know, I must be awfully trusting or terribly stupid to follow you down a dark, hidden passageway in a red light district. But believe it or not, I trust you. If you wanted to sell me or harm me or do anything dodgy, you would have done so already, right, General?"

She's babbling again. Talking too much.

Ah. She is nervous.

I take her hand into mine, stealing a moment in the darkness. "Do not worry," I whisper. "This will be brief. We are here to acquire a means of transportation, as unlikely as that might seem."

"Okay." Underneath the hood, her eyes widen in surprise. I am also mildly surprised, because for once, she doesn't question me. She pushes her hood back momentarily, putting on the dark-vision goggles. Her pale skin glows in the darkness and I lean in, brushing my lips against her forehead. I can't wait to tear all those layers off her.

Things of beauty should not be hidden. But on Kythia, there is no choice. She is Human, and vulnerable to the cold.

I lead her down the stairs and into a cavernous entrance hall that is surprisingly luxurious. My feet sink into plush carpet underfoot. There are ornate Jentian multiglass lights hanging from the ceiling, giving off a muted glow that is refracted into thousands of tiny glowing shapes that dance across the walls. Various cushions and soft padded recliners are placed around the space.

Abbey is silent beside me, but I know her well enough by now. She's taking in the detail, analyzing, making her own conclusions. I do not need to tell her much, because she is as observant as ever.

From behind a curtain, a Kordolian male appears, wearing only silver metal ornaments. He is lean and waif-like, and his artificially curled hair is a lurid shade of blue. A intricate garment fashioned from silvermetal covers his nether regions, leaving little to the imagination. His ears hold multiple piercings and there is a delicate, jeweled chain hanging from his nose, connected to one earlobe.

Beside me, Abbey lets out a soft choking sound.

I am inclined to agree. I try to avoid the pleasure sector at all costs, but every time I come back, it feels as if the fashions have become more outlandish; more ridiculous.

The male standing before us is a *Sensi*, a pleasure worker. Or pleasure expert, as they prefer to call themselves.

His clientele are mostly male, but the occasional Kordolian female may be entertained, as the *Sensi* claim to be skilled in the rarer types of pleasure, whatever that means.

"Eternal greetings, good Sir." He greets me in Kordolian, his yellow eyes roaming over me in a way I don't like. He gives me a suggestive wink. If I weren't trying to keep things low-key, I might strangle him for that. "Master Berad has registered your entry and is waiting." He does that ridiculous Imperial bow, the one I detest. "I see you have brought your servant. It may wait here in the anteroom until you have concluded your business. Please, this way."

I look back at Abbey. She's standing rigidly, her fists clenched. She's not liking this at all.

I would like to offer her some placating words, but that would draw suspicion. I can't bring her in to see Berad, because that would attract even more suspicion. So instead, I point to a recliner. "Servant, sit. Wait until I return."

She's still wearing the dark-vision goggles, but I can feel her icy glare upon me.

And for the first time in a very long time, I feel a sense of unease. I don't understand how this small female can make me feel such things. I have killed thousands of Xargek and other hostile alien enemies. I have been instrumental in colonizing planets, and I have been recognized by Emperor Ilhan as a war hero. My body is near indestructible, a consequence of being the lone survivor of the notorious First Generation Enhancement Trials.

So why do I care about her opinion of me? Why does she suddenly seem so intimidating standing there bundled up in her Szkazajik fur and scarf?

This Human never ceases to surprise.

Strange, beautiful creature.

I do not know what to make of this, so I turn and follow the Sensi. "See to it that my servant is not disturbed," I order, leaving her in the antechamber. She is clever enough not to argue.

A flicker of anxiety over her wellbeing enters my mind. Again, it's strange to have such thoughts. I push them away. Never mind. She will be fine. No Kordolian in their right mind would dare bother the servant of another House.

Abbey

OKAY, I get it. Tarak is keeping up this master-servant act because he doesn't want to draw suspicion. Still, it grates on my nerves. I sigh and lean back against the wall. I'm sitting on an upholstered divan type thing, wondering what the hell kind of business Tarak has in a place like this.

He doesn't seem the type to go and indulge in the sort of thing that this establishment offers.

I should know. He demonstrated his uh, desires, not too long ago, back there in the Veronian freighter.

I close my eyes for a moment, secure in my disguise. The fact that Kythia's so bloody cold is a hidden blessing. It allows me to conceal my Human-ness and avoid the scrutiny of these predatory Kordolians.

Well, all predatory Kordolians except for one.

That particular Kordolian is currently going to talk to a guy about Jupiter-knows-what, leaving me to sit and ponder in this blinged-out waiting room. That particular Kordolian is driving me crazy, in ways both good and bad.

A metallic jingling sound echoes through the room, and I see the mostly naked male escort, or whatever he is, slinking back from wherever he's taken Tarak.

He looks at me with his unsettling yellow eyes and says something in Kordolian.

I ignore him. I can't understand what he's saying, and my dad always told me not to talk to strangers, especially if they're dressed in only a metallic, embroidered loincloth thingy and piercings. Loads of piercings.

He gives me the creeps.

He says something again. I stare back at him, not moving an inch. I want to tell him I don't know, don't care, don't want to have anything to do with him, but he's still giving me that look.

I'm getting the same stalkerish vibe I got from that pervert scientist onboard the Fleet Station.

Seriously, what is it with Kordolians and this psycho mentality? I wonder if it has something to do with their shortage of females.

Ol' Gilded Loins sidles up to me, his skinny, hairless body gleaming under the surreal fractured light that dances across the room. "A female," he says, switching to Universal, his voice soft and lilting. "We do not get many of your kind here, even amongst servants." He leans in close and takes a deep breath. "But your scent is strange. What are you? Veronian? Lamidu? Ka'aran?"

I don't even know what half those are. I ignore him, pretending not to understand.

"Your Master must be quite attached to you. He keeps you quite close. Are you his favorite toy?"

Under the big, fluffy coat, my hand goes to the dagger strapped to my thigh. Just in case.

"Why don't we take a peek under the scarf? Don't worry, little female, I won't harm you. I'm just curious, that's all." He smells weird. Kinda like dishwashing soap. Is that a Kordolian attempt at perfume?

He reaches for my hood, intending to pull it back.

You know what? Before, I didn't know if I'd be able to stab someone, but now, I've changed my mind.

I flick out the dagger, bringing it up to Gilded Loins' neck. "My *Master* will be very upset if he learns you've dared touch me. You saw him. What exactly do you think he's capable of?"

Seriously? Is this escort on drugs? Anyone with half a brain would take one look at Tarak and make sensible decisions, even if they didn't know who he was. Decisions that wouldn't involve shortening one's lifespan. Some guys just have that 'look-at-me-the-wrong-way-and-certain-death-awaits' vibe going on. Tarak's one of those guys.

The thought seems to be a sobering one for the escort, because he freezes, his silvery skin turning pale. So it seems at least a fragment of sense exists somewhere in that crazy blue-haired head of his.

The fact that I've got a blade pressed against his neck seems to aid his decision making process.

He withdraws, offering me a hasty, half-assed bow. "I apologize. It's the hormones. Sometimes I have trouble controlling the urges. Please do not tell him about this." His tone has gone from self-assured smugness to wimpy whining.

"I'll think about it." I shrug, slipping the knife back into its sheath. For a race that's supposedly so fearsome and intimidating, these Kordolians aren't living up to the reputation. Well, apart from you-know-who. But half of them seem to be freaking idiots.

And to think I once wondered whether they'd all be like Tarak and his crew.

My hunch was correct. Tarak is different to these guys. He doesn't realize it, but he stands out. I noticed it when we were going through the Trader's Market. It became even more obvious once we got to the pleasure district.

No matter how much he tries to blend in, he can't help it. It's in the way he stands. It's in the way he walks, with graceful economy, each movement purposeful and without waste. It's in the way he looks and acts military, even when he's wearing plain clothes. Armor or not, he stands like a General and gives orders like a General. He makes even the simple act of shopping sound like he's issuing battle commands.

If we had more time, I'd teach him a thing or two about blending in.

He's always alert, scanning the crowds, watching the exits, looking for the first sign of danger.

I guess he can't help it. It's the way he was wired. And I do rather like him that way.

He's bossy but dependable, ruthless but considerate, hard-as-nails but deeply sensual. A walking contradiction.

He's protective as hell; terrifyingly so.

Gilded Loins doesn't realize it, but I've just done him a massive favor.

And I've just decided something. The General is coming to Earth with me.

He just doesn't know it yet.

Tarak

"IT'S HERE SOMEWHERE." Berad Sokal, brothel-owner, smuggler and unofficial 'boss' of the Fourth Quarter, taps a panel beside his holoscreen. He runs a hand through his darkening hair, tapping one cybernetic foot impatiently. "Ah. Here ya go. Access code for the landflyer. It's unregistered, unmarked, and untraceable. A bit old and slow, but it'll get ya where ya need to go." He narrows his eyes. "Bit unusual for ya to be comin' here unannounced, General. Somethin' up?"

"Nothing for you to worry about, Berad." I study the symbols on the holoscreen, memorizing the access code.

"She's parked two sections from here, in the grey hangar beside the meat shop. Ya can't miss it." He joins me as I stand, walking me to the door. His gait is slightly uneven, a result of having a cybernetic leg replacement.

"Been a while since my military days, but I know when somethin's up, Tarak. I ain't so dumb as to ask, but just take care."

"As always," I reply, briefly clasping his hand in the military way. Despite the fact that he conducts most of his business outside the limits of Kordolian Law, Berad is trustworthy. He served as the First Division's weapons master for many cycles before getting his leg blown off on a remote expedition.

He still knows his weapons. Under my ordinary looking robes, I'm now equipped with two plasma guns and a vicious, short Callidum sword. Even though I miss my long swords and would have preferred a high-powered military plasma cannon, they would have drawn too much attention. These small concealed weapons will suffice. Berad always comes up with the goods.

He will not betray me.

And now that we have access to an untraceable flyer, we can start our journey to the Vaal.

I return to the antechamber to find Abbey sitting with her arms crossed, her entire demeanor hostile. But with her features hidden by the hood and the dark-vision goggles, I can't read her so well.

The pleasure worker has disappeared.

I give her a small nod and she follows me out.

"You were not bothered?" I say quietly, as we go back through the dark entrance.

"Not so much," she replies, but there's a hard edge to her voice.

I wonder if that pleasure worker tried anything stupid. If he did, I am tempted to go back there and fucking strangle him, but Abbey's not saying a thing.

Whatever happened, she's obviously handled it.

We step back onto the throughway and start to head away from the pleasure district. I follow Berad's directions, and we end up in an area lined with storage facilities. Some of the buildings are ridden with ice-rot, their signage faded, the windows cracked. There's a meat shop on the corner, just like Berad told me. It's closed now, the grimy windows darkened. It looks neglected. I can't even tell if it's operational.

Berad must have keyed the entrance to the hangar to my bio-signature, because the large doors open as we approach.

I pull Abbey inside, out of the cold.

"You—"

"Shh." I push down her scarf and press my finger against her lips. I didn't have to. I simply wanted to see her face and feel her sweet, soft skin.

I glance behind.

Just now, I thought I sensed something. I peer around. We're in a large, dark storage shed that appears to double as a hangar. The flyer is in the corner, just as Berad said it would be. It's an older model from the pre-Callidum era, its body a dull silver color as opposed to the Callidum-black of our newer craft.

I look around, my senses stretched taut, listening for even the barest hint of movement.

But there's nothing.

If someone's trailing me and they've evaded *my* notice, that would make them very, very good. A formidable enemy indeed. I need to stay vigilant.

We're not out on the Vaal yet. Despite my best efforts to evade surveillance, the civilized zones of Kythia are full of hidden eyes. There's always the possibility I might have been recognized.

But it's pointless to worry about any of that now. The sooner we reach the Vaal, the sooner I can find Prince Xalikian. He wishes to meet me, but I also have vital information for him. Sensitive information, that can only be given in person. There's no way I'd allow him to enter the civilized zones just to find me.

So we go to him.

The Humans' reproductive compatibility could be the very thing we've been looking for all this time.

And the place we've been searching for? It could be Earth.

Even though the light of their star makes it sickeningly bright. Even though we would have to co-exist with Humans. Even though it's in an inconvenient sector of the universe.

It could be Earth.

"I'm guessing that's our ride?" Abbey's soft voice interrupts my thoughts. With her dark-vision goggles on, she can see perfectly well.

"That is the flyer we're using, yes."

"It's small."

"Yes."

"It has auto-pilot?"

"Of course." These primitive Humans. What kind of flyer doesn't have auto-pilot?

"You'll be looking for a way to spend the time, won't you, Tarak?"

I like it when she says my name like that, sounding both stern and playful. Shaped by her sexy Earth accent, it sounds good. I will never tire of the sound of her voice.

"Any objections?"

"I'll do you a deal. You tell me what you're doing here on Kythia, and I will be more than willing to compromise." She presses a gloved hand against my hardness, feeling me through the thin robes.

"A piece of information, in exchange for—"

"Exactly."

Devious female.

"Very well," I growl, admiring her persistence. I'm pleased with the compromise. The corner of her mouth quirks upwards. "But wait until we are a good distance from the civilized zones. Once we are over the Vaal, we shall talk."

CHAPTER TWELVE

Abbey

Tarak keeps the cabin of the flyer pitch black, and I'm guessing that's because he doesn't want us to be spotted. As we leave the city behind, we become engulfed by darkness. There's nothing to guide us but the glittering stars.

He's at home in the darkness. It's a little unsettling how he can see perfectly well.

Thankfully, I've got the dark-vision goggles. I look out at the scenery below. The flyer has a clear, curving roof that allows a 180-degree view of the sky and surrounding landscape.

The place Tarak calls The Vaal is completely flat.

It's flat and white and desolate.

There's not a single tree or bush or even a blade of grass to be seen.

Occasionally, an outcrop of earth rises out of the plain like an island, but even those are just barren lumps of rock or dirt.

There's nothing living out here at all. It's just frost and ice.

"It's an ocean," Tarak informs me, leaving his seat to come up behind me. He traces his fingers down the back of my neck, sending a shiver down my spine. "When our star died, the seas froze over, leaving flat, endless plains of ice. That is what we call the Vaal."

"And our destination is somewhere out there?"

"There are Kordolian tribes that exist in the Vaal. Animals, too. They have evolved. Adapted. We are searching for one of the Lost Tribes, called the Aikun."

"That's why you guys see in the dark and don't mind the cold."

"So it seems." His voice is a low rumble, his touch warm and certain. Possessive. I shudder, feeling cosy for the first time since we left the freighter.

"So what do the lost tribes have that's so secret and so important?"

Tarak is silent for a while, looking at me with his depthless eyes. Viewed through the lenses of the dark-vision goggles, he's a study in monochrome, his silver skin taking on a pearlescent sheen, his eyes almost glowing.

He looks like something out of a fairytale; a prince of the night.

Look at me getting all dramatic now.

"The Imperial Prince has exiled himself to the wastelands of the Vaal. The Lost Tribes of the plains are loyal to him; they consider him as one of their own. I see potential in Xalikian, and I need to personally discuss certain developments with him, because there is a role I want him to play. These events may impact on the future survival of our race. It is too risky for him to return to the civilized zones right now, because there are many who would rather see him dead. Therefore, I go to seek him out."

Oh. Talk about dramatic. I close my mouth, wondering when my jaw dropped.

Tarak shrugs. "Kythian politics is complex."

"Obviously." I had no idea Tarak was tight with the Imperial family. "You're kind of a big deal around here, aren't you?"

"I've always tried to serve the Empire with distinction." His voice is distant. For a moment, he's quiet, looking out over the empty Vaal. Is it just me, or does he sound a little bit conflicted?

He's curling his fingers around the nape of my neck, stroking the bare skin there. "Does that satisfy your curiosity?" he asks softly.

We're gliding over a frozen sea, alone in a desolate wasteland, and I'm seeing another side to Tarak. It's a rare glimpse of his inner thoughts.

I wonder what this battle-hardened male has seen and done in his lifetime. Some good things, and some terrible things I'd imagine, all in the name of the Kordolian Empire.

My curiosity is far from satisfied, but I don't tell him that. If I have my way, there will be plenty of time to get to know him.

Instead I remove my gloves, taking his hands into mine. I'm sitting in the passenger seat and he's standing behind me, looking out over the Vaal. The flyer's on autopilot, gliding noise-lessly over the icy plains.

It feels as if we're the only two beings on this planet, with millions of miles of vast emptiness surrounding us. It's as if we're stuck in infinity; in darkness.

I get up and walk to him. As I reach him, he takes the dark-vision goggles from my face. Without them, it's pitch black. I can't see a thing, but I'm anchored by the feel of his warm, hard body, pressing into mine.

"I want to see your eyes," he says, tracing his rough thumb down my cheek.

"It's okay," I reply, running my fingers along his jawline, over the tips of his ears, along his cheekbones, down his nose, to his lips. I trust him. And I rather like this perspective, viewing him with a different sense. Touch is so powerful. He takes one finger into his mouth, and my finger brushes against the sharp points of his fangs.

It turns me on.

He sucks on my finger, his mouth warm and wanting. That simple act makes me moan in surprise and pleasure. I never thought such a thing could feel so insanely erotic.

I'm about to reach out and tear his robes off when a deaf-ening blast goes off, and a flash of light tears through the clear roof of the flyer, missing Tarak's head by an inch. Going from darkness to blazing light, I'm momentarily blinded. The bolt of light, or whatever it was, has hit the wall behind me, causing a shower of sparks to fly.

An eerie whistling sound echoes through the cabin. I can't see anything, but it seems like the blast has left a small hole. A stream of freezing air starts to flow inside, causing the temperature to drop instantly.

Tarak spits out a string of vicious sounding Kordolian curse-words.

He picks up my dark-vision goggles. "Put these on." He passes me something; a blaster of sorts. "Plasma gun. Anyone bothers you, push this button here, and pull the trigger. I'm going outside. Someone's out there."

"What?" I look up through the clear roof in alarm. "But—"

I was about to say something silly like: *'it's dangerous,'* but Tarak's throwing off his cumbersome robes and trousers and drawing out his armor, the inky, liquid black stuff coalescing and hardening over his skin.

"I fucking hate being interrupted," he growls, pulling a nasty looking short blade from somewhere, sheathing it at his back. He bends over to kiss me, and I twine my fingers with his. His hand is now covered with a hard, exo-armor glove. It feels totally impenetrable. No wonder the peacekeepers on Fortuna Tau backed off when Tarak and his boys turned up. I really hope they're doing okay, back there.

We'll need to talk about that.

And there's another little discussion I'm going to have to shelve for later. I still don't get how the exo-armor works. The nanites live in his body, or something. Are they symbiotic, perhaps? Even though I've studied biotech inside and out, nano-technology just boggles my mind.

It's way beyond what we Humans are capable of right now.

"Don't move. I'll be back. If you see an intruder, shoot." Tarak turns, and the black stuff glides over his face, forming a menacing helm. I'd hate to be his enemy. He opens a hatch at the top and pulls himself up and out, letting a blast of cold air into the cabin.

For a moment, the wind rushes past, impossibly noisy. Then he shuts the hatch, and everything goes silent save for the thin whistle of cold air that flows in through the crack in the roof.

I hear a thud, then the flyer shakes a little, then there's footsteps. Tarak appears on the roof, a black-armored figure. He's followed by a person dressed all in white. The flyer rocks back and forth, unsettled by their movements.

They're trading blows.

Tarak's attacker is agile and nimble, but Tarak is equally as fast, and their movements become a blur. Tarak has drawn his blade, and the attacker keeps hurling things at him. They look like small throwing knives. The weapons are thrown with vicious intent, but they deflect off his armor harmlessly. Tarak dances out of the way, looking for an opening.

Who the hell is this white-clad person?

He, and it's definitely a *he*, is wearing a mask of some sort, concealing his features. For a brief moment, he looks down, and it's as if he's focusing on me, marking me through the transparent roof. The mask he wears is as creepy as hell; it's got two black, tear-shaped marks where the eyes should be, but it's otherwise smooth and faceless.

That split second of distraction is enough for Tarak to sweep the assassin's feet out from under him. The attacker lands on his back and Tarak tries to stick him with his sword, but the masked guy rolls out of the way.

Tarak stabs again, but again the guy rolls. What Tarak's trying to do looks near-impossible; he's balancing on his feet while the flyer rocks back and forth, cold air streaming past them, the whole thing moving at ridiculous speed.

I'm surprised they haven't fallen off.

The thought of Tarak dropping to the barren wasteland below scares the shit out of me.

There's no way I'm going to just sit here like an idiot while he's risking his life out there. I stare down at the weapon Tarak's left in my hands. It's similar to an Earth-style bolt pistol, but this one obviously fires plasma. I tap the little button the way Tarak showed me and a series of blue lights flickers along one side.

Whoa. It's charging?

Was that the safety?

It's surprisingly light in my hands. I curl my finger around the trigger and walk over to the point where Tarak's attacker is rolling around on the roof. He aims a gun at Tarak, but Tarak kicks it out of his hand, the weapon flying off into nothingness.

I look through the clear barrier, my arm trembling slightly as I raise the gun. I add my other hand, trying to steady my aim.

I've never actually fired a gun before. I guess there's a first time for everything.

I wait, both arms raised, forcing myself to breathe slowly. My heart is hammering inside my chest.

The guy above is moving all over the place as Tarak stalks him, trying to get a hit in.

I wait, because I don't want to hit Tarak. I wait to get a clear shot.

Get out of the way, love.

There.

I pull the trigger, and there's a blinding flash of light. A boom reverberates around the cabin, and the recoil of the plasma gun sends me crashing to the floor.

Did I hit him? I'm not sure.

Tarak

THE ASSASSIN'S head explodes in a spray of black blood, leaving a splatter of black dots across my visor, marring my vision. His death mask disintegrates into thousands of tiny fragments, instantly whipped away by the rushing wind.

I blink, and then the attacker's body is gone, having tumbled to the icy wasteland below.

My vision clears as the nanites forming my armor internalize the organic matter. For the minuscule bio-machines, the blood is a source of energy, nothing more.

I look down through the clear roof of the flyer. It has two

holes now, but the material has not fragmented. Below me, Abbey is lying on the floor, the plasma gun clasped in her trembling hands.

She looks so small and vulnerable, her face pale and luminous against the dark background of the flyer's cabin. Her eyes are hidden by the dark-vision goggles.

This tiny, fragile Human has just taken out a Silent One, a notorious Imperial assassin. They are the most dreaded of killers, feared throughout the galaxy.

She stares up at me, and the most glorious thing happens. She smiles. Her expression is filled with relief, but also with a savage protectiveness I haven't witnessed before.

Crazy Human. She will be a fine mother to our child.

My female is insane, and I am completely, utterly obsessed with her.

To think I once regarded her species as inferior. She has proven herself brave and clever beyond my wildest imagination.

I open the hatch and drop back into the cabin, willing my helm to retract. The outside air is streaming in from two holes in the roof now, causing an infernal whistling sound to echo throughout the cabin.

I take the plasma gun from her hands, reset the safety, and pull her into my arms. It takes her a moment to regain her balance.

She's shivering, and her lips have taken on a blue tinge.

Even at this low flight level, the atmospheric air is much colder than it is on the surface.

Curse that Silent One to Kaiin's nine barren hells. How dare he damage my fucking roof? I look around for a repair hatch. Berad's ex-military. He would have made sure there was one, even on this small craft.

I spot the set of tiny red lights beside the passenger exit. "Wait for one moment, *amina*." I step away, making sure she's able to stand. I turn my attention towards the wall.

The hatch slides out as I press my palm to the activation panel. I open the case and find it fully stocked.

I say a silent thanks to that sly old warrior Berad for keeping his craft properly maintained and resourced.

I find what I'm looking for easily; a tube of polymer putty. I snap the tube in half, activating the chemical compounds inside. The putty heats up in my hands, turning from red to grey. I split it in two, making two balls.

Reaching up to the clear roof, I slap a ball on each hole. The polymer molds to the defect and hardens instantly, becoming transparent.

The irritating whistling sound stops, and silence surrounds us, save for the low hum of the flyer's engine.

"You didn't tell me about the recoil," Abbey says dryly, tucking her hands into her coat. "That thing has a hell of a kick on it. How do you handle it?"

"Training." I shrug. Add to that the fact that Kordolians possess far greater natural strength than Humans. My species has evolved to hunt wild creatures across the dark, icy wastelands of the Vaal.

I pull her against me, unable to contain myself any longer. "What were you thinking, female, shooting that thing through the roof? I did not ask you to help me win my battles."

"No, you didn't. And I've seen what you do. I know you're quite capable of kicking ass. It's actually scary, how capable you are. But when I see you out there in the cold, fighting some masked weirdo on the roof of a flyer traveling at high speed, what do you expect me to do? Sit back and watch? What if you'd fallen?"

"I never fall," I growl, the mere thought causing my irritation to spark. My footing was sure, my weight perfectly balanced. I was stalking that assassin patiently, wearing him down, waiting for him to make a mistake.

It was only a matter of time before I ran the sightless bastard through with my blade.

Imperial scum. The Silent Ones are brainwashed tools of the Noble Houses. That's all they are.

"I-I'm sure y-you don't." Her teeth are starting to chatter. "Bbut I'm not the sort to sit around and tempt fate. Especially when it comes to you."

"Come here." I take her into my arms, willing the exo-armor to retract, the nanites dissolving, re-entering my body through the pores of my skin, leaving me naked. I press my body against hers. Even though she's wearing the coat and the thermowear, her temperature has dropped. Her hands are cold underneath the gloves. I take them into mine, willing the heat from my body to seep into her.

The thought of my female trying to protect me is strangely pleasing.

Others don't usually concern themselves with my safety.

"You are cold," I remark, placing her hands on my torso. I slide my arms underneath her coat, wrapping them around her waist.

"All of bloody Kythia is cold," she grumbles, curling up against me. She's shivering. I press my lips to hers and find them cold.

This will not do.

"Then we shall make our own heat," I murmur, between kisses.

Abbey

HE'S AT IT AGAIN. But my goodness, he's toasty warm and this time I'm not complaining. He's also naked. Again.

Our flyer glides along through the darkness, skimming over desolate nothingness. Tarak has sealed the holes in the roof, but the cold air that entered the cabin has caused the temperature to plummet. Luckily, I have my own personal heater, right here.

Any sane person might be asking questions right now. A sensible person might be wondering why a lethal, masked weirdo was chasing us. That assassin looked at me too, showing me that creepy, blank face. I don't know how he was able to see anything with that thing on his face.

Was he after me, or Tarak?

It doesn't matter now. He's dead. I shot him in the head.

I can't believe I did that.

Surprisingly, I feel okay. I thought I'd be a mess, but instead I'm relieved. Maybe this is one of these things where the shock will hit me afterwards and I'll turn into a blubbering mess at some random moment.

Tarak is standing with his arms circled around my waist. He's placed my hands against his bare torso, and through my thin gloves I can feel the rigid muscles of his stomach. They move back and forth, ever so slightly, to the rhythm of his breathing.

He's deliciously warm. I'm like an iceberg, and his heat is thawing me out.

He's just been fighting an attacker on the roof, a guy who had his brains blown out in front of him, and now he's all over me, and it's as if the entire thing never happened.

I've stopped shivering now, thanks to Tarak's internal heater. As I look up at him through the dark-vision goggles, he smiles.

I don't think I've ever really seen him smile like that before. It's glorious. It transforms his hard features, and for a moment, he almost looks Human. Not that I'd prefer for him to look Human. I like my big, bad Kordolian just the way he is.

"You did well, my female," he rumbles approvingly, sliding his sneaky hands down my lower back, slipping his fingers under the waistband of my pants, tracing the curves of my ass. "Although I would have managed without your help."

"Of course you would have," I say sweetly. "I just felt bad for you, battling the elements and that psycho on your own."

He snorts in amusement. "I have dealt with worse."

"Hm." I'm too distracted to come up with a witty reply. My hands are warm enough now, thanks to his very useful, very delectable abs. I pull off my gloves, allowing them to drop to the floor.

He pulls me towards him, and I feel his erection brushing up against me. I take his cock into my hands. There's wetness at the tip, and I caress that sensitive area, eliciting a low growl.

Tarak's grip on my ass tightens. He looks at me with a raw, hungry gaze, the points of his fangs just visible as he leans in and inhales my scent.

"I want to see your face while I fuck you," he whispers, his voice low and hoarse. I shiver, and not because of the cold. His warmth has spread through me, right down to my toes, and any trace of the chill I felt is gone.

He removes one hand from my ass and pulls the dark-vision goggles from my face, submerging me in darkness.

"Now let us pick up where we left off, before we were so rudely interrupted." The sound of his voice and the feel of his hard body against mine anchor me in the darkness. I close my fingers around his hard length, applying a little pressure, pumping up and down.

He moans, a low, primal sound, moving in to plant soft kisses at the top of my ear, taking a moment to nip and suck at the sensitive skin. He trails kisses down my cheek, across my jaw, all the way to my lips. His tongue meets mine, insistent and wanting.

Then he's undressing me, slipping the Skaz-thingy coat off my shoulders, pulling off my silver jacket and the stretchy thermo top underneath. I raise my arms as he lifts it over my head, my breasts coming free. He leans in and circles his hot tongue around one nipple, growling in approval as it becomes hard. He does the same to the other nipple, before trailing a line of warm, sucking kisses down my stomach as I release his cock from my grasp. He must be down on his knees now, but I can't tell for sure. I can't see a thing.

"What are you doing?" I gasp, as desire overwhelms me. A feeling of exquisite, erotic tension starts in my core and slowly unfolds, causing a gentle ache between my legs.

"The female body should be worshipped," he says in a low voice. "Yours especially."

Ooh. The General knows exactly what to say. I let out a gasp of anticipation as he slips my pants down and pulls both of my boots off with the greatest care.

He's completely undressed me. I stand naked in the cabin,

surrounded by inky blackness, save for the flashing of a few random instrument lights.

We're flying over a frozen sea, and I'm naked.

I can't see his face; I can't read his expression. All I know is that he's watching me from the darkness.

His hands are gone and his mouth is gone. I need his touch. Just when I'm unable to stand it any longer, he comes up behind me, wrapping his big, warm frame around me.

His erection presses against the small of my back, and he pulls me into him. Our bare skin touches, sending a thrill through me. I'm completely naked, but I'm not feeling the cold at all.

His devious fingers part the lips of my pussy, going in deep. He uses two fingers, stretching me, finding me wet and ready. He rubs my g-spot, and I squirm against him. He wraps his other arm around my waist, his muscles bunching as I cry out in pleasure, arcing my back. He strokes me harder, faster, until I'm in sensory overload, overwhelmed, my body trembling.

Just as the stirrings of a climax begin, he withdraws and pulls away from me, disappearing into the darkness, leaving my body wanting.

"You and your unfair advantages," I groan. I can't see him; can't hear him. Where has he gone? That sneaky, underhanded male. How can he leave me hanging like this?

I reach out in front of me, but my fingers find only cold air.

"You—"

Tarak kisses me down there, at the entrance to my pussy.

Oh Jupiter, what's he doing now? Is he kneeling in front of me? I reach down and touch his head, my fingers brushing through his soft, short hair. His tongue flicks in and out, circling my clit, penetrating deeper between my folds, then back again.

Back and forth; it feels so good, and I am in heaven right now.

He sucks gently on my clit, and the tightness in my core builds. He's drawing out my pleasure, teasing my sensitive flesh, his tongue gliding over it with tiny, measured strokes.

His rough hands caress my hips and I tremble as he drags me willingly to the edge.

He's touching *that* spot with just the right amount of pressure, coaxing my body to respond.

I never imagined it could feel this good.

I can't see him in the darkness, but the sheer feel of him and his rich, masculine scent inundate my senses. I'm drowning in sensation.

I reach the tipping point. I'm no longer in control of my body. Waves of bliss crash through me, each one bigger than the last, and I'm barely hanging on as my legs turn to jelly, my body becoming a quivering, helpless, wonderful mess.

I'm thankful we're gliding over the middle of nowhere, because when I come, I scream.

It's loud enough to blow the roof off this bloody thing.

Tarak

MY FEMALE VOICES HER PLEASURE, and it's a most satisfying sound.

I rise, savoring the lingering taste of her on my tongue. She collapses against me, warm and soft and undeniably female. I breathe in her rich, complex perfume; the heady scent of her arousal.

"You're mine," I growl, enjoying the sight of her. She stares into the distance, her eyes unfocused in the darkness. I can see her perfectly well, but she can't see a thing. She is glorious, and she is mine to enjoy. I hold her in my arms, appreciating the sight of her. A red flush has crept along her cheeks, and her lips are slightly parted. Her chest rises and falls, her breathing rapid, her ripe breasts moving to a gentle rhythm.

She is incredibly responsive to my touch, and that pleases me.

I'm aroused to the point where it's almost painful, and I am tempted to take her now, to fuck her savagely and satisfy my lust, but I pull back, wanting to draw out the occasion.

I guide her across the floor as I move to the pilot's chair and sit down.

Abbey gets the idea, swaying her hips suggestively as she climbs on top of me. She guides herself using touch, bringing her hands up to my face. Her small, nimble fingers trace across my cheeks, and she places two fingers in my mouth. I suck on them, and she grins.

Her expression, both devious and charming, is incredibly sexy.

She's aware of the powerful effect she has on me. She's self-assured and confident. I have never seen anything more beautiful.

One of her hands drops below, to her moist sex. As I suck her fingers, she pleasures herself, sighing, her hips moving back and forth. It makes me want her even more.

Is such a thing even possible?

My erection strains, becoming sublimely unbearable. She hasn't even laid a hand on me and I'm like this. I let out a low, deep, growl, expressing my hunger.

"Steady, big boy," she teases. She moves in close and guides me inside her. I groan as I enter her.

The feeling is indescribable. It's everything I'd imagined, and more. She takes control, moving her body to a slow, pulsing rhythm. I close my eyes and let her take over.

She knows exactly what to do.

Soft gasps escape her lips as she increases her speed, and I grab her ass, guiding her movements. She finds the sensitive points of my regenerating horns and caresses them, taking me to the next level of pleasure.

We move as one, and I know nothing anymore save for the feel of her, the sound of her, her scent, her taste.

I know nothing but my own savage need.

I rise and draw her against me, our bodies still entwined. I'm deep inside her as I lift her with ease, her legs curling around me. I turn and fuck her against the instrument panel. She's panting, her sweet voice hoarse with pleasure.

I push her hair back and stare into her face, captivated by her remarkable eyes. My dark-vision is sharp, but with only a trace of starlight refracting through them, her irises appear depthless.

I watch her face as I thrust harder and deeper. A universe of emotion is captured in her expression. She is vulnerable yet strong, complicated but pure.

She's so very Human.

The climax starts from deep within me and builds, consuming me, making me cry out as I reach a place I never knew existed.

Her sweet voice joins mine as I come inside her, my seed spilling forth.

She is mine, and I belong to her.

CHAPTER THIRTEEN

Abbey

Holy, moly. I'm raw and tingling, but in a good way. Tarak is navigating the flyer now, preferring to fly manually as we near our destination. He looks awfully pleased with himself.

And so he should be.

What the hell just happened? He did it again, that's what happened.

This is starting to become a pattern. That's the problem when you're stuck in a confined space with a big, sexy, silver alien. You get cosy, really quickly. *Too* quickly.

Not that I'm complaining.

Far from it.

As far as I'm concerned, the General can carry on with his distractions, but he needs to be a bit more forthcoming with information, especially since I've gone to the trouble to accompany him to seek out some crazy Prince who lives in an icy wasteland. Not that I had much of a choice.

Now seems like as good a time as ever to ask the important questions.

"Ta-rak," I say slowly, watching him through my dark-vision

goggles. Questions; I have so many questions. Where to start? *Take a pick, Abbey.* "What's with the suit?"

"Hm?" He's staring at me again, even though I'm now bundled up in the Skaz-coat.

"You have these freaky black nano-things that live inside you and come out of your skin. What's up with that?" Now I've been around space a little bit. I know there are things out there that are beyond the capability of Human science to explain, but this seems a little far-fetched.

I wouldn't believe it if I hadn't seen it with my own eyes.

"Virulent nanites." He shrugs as if it's no big deal. "They are made from Callidum and infected with a virus that has integrated them into my bloodstream. The armor is a prototype that was programmed into them. They are keyed to my neural signature."

That didn't make a whole lot of sense, but my semi-scientific brain is able to understand at least a fragment of his explanation. My major was plant biotech, not advanced alien nano-bio-engineering, or whatever it's called.

"Not all Kordolians have these, er, nanites, do they?"

"No. Only myself and the soldiers of the First Division survived the trials. The project was abandoned soon afterwards. I was the sole product of the first generation experimental phase."

"Oh." I hesitate, unsure of what to say. His expression is frosty cold right now, desolate and bleak like the frozen sea we're traveling over. I'm treading on sensitive ground.

"You don't have to feel sympathy for me, Abbey. I survived, others did not. I'm an aberration."

"No you're not," I blurt, without even thinking. "Which stupid idiot coined that term? That so does not apply to you. You're a decent ma… uh, Kordolian."

Tarak blinks, and gives me a long, scrutinizing look. Then, the corner of his mouth quirks upwards. "It takes a Human to tell me such things."

"I speak my mind. You should know that by now."

"Hm." His attention is diverted for a moment as he banks the flyer. A large, hulking shape comes into view. As we near, I realize it's a landmass; a mountain with a crater at the top. It rises out of the frozen sea, black and forbidding.

Tarak narrows his eyes as he glances back at me, his fangs peeking out just below his upper lip. Some might find that expression rather menacing. I think it's adorable. That's just how he looks when he's thinking.

"Prince Xalikian will like you," he says eventually, as we descend, heading towards the large crater. It looks like an extinct volcano.

Tarak's little statement doesn't exactly inspire confidence. "This Prince of yours; he's not crazy like almost every other Kordolian I've met, is he? Present company excepted, of course." The thought of meeting some strange Kordolian out in the dark, icy wilderness makes me uneasy. I'm rather sick and tired of various Kordolians trying to hunt me for my Human flesh and organs.

At least I've got Big Bad here on my side. That's the main reason I'm not terrified out of my wits right now.

Tarak's face is annoyingly blank. "Kordolians think he's crazy."

I don't know if that's a good thing, or a bad thing. Is he crazy as in relatively sane, or crazy as in too crazy for even Kordolians?

"So you and this Xalikian guy are in cahoots together, and he's in exile. Are you planning a coup?"

Tarak stiffens. "I have vowed not to start war on Kythia. The future of our species is already tenuous. We would not survive a civil war. However, other options have presented themselves."

"And what might these 'other options' be?"

"Nothing is certain yet, Abbey. Once Xalikian and I have decided on a course of action, you will be made aware."

I sigh. He's as cryptic as always, keeping his cards close to his chest. "So when you're done with your secret fate-of-the-Empire business, we can go back to Fortuna Tau, right?" I say it half-jokingly and half-hopefully, taking advantage of Tarak's rare chatty mood.

"Perhaps," he says nonchalantly.

My jaw drops. What did he just say? Did he just hint at taking me back home?

And Tarak's not the sort to joke around.

I try to conceal my surprise. "You know you're coming with me, right? You'll love Earth. We have sunshine there, it's warm, and there's chocolate. It's even better than Veronian food. I swear, you'll love it."

Tarak frowns. "I dislike ultraviolet light. The light from your star is particularly irritating. It hurts my eyes. And I hate sweet things." Party pooper. He hasn't even been to Earth and he's grumbling already. Tarak pushes the flyer into a steep descent, and we swoop down into the crater of the mountain. "But your planet may be of interest to us in other ways."

"What other ways?" I ask suspiciously. "And what do you mean by 'us'? What are you planning? Don't you dare think about colonizing us, Tarak. We are not going to end up becoming a giant pineapple farm for Kythia. I forbid you from colonizing Earth."

Tarak inclines his head. "You forbid me, Human?" He raises an eyebrow, his voice low and dangerous. His lips are curved, ever so slightly. Is he amused? I find his expression devastatingly sexy. It's that magnificent mixture of menace and irony that only he can pull off.

Damn this male. I can't tell if he's being serious or if he's messing with me.

"You know I can't stop you from doing anything, General. But you know what they say. Happy wife, happy life. And trust me. If you guys come and take over Earth, I am *not* going to be happy."

"Noted." He pulls the flyer into a sharp curve, once again focusing on the descent. "I do not understand the relevance of this 'pineapple' you speak of, but if the idea of Kordolians ruling Earth displeases you, then I will consider alternatives." He looks ahead, concentrating as he circles the giant crater, reducing our speed. "But only because it's you who's asking, Abbey of Earth. I will do it for you, but not for anyone else. The welfare of other Humans doesn't concern me."

Urgh. He's gone all Kordolian on me again. If we do end up going to Earth, we're going to have a little chat first, because I don't want him just barging in and messing everything up. Badass General or not, on my home turf, he'll play by my rules.

Tarak

AS WE LAND, a group of Kordolian males emerges from behind a cluster of large boulders. They're mostly young, their appearance typical of the Aikun. Unlike the Kordolians who dwell in the civilized zones, these males are fit and lean-bodied, their expressions hard and suspicious.

The Aikun are one of the Lost Tribes that exist in the Vaal, and they possess an innate mistrust of everything that comes from the Empire. Over hundreds of cycles, the Empire has stolen so many of their children that they've become secretive and withdrawn.

It's no wonder the Wild Prince has adopted them as his people. Xalikian's rejection of the Empire comes from the fact that he was raised in the belly of corruption.

With a mother like Vionn, it's no wonder he's left Kythian society to live in the Vaal.

Apparently, the Lost Tribes are my people too, but I have no recollection of such things. My memories of childhood were taken from me, as part of my conditioning. I have flashbacks now and then, but I have never been one to dwell on the past.

Beside me, Abbey has dressed and concealed her face with the scarf, in anticipation of the outside temperature. She is staring intently at the Aikun. "They live here?"

"Yes."

"They have horns," she gasps.

"All Kordolian males have horns," I inform her. "The Aikun refuse to file them off."

Their twin black horns rise from their temples, curving slightly. All of the Aikun males have grown their hair long, and they wear it in a range of styles. Some have fashioned their hair into intricate braids, while others leave it loose and untamed.

They wear nothing save for simple loincloths, and their bodies bear scars that they display proudly; hard-fought reminders of their battles with the dangerous creatures of the Vaal.

They are both savage and dignified in appearance.

As we exit the flyer, Abbey nudges me in my side. "You should grow your horns," she whispers suggestively.

"They are impractical," I growl, wondering how she can be thinking of such things at a time like this.

"But they're very sensitive, aren't they?" She pauses. "Erotic, even."

Mischievous female.

"Abbey," I snap, although I'm far from annoyed. What she suggests is interesting. "We will discuss this another time."

She walks by my side, staying close to me as we cross the clearing. For her, this is the safest place in the universe. I will let no harm come to her. The Aikun can be vicious fighters, but they are no match for me. In order to appear less threatening, I have worn my robes and left my weapons concealed.

I do not wish to fight them.

"What business do you have here, Lost One?" One of the males, a young Kordolian with a vicious scar running from the corner of one eye to his jaw, steps forward, an ancient looking plasma cannon aimed at us. He speaks Imperial Kordolian with a heavy accent.

It is ironic. Kythians who live in the civilized zones refer to the Aikun and their like as the Lost Tribes. In turn, the Aikun call us the Lost Ones. They feel we have strayed too far from the teachings of the Goddess.

I'm not religious by any stretch of the imagination, but the value system of the Aikun intrigues me. They do not conquer or take more than they need. They simply exist.

After so many cycles waging war on other planets in the

name of the Empire, the cause has become tarnished. I can no longer blindly serve my masters, who sit on their thrones in civilization and shield themselves from the realities of the universe.

I have even taken a mate; a Human. I never would have thought such a thing was possible. It is as if she has been created for me.

Prince Xalikian must agree to my plan, or else I will be half-tempted to take myself to the other end of the universe and be done with the Kordolian Empire for good.

I spread my hands wide, showing the Aikun that I'm unarmed. "I bear no ill will. I seek our mutual brother. He is expecting me."

"I do not know who you speak of." He narrows his eyes, his attention diverting to Abbey. He sniffs the air, trying to identify her scent. I suppress the warning growl that threatens to erupt from my throat.

The Aikun are being cautious, trying to protect Xalikian from outsiders. They don't recognize him as a ruler, but as an equal. I can understand their reticence, especially when the High Council would see Xal's severed head displayed in the forecourt of the Palace of Arches, a warning to all who would consider betraying the Empire.

That is what happens when one tries to kill the Empress, even if she is his own mother.

When news of his actions was transmitted throughout the Empire and he was denounced through the Nobles' propaganda machine, Xalikian became a cult figure in the eyes of the ordinary classes.

He'd already earned their respect through his advocacy and his charity; this just sealed the deal.

The Aikun males draw nearer, their weapons raised. They carry an odd assortment of blades, guns and spears. Some are made from Callidum, while others gleam silver in the faint starlight. Beside me, Abbey is still, watching from behind her dark-vision goggles. I sense no fear from her. She is calm and steady like a seasoned soldier.

She is brave; a worthy mate.

She trusts me. I must do right by her.

I could threaten them right now, but that would bring tension and violence, and might result in unnecessary deaths. Theirs, of course.

There is a better way to convince these tribesmen that I mean them no harm. I drop to my knees and recite a short prayer to the Goddess. I speak in the secret, musical Aikun tongue.

It's one of the few memories that remain from my life before the experiments.

I remember a soft female voice. She sings the words in a low, melodic tone. Her arms are around me, cradling my small body.

Fragments of memories are all I have left from my childhood.

The Aikun males respond by following my words with a deep, rhythmic chorus. The male with the scar on his face steps forward. "You are a stolen child," he says, his eyes wide.

"Now can you understand that I mean our brother no harm?"

"And what about your companion, who is not of our world?"

"She is my mate," I snarl, my sword hand twitching. "That is all you need to know."

Abbey can't understand what we're saying, but she edges closer to me, sensing the tone of the conversation. She's staring up at me. I'm not letting her out of my sight.

I sigh. "I understand your hesitation, Aikun, but the fact that I have come alone with my mate should be proof enough that I mean no harm."

The Aikun males confer for a moment, muttering softly amongst themselves. The lead male turns back to me. "He is out on the plains, hunting beneath the ice."

"We'll go to him," I say, and the Aikun laugh.

"You may have some difficulty traversing the mountain, Kythian. We can escort you, but your people aren't familiar with the terrain." The lead male's tone is slightly condescending. "Would you not rather wait?"

"Don't worry about me, Aikun. Worry about whether you

can keep up." I resist the urge to smirk. These Aikun have no idea of the conditions I've had to fight under; of the harsh planet environments I've fought in.

Navigating the mountainside is nothing for me.

It is time to take my Prince from his comfortable life on the Vaal, even if I have to drag him by his infernal horns. The future of our people is at stake, and he is the catalyst.

And somehow, this tiny planet called Earth, which had escaped our notice until now, could become our sanctuary. It's blindingly bright, and Humans are irritatingly contrary, fragile beings, but they can also be brave, resourceful and clever.

This female beside me has clung onto life tenaciously, despite all that's been thrown at her. And she's brought me, a proud Kordolian General, to my knees.

Of course, I will never tell her such things.

I cannot have her becoming too comfortable now, can I?

Abbey

SOMEHOW, I've ended up in Tarak's arms, and we're careening down the side of a black mountain at terrifying speed.

I must be light as a feather to him, because he's running down the rocky slopes like a goddamn mountain goat, never missing a step.

The tribal guys are lagging behind. Tarak laughs, his deep voice distorted by the wind. It's rare to hear him laugh with such careless abandon. It's almost as if the act of running down a dangerously steep mountain with a woman in his arms has unleashed some kind of childlike joy.

"What's so funny?" I curl into his broad chest, enjoying his warmth and his scent.

"Those Aikun males thought they could outrun me."

"They haven't figured out that you're a freak of nature, huh?"

"It's true; I have enhancements that make this an unfair contest."

Bits of gravel fly around his booted feet as we reach the base of the mountain. It ends abruptly and the flat, white, endless plains of ice stretch out before us.

"So where exactly are we going?"

"Prince Xalikian is fishing in the ice, so we go to find him."

"And then?"

"We talk, we decide on a course of action, and we follow it."

"To Earth?"

"Probably."

Okay, that seems like progress. We've gone from 'perhaps' to 'probably'. I still can't figure out what's going on in this infuriating male's head, but at least he's starting to become a little bit more open with me.

He needs to be, because I didn't understand a word of what just went on between him and those tribal looking guys. It was the strangest thing. In the middle of a macho male-off between Tarak and the tribal guys, he suddenly knelt down and reverently recited something in a different language. It was soft and melodic, so different to the harsh Kordolian tongue.

After that, they all suddenly became cool with him.

Urgh. There's so much I still don't understand. Such as, who are these wild looking Kordolians who amazingly seem to be able to survive in the middle of the most barren place I have ever been to?

When I was a kid, I went on an Antarctic tour with my dad. I thought that place was cold. The entire trip, I couldn't wait to get home. This is ten times worse. How do they manage to live out here? The chill doesn't seem to affect them at all. I would love to have access to a text on Kordolian physiology right now.

Again, and this is starting to become a recurring theme, those young Kordolian males behind us are barely dressed, wearing simple loincloths and not much else.

They look like characters out of some ancient, dark fairytale, with their wild, long hair and menacing black horns. Like all Kordolians, their eyes are varying shades of fire, from deepest red to striking yellow.

Now I understand what those little bumps on Tarak's temples are supposed to be.

The horns are unearthly and beautiful.

Why the hell would any Kordolian cut them off? When we're back in relative civilization, we are going to have a talk about that.

We sprint across the flat, icy surface, Tarak slowing a little so the others can catch up. He's not even out of breath. They shout at him in Kordolian, and he yells back. It sounds like playful banter.

Now, they've become totally chilled.

Maybe it had something to do with Tarak's approach. Instead of his usual threaten-first-ask-questions-later style, he went softly, softly on this one.

I was rather impressed. There's hope for him yet.

We reach a defect in the ice. It's a large square-shaped hole. Tarak sets me down and I peer over the edge, fascinated.

There's water at the bottom. It's black and sinister and totally flat. I get the shivers just looking at it.

The ice must be about twenty feet thick, and somehow they've cut a hole in it. A metal ladder stretches down from the surface of the ice to the water, and there's a small floating platform at the bottom.

"What's that?" I ask, mesmerized by the dark water.

"Waterhole," Tarak replies, staring down into the depths. "So they can hunt what's beneath the ice."

"And that just happens to be—"

Before I can finish, something black and sleek breaks the surface for a second, before disappearing into the depths again.

"Lamperk." Tarak nods towards the water. "Watch."

The black thing surfaces again, and this time I see its giant, gaping maw. It has teeth. Lots of sharp, white teeth. No eyes, no face, just teeth. It's like a massive, underwater leech.

Alongside the lamperk, a flash of sliver appears. There's a Kordolian swimming around down there.

"Oh shit, there's someone down there! That thing's going to kill him."

Tarak just laughs.

I stare at him in disbelief. "Aren't you going to help him?"

"Of course not," he shrugs. "Wait and see."

The water starts to churn, becoming a chaotic, turbulent mess. I see intermittent flashes of silver and black as the two bodies twist and turn in the water.

A plume of white liquid appears, clouding the water, contrasting with the inky blackness. Ew. Is that some kind of bodily fluid? The creature's blood, perhaps?

The Kordolian seems to be gaining an advantage, because the lamperk's thrashing is becoming less savage. Then all of a sudden, it goes still.

The Kordolian swims around and sticks a giant hook through its mouth, the sharp barbed end breaking through the creature's black skin on the other side. A trickle of white blood streams down its skin where the hook has pierced it.

Is this guy the Prince Tarak was talking about? He doesn't seem very, uh, princely.

The Kordolian swims through the water, dragging the limp beast towards the floating platform. With one hand, he hauls himself up, dragging the dead lamperk after him. The creature flops onto the hard surface with a loud squelching sound. It's huge. It has to be about six feet long.

It looks as disgusting as I'd imagined. Its face, if it can be called that, consists mostly of a huge mouth, with hundreds of tiny, razor-sharp teeth. Its head is bulbous and eyeless, tapering into a long, glistening, snakelike body.

"Lamperk are a delicacy," Tarak informs me. "They make for good eating."

The thought of eating a piece of that thing makes me nauseated. My attention turns to the hunter, who's shaking his head, droplets of water cascading around him.

Like the other tribal guys, he's impressively built. His silver skin gleams with moisture, emphasizing his rippling muscles. His snow-white hair is long and wild, crowned by a pair of curving black horns. He brushes a slick of wet hair back from his face, revealing his aristocratic features.

If Tarak is a dark elven warrior, then this guy is the fucking Fae Prince.

Predictably, he's totally butt-naked. I sigh.

Besides Tarak and myself, the other tribal guys are now standing at the edge of the hole, peering down. The Prince looks up, sees us, and shouts an exuberant greeting in Kordolian.

Hauling the monster over his shoulder as if it's nothing, he starts to climb up the ladder, grinning, his body wet and glistening.

These guys really must enjoy the fact that they're totally immune to the cold.

Tarak and I are the only ones who seem to be wearing clothes around here.

As the Prince reaches the top, he throws his catch onto the hard, icy surface. Its weird milky blood spills around it, starting to freeze as it touches the ice.

He sees Tarak, lets out a stream of rapid Kordolian, and then proceeds to punch him in the face. Tarak doesn't even flinch.

"What the hell?" I gasp, without even thinking, moving to step between them, reaching for my dagger. Tarak curls one arm protectively around my waist.

"Do not worry," he whispers. "It's a traditional Aikun greeting."

Traditional, my ass. What kind of numbskull says hello with his fists?

Tarak's grinning. The crazy idiot. That Prince is crazy, too. All Kordolians, I've decided, are crazy, and I've just happened to become very attracted and attached to one of them. Therefore, I must also be crazy.

I feel for the black knife strapped to my thigh, my fingers curling around its familiar, reassuring shape. For the most part, it looks as if Tarak has things under control, but this is Kythia, and these are Kordolians.

One just never knows what's going to go down.

Tarak throws off his robes, carefully placing his weapons beside them, but to my relief, keeps his pants on. He stretches, the taut muscles of his back and arms flexing.

Then he returns the punch, his fist slamming into the guy's nose. The Prince smiles back, and then, even more confusingly, they hug, with lots of masculine back-slapping.

Tarak moves across and puts a gentle hand on my shoulder. "Relax, *amina*. This is perfectly acceptable. It may seem strange to you, but amongst the Aikun, fighting can be a show of affection." He squeezes my shoulder, then turns to the Prince.

What happens next makes me roll my eyes in exasperation. They both move away from our group, giving themselves a little space.

The Prince, still wet and dripping from his underwater escapade, tries to get another punch in. This time, Tarak dodges it, feinting to his left. He responds with a blow of his own, his fist connecting with the other Kordolian's jaw.

It's not a hard punch; I get the feeling Tarak's holding back. The Prince launches into a flurry of blows, trying to get a hit on Tarak. They weave and dodge, using some impressive footwork. Some glancing blows land on Tarak, but the Prince can't really get a good hit in.

The attack picks up pace, and it's the Prince on the offensive, with Tarak blocking and dodging.

They're both grinning, their expressions reminding me of children who are playing with their brand new Christmas gifts.

Males. I sigh as this ridiculous spectacle unfolds before me.

It's obvious that Tarak's the better fighter, but the Prince is putting in a solid effort. In other circumstances, he'd be considered an excellent fighter. A Human wouldn't stand a chance against him.

But with Tarak, it's like the master schooling the pupil.

He lets the guy attack. He dodges, blocks, and doesn't give an inch. He doesn't go easy on him, but he's not fighting back, either.

The tribal guys are cheering them on with loud, raucous cries.

If the whole thing weren't so stupid, it would be an impressive thing to watch; two large, bare-chested Kordolian males at peak physical fitness, battling it out.

Tarak and the Prince keep at it for a while, but eventually the Prince starts to tire, and Tarak executes some kind of swift grappling move that leaves the guy flat on his back and breathless.

The Prince grins like a madman as Tarak extends a hand to help him up.

They start chatting as Tarak returns to my side. The Prince sets eyes on me for the first time and he raises both eyebrows, tentatively sniffing the air. His amber eyes go wide.

"Human," he murmurs, his voice full of wonder. He babbles something to Tarak in Kordolian.

"Universal, Xalikian. Speak Universal so she can understand." He slides an arm around my waist. He's warm from the exertion of their little tussle, and he feels good. "She is my mate," he proclaims fiercely.

The way he says it is unexpected; he actually sounds proud. A delicious, warm, satisfying sensation courses through me. Mate, huh? I think I'll go with that.

Still, Tarak needs to learn how to make proper introductions. I'm not going to go around being referred to as 'mate'. I pull the scarf from my face remove my hood, the cold air slapping me in the face. I ignore it, putting on my most winning smile. I hold out a gloved hand. "Abbey Kendricks, of Earth. Pleased to meet you."

The Prince smiles, revealing his fangs. It's a genuine smile that reaches his eyes. "Abbey of Earth, I am most honored to meet the female who has tamed the great General." His accent is urbane and cultured. It's definitely not what I was expecting from a guy who has just brutally killed a giant underwater slug.

I cast a sidelong glance at Tarak, who's reverted to his usual stony expression.

The Prince does a funny little bow. I've seen a more elaborate version of that bow directed at Tarak before, but until now, no Kordolian has ever bowed to me. "I am Prince Xalikian Kazharan." He winks. "But you may call me Xal."

"Nice to meet you, Xal."

He stares at my outstretched hand, then at Tarak, then back at me, uncertainty creeping into his expression.

"Uh—"

"On Earth, shaking hands is a way of greeting," I inform him, realizing that Kordolians probably have no idea what a hand-shake is.

Beside me, Tarak stiffens. Xal glances nervously at my hand, then takes it, his fingers brushing ever so briefly against mine. "Interesting gesture," he remarks, unconsciously taking a step back.

What's got him so jumpy all of a sudden?

Is it because the big guy is staring at him so intently? Tarak reaches down and throws Xal his robe. "Put this on, Xalikian. It is not appropriate to be such a way in her presence."

Of course, he's referring to Xal's naked state. I've become so used to seeing Kordolian males traipsing around in their birthday suits that I didn't really think much of Xal's appearance. It's as if I've become desensitized to male nudity.

Xal takes the robe and dresses, giving Tarak a wary sidelong glance.

Looking up, I see that the little vein at Tarak's temple is twitching. His pointed ears flicker, and he narrows his eyes at Xal. He's annoyed.

My mouth opens wide in realization. Is the big guy jealous of the Fae Prince?

Oh, my. He *is* a possessive male.

Doesn't he understand that he has nothing to worry about?

I snuggle into him, taking his hand into mine. To my relief, he seems to relax, the tension draining out of his body. Sensing the change, Xal looks visibly relieved.

"I sent a message through the Soldar that I wanted to see you, but I didn't expect you here so soon." Xal glances over his shoulder and says something to the Aikun in their tribal language. One of them unsheathes a big knife as the other pulls a round black device from a bag at his waist. They haul the lamperk over and start skinning it. Its raw, meaty smell drifts to me on the wind. It's not unpleasant, just very, uh, fresh.

"There have been developments," Tarak says. "I did not want to delay any longer."

"I'm guessing this has something to do with the ruckus you caused with the High Council. And *she's* at the centre of it, isn't she?" Xal looks at me with a thoughtful expression. "My sources told me as much. It's the reason I wanted to meet with you, actually."

I disentangle from Tarak, crossing my arms. "Ta-rak," I say, my voice low and dangerous. "What is he talking about? What exactly am I at the centre of?"

I know those creepy scientists were after me because they wanted my Human body for some kind of experimental research, but I had no idea I'd become some sort of political football. And even Xal, who lives in the middle of nowhere, knows about it?

The General has some explaining to do.

Tarak shifts uneasily, but his expression remains carefully blank. I watch his wine-dark eyes, for once refusing to be distracted by his bare torso.

"I was protecting you," he mutters eventually, shooting Xal a dark glare. "The rulers of Kythia demanded I give you to them. I refused."

Oh. Tarak protected me from the Powers That Be. I resist the urge to hug him. He might look scary, but that hard exterior hides a tender, protective heart. However, all this handing-over business sounds quite serious. "General, what exactly makes me so valuable to you Kordolians? As a Human, I assumed your people wouldn't give me a second glance." I'm not liking where this is going.

Tarak turns his back on Xal. He puts his big, warm hands on either side of my face and meets my gaze. His red eyes are wide and clear; I sense no deceit there. "When you got the nanograft, back on the Fleet Station, they did some tests without my knowledge." His voice is soft. The wind picks up, whipping at my hair, chilling the tips of my ears. "They found something quite remarkable."

"What, Tarak?" My voice cracks a little.

"Humans and Kordolians are compatible."

"What do you mean?"

"We can have offspring together."

"Oh." My heart skips a beat. He runs his rough thumb gently down the side of my face, from the corner of my eye to my jawline. The sensation sends shivers up my spine. I don't know what to feel right now. I don't know whether to be angry and shocked that he omitted that particular detail, or overjoyed. Oh, the children we're going to have together. "Is that why you're keeping me around?"

"No." He rests his thumb under my chin, tilting my face upwards. He almost seems angry. "You are not a female whose sole purpose is to bear offspring. You are my mate, and I need you by my side. I *need* you. I am not going to let you fall into the hands of those who would tear you apart and use you; those who would destroy you. Do you understand, Abbey of Earth? You are mine, and no-one, Kordolian or otherwise, is going to take you away from me. I will do everything in my power to protect you, even if I have to wage war against my own people."

Oh, my. My heart, seemingly on hold, flutters back to life.

"You're *not* going to start a war because of me," I whisper, as the wind starts to howl. Behind us, the Aikun males are babbling on in their own language, and I hear the sound of lamperk flesh being chopped. "Although that's very sweet of you," I add, almost as an afterthought. Only Tarak could make the idea of starting a war seem romantic.

"No," he shakes his head, much to my relief. "A war on Kythia is not my intention. I have devised a more suitable plan."

"Of course you have," I say gently. "That's why we're out here in the middle of the badlands, meeting a Prince who doesn't want to be found, but who somehow still has his ear to the ground. We're about to discuss the fate of the universe, aren't we? And he's somehow involved, and you have cryptically mentioned Earth a few times now. We're going back there, aren't we?"

"We are." He shakes his head, half-amused, half-astonished. "Astute female. That is why you're my mate."

He's such a sweet, stubborn, infuriating male. "Well, let's hear this plan of yours then, General."

Tarak

I GESTURE TOWARDS XALIKIAN, indicating he should join us again. He was perceptive enough to give Abbey and I a moment of privacy while I discussed a certain issue with her.

It was the least he could do, after tactlessly bringing it up in the first place.

It went better than I had hoped. But that is how she is. She speaks her mind, but she's thinking on her feet, always adapting. She has observed and listened and come to her own conclusions. She does not carry on with drama and angst like those cloistered Kordolian females.

I am fortunate.

The Aikun males have dissected the lamperk. They have skinned it and kept the black hide for curing. The soft white flesh has been cut into small cubes. They are busy setting up the heat source for cooking.

The Prince looks at Abbey and I curiously as he nears. He has wrapped himself in my black robes, covering his naked body. I do not have problems showing my body to her, but suddenly, I don't want her to see other naked males. Besides, Humans seem to be sensitive about such things.

I haven't seen Xalikian for several cycles, and he's changed since he escaped the Palace. There is a hard edge to his gaze now, and even though he's lost none of his charm, life in the Vaal has made him lean and tough, like the tribesmen he considers his brothers.

The resemblance to Vionn and his late father, Ilhan, is striking. He's inherited his mother's haughty, aristocratic bearing and his father's compelling amber eyes. His charm and cunning seem to be his own. I hope he hasn't inherited any his parents' madness.

"You have heard the latest from the High Council, then," I say, pulling Abbey close. "Sooner or later they will be heading for Earth, looking to take Humans for their experiments."

"I have my sources." Xalikian wears an enigmatic expression. His tone changes, becoming bitter. "My mother's behind this. She sees all other races as animals. She believes in the supremacy of the Kordolian race, and she won't spare anything or anyone in her quest to produce the perfect lineage, even if it means extracting biological material from other species. The next time I see her, I will make sure I finish what I started. She will die by my hand." His golden eyes are as cold as the frozen sea we're standing on. It doesn't surprise me. Xalikian has suffered so much at the hands of his mother, the Empress.

I shake my head. "Vionn is a lost cause. You are better off concentrating on what needs to be done now." I wrap my hand around Abbey's smaller one, our fingers entwined. "I have decided to withdraw my entire fleet and the First Division from the High Council's jurisdiction."

Xalikian blinks, staring at me in shock. "They'll sic General Daegan and his soldiers on you if you break away, you know that."

I let out a derisive snort. "Daegan is an idiot. Let him come. If he is stupid enough to take me on, I will destroy him." Daegan is a Noble who rose to the rank of General through connections and favors. He hasn't seen real combat in his lifetime. He's the sort who commands battles remotely, hiding behind strategy advisors and officers. I am not afraid of Daegan. His fleet is comparable in size to mine, but my soldiers are in a different class.

The only ones who would suffer in a war between military factions would be the ordinary classes, Kordolians who don't have the backing of a Noble House. The High Council would hastily conscript them into a pointless war.

"Anyhow, the High Council can't wage war if they can't find us."

Both Abbey and Xalikian stare at me, looking perplexed.

"I have ordered my commanders to make the Fleet Station untraceable, cutting off all communication with Kythia. All non-military personnel have been ejected, and it is being moved as we speak. A holographic representation has been left in its place. They won't know until it's far too late."

Unexpectedly, Xalikian laughs. "That's genius, General. You're stealing half the fleet from right under their noses."

"I can't steal what already belongs to me, Prince." The Fleet Station is mine, and all the soldiers on it are under my command. The fighter craft on it are mine to command. There is no fucking way I'm allowing such artillery into the hands of the Nobles.

Abbey squeezes my hand, turning towards me, so her face is protected from the wind. Her cheeks have become flushed again, a faint pink color spreading across them. So that happens when she's cold, as well.

"You mentioned something about Kordolians heading towards Earth to take Humans," she says, suspicion clouding her voice. "Please tell me you have a plan to stop that."

"I was coming to that." I meet Xalikian's gaze. "Earth is habitable. Humans and Kordolians can have offspring. It seems like an ideal location for the scenario we have previously discussed."

"A Kordolian settlement, outside Kythia?"

"A breakaway. For any who wish to be free of the Empire and the corruption of the Noble Houses. For those who would consider taking a Human mate. Some of us would rather see our entire race die out than take a non-Kordolian mate. They are obsessed with outdated ideals; with purity. I am not one of those."

"What's my role in all this?"

"We need a figurehead. You are popular enough amongst the ordinary classes, a cult figure to ordinary Kordolians and alien servants alike. Kordolians would follow you, even to Earth. I'm just a soldier. A war hero in their eyes perhaps, but I can't inspire loyalty in civilians. You, on the other hand, have had diplomacy training. You can open negotiations with the Humans and apply for asylum on Earth."

"I never expected to leave Kythia," Xalikian says cautiously. "Even though I'm out here in the Vaal, I'm not entirely disconnected from the civilized zones. There are things I'm working on here, and Earth is impossibly far. It's a six-cycle trip, isn't it?"

Abbey holds up a hand. "Hang on just a second." She gives both Xalikian and I a pointed look. "Planning an invasion of Earth is all well and good, but as the only representative of Earth here, I'd like to bring a few negotiating points to the table."

The Prince inclines his head. "Certainly, Abbey of Earth. Unlike my mother, I don't believe in haphazardly colonizing planets, and I recognize your right to speak on behalf of your people. What are your concerns?"

"Firstly, I get the feeling there are two sorts of Kordolians. Insane, and not-so-insane. You and Tarak here obviously fall into the latter category. I don't even want to think about what the batshit-crazy ones would do to Earth, and to Humans."

She has a habit of using Earth words I do not understand, such as this 'batshit.' I shrug. "We would defend Earth against any Imperial takeover."

"You'd better." This tiny, delicate female is standing between two Kordolian males who tower over her, and dictating terms. She glares up at me, hands on her hips. She's both utterly adorable and indomitable at the same time. "Secondly, what about those insect monsters and Fortuna Tau? We just left them there, and we haven't heard anything since."

My ears twitch. It is an annoying, involuntary habit I cannot control. It only seems to happen when I'm with her. "I sent a retrieval craft shortly after we arrived on the Fleet Station. I am not worried about my First Division. They are beyond competent, and they have dealt with much worse without me. I am certain they already have the situation under control. I am sure the Humans will also be calling their people for assistance."

I'll admit, my decision to leave the mining station was a bit preliminary, and certainly not within protocol, but I had a most compelling reason.

"They'd better not let those things get to Earth."

"It's highly unlikely. And even if they do, only the First Division and I are equipped to handle them."

"Are you trying to suggest that Humanity might need you,

General Tarak?" She gives me a sly, sidelong glance. She almost sounds amused.

"If the Xargek ever reach Earth, then yes." What is certain is that I need her.

Abbey gives me a long, hard look and seems to come to some sort of conclusion. "Fine. You guys can come to Earth. But no colonizing, no using Humans for medical experiments, and you have to promise that you'll exterminate any oversized insects that try to eat us. Oh, and in public, you have to wear clothes. It's a cultural thing."

Humans and their strange customs. I shrug. "I can abide by those conditions." Of course, I have certain conditions of my own. She is my mate, and she will allow me to ensure her happiness and protect her. In return, I won't stage a hostile takeover of Earth. I will do something I have seldom done throughout my military career.

I will negotiate.

I will be open to discussion with the Humans. They are fortunate to have her as a member of their species, because otherwise I would just take their damn planet and be done with it. However, her happiness is important to me.

Therefore, I will show restraint.

The scent of roasted lamperk meat reaches my nose, drifting to us on the icy wind. Both Xalikian and I look towards the skies as a faint roar reaches our ears.

The Prince shares a knowing gaze with me. "They have found us," he says grimly.

That roar is the distant sound of an Imperial destroyer. "Warn the Aikun," I snap, scanning the skies. The black, starry backdrop doesn't reveal a thing. I do a quick mental calculation, estimating its distance based on the sound.

"They will want to take Abbey alive. The rest of us, they want dead."

"How did they find us?" Xalikian's white hair whips around his face, the dark robes fluttering. The sound of engines is becoming louder.

I don't answer his question, because I don't know. Perhaps

the assassin tipped them off to our location before Abbey killed him.

My mate looks up at us in confusion. I sometimes forget that human senses aren't as acute. She probably can't hear it yet. "What the hell's going on, Tarak?"

"Imperial forces. You have to go, now." This situation is most dangerous for her. Her body is fragile. She can't slip into the hole in the ice and hide under the water like the Aikun.

I will have to create a diversion. No matter; I will draw them out. I retrieve the short sword and the plasma gun from where I left them on the ice, and draw out my armor.

"Take her into the crater," I order, as the exo-suit molds over my body. The Aikun males are staring at up at the sky, their feast of lamperk forgotten. They glance at me in shock, probably startled to realize I'm suddenly wearing the armor of an Imperial soldier.

Xalikian nods, his eyes on the horizon.

"If anything happens to her, I'll kill you, Highness."

"Noted, Sir," he replies, a trace of irony in his voice.

The destroyer is in view now. It's gaining quickly, appearing larger as it nears. It's a medium-sized Alpha-class craft, one of the later models designed for both atmospheric and space travel. It's powerful, but it lacks maneuverability. The pilot is going to have a hard time pinpointing me.

I'm sure General Daegan is behind this. It's so typical of him. That pompous idiot always tries to win his battles through firepower, without understanding the conditions. He's fought too many easy wars, whereas my troops are always sent to handle the difficult planets. He's too used to winning to be able to strategize properly. And sending only one destroyer? That's just plain arrogant. How the fuck does he expect to blow us to smithereens and take Abbey alive with that thing?

I do not enjoy fighting our people, even if they are Daegan's soldiers, but if they threaten my mate, I swear to Kaiin I will take them down.

Abbey

I'M LOOKING AROUND, wondering what's got the males all riled up when I hear the noise. It's a faint rumble at first, then it grows into a roar. Tarak has activated his armor, and I get the feeling all hell's about to break loose.

The Aikun males have disappeared, slipping down the ladder into their ice hole, abandoning the white meat of the lamperk.

Tarak growls at Xalikian in Kordolian, much to my annoyance. I'm struggling to get a grasp on what's happening.

Xalikian taps me on the shoulder. "We have to run," he urges. "A battleship is coming." I look across to Tarak, who's activated his exo-armor. "What's he doing, then?"

"He's going to do what he always does. He's going to deal with it."

Of course he is.

"Don't you dare do anything stupid, Tarak," I yell, as Xalikian guides me across the ice. "And you're not allowed to die, General."

"Don't worry, *amina*. This thing can't kill me." Typical Tarak; he's as arrogant as always. But with him, it's not all false confidence. If he says it won't kill him, then it won't kill him. He grins then, a fierce, fearless grin, his crimson eyes filled with bloodlust. I've never seen anything more beautiful and more intimidating in my life.

And this bundle of savage, silver badassery is all mine.

"Let's go." The Prince is beside me, pointing in the direction of the black mountain. "Back to the crater. We'll hide in the underground. He will be fine. Trust me, he's seen and done worse. Can you keep up, or do you want me to carry you?"

"I think I'll be fine." I've got this newfound speed, thanks to the nanites the Kordolians used to repair my legs.

I wrap the scarf around my face, protecting myself against the wind-chill. We set off as the roaring sound becomes louder, Tarak sprinting in the opposite direction. Sweet male. He's creating a diversion.

Despite the bulky Skaz-coat, I'm able to keep up with the Prince easily.

These new legs of mine are totally sweet.

As we reach the base of the mountain Xal turns, holding out a hand. "Need a leg up, or can you do it?"

"I'll give it a try." When it comes to hills and mountains, even on Earth, I've always found going up easier than going down. It's something to do with balance and momentum. I start to run up the steep, rocky slope and find I can manage just fine.

We scramble up the hillside and I bend forward into the wind, gaining momentum and using the weight of my body as a counter-balance. About half-way up, I start to get winded and a dull ache begins in my legs.

I ignore it and keep going. Beside me, Xal's easily keeping pace.

I'm starting to breathe heavily.

"Are you all right, Abbey?"

"Fine," I grate, forcing myself to ignore the pain. The lip of the crater is in sight now, and I look for easy footholds, each step becoming harder.

Despite the fact that it's absolutely freezing, I've broken out in a sweat. I take a deep breath, the air slow to fill my lungs through the thick scarf.

The top is just a little bit further.

The wind is beating at my back, almost pushing me up the slope. Behind us, the roar of engines becomes deafening. A series of explosions rocks the ground.

I'm dying to look back, but I don't dare. I have to trust Tarak's judgement on this.

He told me to run, and that's what I'm going to do. I'm not going to rush back there like an idiot and put myself in danger. That would just weaken his position and make him vulnerable.

I'm not going to do that to him, so I just have to trust him.

We're almost at the top now, and my legs are burning. But I've come this far, and death-by-spaceship is not something I have on my bucket-list, so I let out a scream, willing my body beyond its limits, and haul myself over the edge.

I find myself hanging.

What the hell?

Xalikian is grabbing my arm, and I'm staring down at an impossible drop. My heart flips into my throat.

The lip of the crater ends abruptly in a steep cliff, and the bottom is hundreds of feet below.

This isn't the way Tarak went when we ran down this mountain the first time.

"Next time you're going to jump over the edge, warn me first, Abbey!" Xal is looking down at me, his eyes wide with shock. He mutters something under his breath in Kordolian. It sounds like the same curse-words Tarak uses. "The General would rip my head off if anything happened to you." He's visibly shaken.

With one arm, he hauls me back up, and I scramble onto a solid bit of rock that's shaped like a little platform, my heart pounding. I realize I'm shaking. "S-sorry. I thought there would be a ledge, like the place where we came up."

I take a moment to catch my breath, stealing a look at the wasteland below.

A sleek triangular-shaped battleship has appeared. It's matt-black and about half a football field long. An impressive set of artillery bristles from its underside and I cry out in dismay as a bolt of plasma strikes the icy ground, causing chips of ice to fly into the air. It leaves a huge, glistening crater on the white surface.

Where the hell is Tarak?

"There," Xalikian points, and I make out a tiny black figure running around on the ice. From up here, he looks so insignificant; almost ant-like.

The odds against him seem impossible.

Tarak switches direction and the ship tries to follow him, turning around. But it's slow and cumbersome.

Ah. That's where Tarak has the advantage.

He can run really, really fast.

"He'll be fine," Xal reassures me, taking my hand. "We need to get out of sight. They will have heat sensors onboard that thing.

They may have spotted us already. If you move ever so slightly to the left here, you will find a set of footholds."

I peer into the darkness and see what he's talking about. There are pieces of metal jutting out of the cliff face, leading down into the darkness. They're about the length of my arm, forming a precarious looking ladder.

"So we have to climb down that thing." At least my phobias are limited to closed-in spaces, and not heights.

"I'm afraid so."

"Let's go, then." I swing over the side and my feet find the first rung. Xal follows me and we descend into the inky blackness, climbing down this odd, makeshift ladder.

From a distance, I hear an almighty crash. The mountain shakes a little, a few pebbles dropping onto us from above.

What the hell is Tarak doing out there?

"The ship's crashed," Xal says softly.

I want to go back up there and see. I want to make sure Tarak's okay. But I force myself to continue the descent.

Everything's gone eerily silent now, save for the sound of my labored breathing and the howling wind swirling down into the crater. Eventually a stone ledge appears, and Xal and I stop to rest.

There's a bit of light here. I look down and see another ledge below us. From the side of the cliff, a waterfall has appeared, sending a fine mist across a forest of giant, glowing blue mushrooms.

If we weren't in a life-or-death situation right now, I'd stop to appreciate the stunning beauty of the scene below. It's the first sign of vegetation I've seen on this bitterly cold and dark planet. I really can't wait to get back to the sunshine.

"There's a cave past here," Xal informs me, pointing towards a dark hole in the rock face. "We will be safe there."

This mountain is full of surprises.

We enter the cave and I fight with all my willpower against the sense of panic that threatens to overwhelm me. There's nothing like ending an escape from almost-death with a descent into a dark crater, followed by a retreat into a mysterious cave.

For some reason, my dark-vision goggles don't work as well in here. Everything is shadowy and indistinct.

"There aren't any monsters in here, are there?"

Xal is quiet for a moment. That's not super reassuring.

"Xal?"

"There shouldn't be," he says cautiously. Great. He goes silent for a bit. "I can see why he chose you as his mate," he says eventually, his rich voice echoing throughout the empty space. From somewhere deep inside, I hear the steady *plop, plop* of dripping water. "You are brave, Abbey of Earth."

I shake my head. "I'm just surviving. There's nothing brave about that. I should be out there helping Tarak in some way. But I can't do anything right now."

"Oh but you have helped him." Xal gestures towards a big flat boulder, and we both sit down. "He's different, somehow. Before, he would allow himself to be dictated to by the Empire, even though he holds a lot of power himself. But now, something has given him the strength to seek change. I'd say that something is you."

"Don't be silly. He's the sort that's going to do what he wants, when it suits him, each and every time."

A soft laugh escapes Xal. "You see, that's what I'm talking about. There's no-one else on this planet who would dare say that about him. It's so rare that anyone will challenge him to his face. You're exactly what he needs, Abbey of Earth. Someone has to keep him, one of the most dangerous beings in the universe, in line. And he's totally besotted with you. I've seen the way he looks at you. It's remarkable."

"If that's the case, then it's a two-way street." I shrug. "And what about you, Prince? Why are you here, hiding in caves and hunting ice-monsters, instead of ruling your people? And why do you let the General boss you around?"

Beside me, Xal stiffens. "It's complicated," he says, and his friendly tone disappears, his voice turning cold. "Let's just say that not is all it seems on Kythia. As for the General, he once had orders to kill me. He refused, for reasons known only to him. And ever since, we've stayed in touch."

"As I said, he does what he wants." I bring my knees up against my chest, curling up into a little ball. I thought the cave might be a little bit warmer, because there's no wind in here, but just like everywhere else on Kythia, it's freezing. "I wonder why you guys are different. I mean, no offense, but I've run into some Kordolians who are downright evil. You and Tarak on the other hand, you guys seem to have standards." It's more of a loose statement rather than a question, but Xal makes a noise of agreement low in his throat.

"You know, I've often wondered the same thing."

"So, are you coming with us to Earth, or what? It sounds like the future survival of your people is at stake. And we have females, Xal, lots of them. The ladies would go nuts over a guy like you."

Xal sighs. "It's increasingly looking like the only option. I'd better get out of the Vaal before the High Council starts causing the Lost Tribes a great deal of trouble. They shouldn't suffer just because they're sheltering me. And somehow, I get the feeling Akkadian will drag me to Earth by the horns if I refuse his offer. He really wants an out, and he's genuinely concerned about the welfare of our race. So he'll do whatever it takes to get me there. He's just asking me first so I can preserve my dignity."

"Exactly. You know how he gets."

"And I *am* still looking for a mate." A cynical laugh escapes him. "I would rather jump into the boiling lava pits of Keldork than hitch myself to one of those vicious Kordolian females from the Nobility."

"Well, there you go."

Agreement reached; mission accomplished. Tarak can thank me later. Now, we just need to sit and wait for him to single-handedly take down a Kordolian battle cruiser.

Abbey

I MUST HAVE FALLEN asleep at some point, because I wake to

the sound of soft voices murmuring in Kordolian. Where the hell are we? Oh yeah, the cave. I remember waiting in the darkness, chatting with Xal, speculating, and worrying.

Tarak's low rumble is music to my ears. That means he's alive and safe.

I curl up into my Skaz-coat, feeling toasty and warm, drifting back into a half-sleep. The events of the past few hours float through my mind in a confused, hazy mush, almost as if this were all a dream.

Then warm, rough hands are tracing along my neck, tenderly caressing the side of my face, brushing through my hair.

"What the hell did you do, Tarak?" The words come out as slurred, mumbling sleep-talk. My eyes flutter open, but all I see is blackness. Someone's removed my dark-vision goggles. "I heard a crash."

"If a destroyer tries to change direction too quickly, it stalls. It's the first thing we learn in flight school. I simply made them change direction too fast, drawing them into the error. But then I took pity on the soldiers and gave them a choice. Run back to the civilized zones, or die. Naturally, they knew who I was, so they ran. It's not their fault if their commander is stupid."

"Oh." I bask in the sensation of his gentle caresses. "You *are* a clever male. Well done."

"It was nothing," he says gruffly, awkwardly, as I sit up, leaning into him. "But we have to go quickly now. There will be others coming for us."

"Where are we going?" I blink, and feel around in the dark for my goggles. Tarak presses them into the palm of my hand.

"Earth," he says, with absolute certainty. A thrill of excitement shoots through me. "Come, *amina*."

"You keep calling me that."

"Hm."

He stands, and I put the goggles on. "A term of endearment?"

"It means 'loved one' in Aikun." He brushes my hair out of my face and lifts my hood. "Imperial Kordolian does not have an equivalent word."

"Oh." Oh, indeed. The General just keeps on surprising me. I decide I like this lyrical little pet name.

I follow him out of the cave and Xal joins us. The three of us look up to the sky. The dark walls of the crater surround us, but at the top, there's a patch of pure, uninterrupted space, a river of stars glittering across the black, impenetrable canvas.

We say nothing as we climb back out of the crater. As we reach the top, I see a big black shape down below.

The destroyer has crashed into the ice, leaving a giant gash in the hard surface.

The wind whips and howls around us and Tarak moves behind me, shielding me.

"That's our way back," he says, nodding towards the stranded ship.

"It will still fly?"

"Of course. Its body is made of Callidum, and nothing destroys Callidum except for Callidum itself."

"Massive tongue-twister," I say, as both Tarak and Xal give me a strange look. "Never mind." I shake my head. There will be plenty of time on the flight to Earth to teach these Kordolians about Earth humor and Earth customs.

And Tarak and I will have plenty of time to ourselves. Oh, yes we will. I smile underneath my scarf, feeling a little giddy. What started out as a misguided, terrifying, but well-intentioned abduction has turned into a fantasy beyond my wildest imagination.

I'm going home with my very own growly, arrogant, domineering Kordolian male.

It turns out he's not so bad after all. There are people on Earth who are going to have major problems with the idea of Kordolians coming to live with us, because the silver-skinned guys can be as scary as hell when they want to. But we'll deal with that headache when it happens. The universe is changing, and if these guys don't find mates in this generation, there won't *be* another generation of Kordolians.

Right now, the Kordolian Empire is desperate, and desperate individuals can do terrifying things, like enslave other species.

I'd much prefer Tarak and Xal's approach, especially if they can protect us from evil Kordolians and disgusting insect-aliens. Earth *is* ripe for the picking; we've just been lucky so far.

I yelp as Tarak lifts me into his arms, and all of a sudden we're barreling down the mountainside again, going so fast that everything becomes a blur.

As we reach the bottom, waiting for Xal to catch up, Tarak lowers me to the ground. He pushes my hood back ever so slightly and pulls down my scarf. He bends down, his lips brushing against my ear. "The journey to Earth is long," he whispers, his warm breath tickling my skin. "You Humans live in such an insignificant part of the universe that it will take almost six cycles to get there."

"Is that going to be a problem?"

"I will teach you a thousand and one things in that time, my *amina*." His deep, resonant voice is filled with hunger, causing me to shudder. "So it will not be a problem for me at all."

Oh, no. He's doing that thing again, where I get all warm and fuzzy inside. Can't he at least wait until we're alone? Devious male.

"I also have things to teach you, General," I say softly, as he pecks at my earlobe with his warm, sensual lips.

"I am full of anticipation, Abbey of Earth."

Suddenly, the trip back to Earth doesn't seem so long. Tarak takes my hand, squeezing it, and we start to walk across the ice as Xal catches up to us. The place is eerily silent, the crashed black ship rising out of the ice like a strange, brutal sculpture.

It's so Kordolian in appearance, just like my beautiful male.

So here we are; the most lethal soldier in the universe, the future ruler of the Kordolian Empire and me, Abbey Kendricks, chocolate lover and bioscientist, heading for Earth.

We're opening up the pathway for the survival of a species, and I just can't *wait* to show Tarak around my home planet.

Kordolians and Humans, who would have thought it?

If Tarak and I are anything to go by, there may be hope for the universe yet.

EPILOGUE

Tarak

I wake and find her side of the pod cold. The sheets are tangled and her scent lingers in the air, but she is not beside me.

We are entering Earth's orbit; the final leg of our long journey. Following Abbey's advice, Xalikian has initiated contact with the Humans and found them surprisingly receptive. Perhaps it has something to do with the fact that my First Division have made it to Earth after rescuing the Humans from the Xargek infestation on Fortuna Tau. Diplomacy is not their strong point, but they must have made some sort of an impression.

I am looking forward to the debriefing.

The sound of retching reaches my ears. I pad across the floor and find her bent over the toilet.

"What's wrong, *amina*?"

"I feel sick." Abbey turns to me, her face pale. "I've been queasy these past few days, but this morning has been the worst. You know what this means, don't you?" Her eyes are full of meaning, but I am lost.

"You are not well," I state, coming behind to push her hair out of her eyes. It has grown longer during the trip to Earth, and it is lush and beautiful, a glossy, light brown color, streaked through with hints of gold. I like it this way. "You must rest, and I will get Zyara to see to you."

"Tarak." She shakes her head, a flicker of amusement breaking through her misery. "I'm sick in the morning, and I've missed my last period. My contraceptive implant's due to be replaced right about now."

I blink as these details filter through, trying to process them. Contraception? Period? These are things Human females are familiar with. I'm just a simple Kordolian General, who is about to introduce our species to Earth. I am not trained in such complex things.

Abbey gets up and activates the shower. She steps out of her robes, letting them fall to the floor. Underneath, she's completely naked.

Unable to help myself, I let out a low growl of appreciation.

She is perfection in every way. Her soft Human skin has become lighter during our journey, a consequence, she tells me, of being away from the sun. Humans are like plants, apparently. Without the sun, they will eventually wither and die.

She will be enjoying the sunlight soon.

Her hair cascades down her shoulders, curling at the top of her breasts, which are perfectly round and full, her dark, delicate nipples contrasting with the paleness of her skin. Her waist is narrow and her hips are curved and generous, cradling her delicate sex.

She beckons to me as she steps under the stream of the shower. She has set it to warm, which is her preference. Steam begins to fill the cubicle.

Naturally, I have no clothing to discard. I follow her as she turns her face up into the cascade of water.

She faces me as my arms circle her waist.

"I think I'm pregnant," she says, and the effect on me is more powerful than a twenty-megakorr fission bomb.

The first emotion that courses through me is happiness; fierce, unbridled happiness, of which I have never known the like. The second is pride; I am proud of my female, and she will be a magnificent mother to our child. The third is protective-ness; I will kill anyone or anything that threatens her and our unborn child.

I say nothing; I simply lean in and kiss her deeply. She responds, her mouth hot and wanting.

And then?

Panic.

I lay a hand on her stomach, and for the first time in my life, I am uncertain, and unsure what to do. "You are with child?" I pull her close. "I must summon Zyara. You need to have a full medical check-up, and then you must rest. You can stay here while Xalikian and I begin the negotiations with the Humans. I will not have you exerting yourself. Do you wish for anything? Food? Drink? I will—"

"Tarak." Her soft voice breaks through, and I realize she's said my name a few times. "Relax." She places a hand on my chest. "I'm touched by your concern, but I'll be fine. Even if I am pregnant, and this is still an *if*, although I'm fairly certain, it doesn't mean I suddenly become an invalid. I will continue doing normal things, and you will treat me normally and not wrap me up in cotton wool. We will be fine."

She smiles, her luminous skin glistening with moisture. She is remarkably calm and self-assured, the very representation of the Goddess herself.

My racing heart slows. If she is with child, I have no need to be concerned. She is in control and there is nothing more for me to do except protect her.

That is a given.

"You are beautiful," I say, enjoying the feel of her warm, wet skin against mine. My erection rests against her belly, and she brings her arms around my neck.

"You're incredible," she replies huskily, and I can bear it no longer. I take her into my arms, her body silken and wet and gleaming. I carry her out of the cubicle and into our sleeping pod.

She laughs; a sound pure and light like starlight, and I kiss her fiercely.

A sudden thought causes me to hesitate, and I release her lips. "I don't want to harm the—"

"Don't be silly," she says, putting a finger to my lips. "As I said, you don't have to walk on eggshells around me."

I raise an eyebrow. It's another Human phrase I don't understand, but I get the gist of it.

"I have little experience with such things," I admit finally. Females and young ones and such things are not my area of expertise.

"Don't worry, my big, bad General. I've got this." She pulls me down, aggressively, hungrily, and I enter her, finding her tight and wet and wanting. I gasp as pleasure overwhelms me.

She is perfection.

And up here in space, on the verge of reaching the planet Earth, the realization hits me.

I am home.

Made in the USA
Monee, IL
26 December 2020

55575776R00135